DESIRE'S CURSE

MARICCA WOOD

Copyright © 2024 by Maricca Wood

All rights reserved.
No part of this book may be reproduced, distributed, or transmitted in any form or by any electronic or mechanical means, including information storage and retrieval systems, without written permission from the author, except for the use of brief quotations in a book review and certain other noncommercial use permitted by copyright law.

This book is a work of fiction. Any resemblance to actual persons and things living or dead, locales, or events is entirely coincidental.

Desire's Curse:
Cover Design: Books and Moods
Editor: The Havoc Archives

Repeat after me… Stalkers. Are. Bad.
Most of the time…

TRIGGER WARNINGS

Dear Wicked Readers,

Before immersing yourself in this roller coaster of emotions, please be aware that this book is indeed a dark romance. Our female main character is forced to deal with the realities and harsh repercussions of online dating.

This book contains conversations, actions, or situations that might be triggering and not suitable for some readers. 18+ is advised. Some triggers include manipulation, mental/physical abuse, stalking, attempted rape, kidnapping, graphic violence, guns, PTSD, masturbation, explicit sexual scenes, murder, death/dying, and bodies/corpses.

With all that being said, there may be some triggers within the book that I have not listed. Things will not be easy for our female lead, so strap in for her crazy and twisted journey.

-Enjoy

PLAYLIST

I love u – Loving Caliber

She's Got It All – Kenny Chesney

What the Hell – Avril Lavigne

Monster - Skillet

Sk8er Boi – Avril Lavigne

It Wasn't Me – Shaggy, Rik Rok

Dirty Little Secret – The All-American Rejects

What's It to You – Clay Walker

Coming Undone – Korn

Master of Puppets - Metallica

CHAPTER 1

Just do it, Amarah, she coached herself as she sat at her work desk, staring at her computer screen. Her finger trembled over her wireless mouse, and the cursor blinked mockingly over the "finish" button as though daring her to click it. Her sister-in-law, Sandra, had suggested she try her hand at online dating.

Amarah had been intrigued, yet equally hesitant. Intrigued with the new avenue in which to possibly meet the man of her dreams. Hesitant because of all the horror stories she's heard over the years about online dating. Not to mention, she preferred to meet people the old-fashioned way, through friends or out and about somewhere. However, that approach had gotten her nowhere. She was twenty-two years old and still depressingly single.

There were no shortage of men who hit on her, of course. Her long, golden hair, deep blue eyes that would put any sapphire to shame, and a fit but curvy figure garnered plenty of male attention, but when a man showed interest in her she always asked herself if she could see herself married to him one day. The answer was almost always a resounding *no*.

Her deflated sigh was the only sound that could be heard in her small office. Maybe she was being too picky. A girl can have standards, right? Standards that she just wasn't willing to compromise on. For example, saving herself for the right man. However, when the men she dated discovered that she wasn't going to hook up on the first date, or second, or even the third, they would be gone, unwilling to wait.

She would always tell them up front that she wasn't ready for anything physical besides hot, intense make out sessions, but they never believed she was serious. They were even shocked and sometimes angry when they finally realized that she meant what she said. As a result, her longest relationship lasted exactly two months and six days.

Her mother had always told her to be the kind of woman a man wants to marry, not date. To only give them a taste, not the full meal. She needed to give them a reason to come back. It was wise advice as far as Amarah was concerned. It weeded out the players and… well, every other man she had dated.

Was she setting herself up for failure from the beginning? Any man Amarah found attractive or was interested in, she found herself subconsciously comparing them to her older brother Travis's best friend, Liam Godrik. She met Liam over a decade ago when she was eleven and he was seventeen, developing a crush on him as she watched him grow from a boy into one hell of a man. Now he was the measuring stick that she held any would-be suitor against, and always found them wanting.

Despite how she felt, nothing had ever happened between them. He had always treated her like a little sister. After she graduated high school, there had been some innocent flirtatious banter between them periodically, but nothing that would make her question their relationship or where she stood with him. She knew she needed to accept that her childhood crush would never want her the way she wanted him. At least she had him in her life as a friend. That was better than not having him in her life at all.

Swallowing her pride and fear, Amarah clicked down on her mouse and finished her online profile for the dating site, Desire.

This is so stupid. Not to mention, sketchy.

She didn't want to go through all this and possibly get her hopes up about a man just to get catfished—or worse, murdered and thrown in a ditch somewhere. After a calming breath, she squared her shoulders, trying to remain optimistic. Who knows, maybe she'd finally meet Mr. Right.

Highly unlikely, she thought. *I've already met him, but I'll settle for Mr. Almost Right.*

Amarah closed out of the website and downloaded the mobile app on her phone before she got back to work combing through emails and financial documents. She had always excelled in school, ranking in the top ten percent of her graduating class, earning herself an academic letterman jacket and a full scholarship to the University of Oklahoma.

She applied to Conner Finances right after graduating high school. She started out working at the front desk, but her hard work and determination paid off, and by the end of her first year there, she had moved to the position of credit analyst, gaining her very own office. Numbers had always been second nature to her, so she pursued a degree in finance. Despite having to work full-time for food and spending money, she buckled down, pulled a lot of all-nighters, and managed to graduate with her bachelor's degree in only three years.

Her office wasn't large or extravagant, but she didn't mind because it was her own space. It contained an L-shaped desk that ran along the back left corner and extended down into the middle of the room. She didn't like clutter, so her desktop was sparse, containing only her dual monitor computer, a purple and white wireless keyboard with a matching mouse, a stack of sticky notes, a tall marble cylinder that housed various pens, highlighters, and pencils, and a few picture frames that always made her smile, despite if she was having a bad day.

A black four-by-six-inch frame housed a family photo containing her father, mother, brother, and herself at Christmas time a few years back. The second picture frame housed a photo of Travis, Sandra, Liam, and herself at the ceremony the day Travis and Liam received their Trident pins and officially became Navy SEALs. The third picture— and by far her favorite—housed a photo of Liam and herself from that year's New Year's Eve party.

Her brother and sister-in-law had hosted a small party to celebrate the new year, and as the ball dropped at midnight, all the couples began kissing. Liam and herself were the only ones who didn't bring a special someone, so Liam walked over to her, leaned in, wished her a happy New Year, and kissed her lightly on the cheek. Sandra happened to sneak the photo and sent it to her the next day. She was unsure if Liam even knew the photo existed. It was a wonderful little secret that Sandra and her shared.

Amarah lost herself in work for about half an hour and jerked when her phone dinged, pulling her attention away from the spreadsheet she was working on. When she checked her phone, a notification from Desire was waiting. Her profile had been viewed and someone wanted to start messaging her. She could either accept it, opening up the communication channel between them, or deny it and that person would no longer be able to view her profile again.

When she clicked on the notification, she was met with a profile photo of a blond-haired hunk of a man with a straight white smile that she was sure could get him anything he wanted from the ladies. His hair was cut short on the sides, longer on top, and brushed back like he had just run his fingers through it. He was clean-shaven, so there was nothing to hide his strong jawline and the sun-kissed skin of someone who spends a lot of time outside.

The photo—a selfie—showed him shirtless, standing on the edge of a rocky cliff, with the ocean as blue as his eyes in the background. He had the nice, muscular, tanned torso of someone who clearly lived an active lifestyle. She sighed as she gazed at the sexy man in the photo, very much liking what she saw.

Amarah read through his online profile. His name was Derick. He was twenty-eight years old and local, which was a plus. She didn't want to mess with long distances. She also liked that he was older. She had never been attracted to men her own age. His "About Me" section read, "Just a simple man, living life outdoors as much as possible." Her brows scrunched together as she couldn't help but think that seemed pretty generic and suspiciously vague.

She chided herself for being such a skeptic. Who knew? Maybe Derick was an actual human male who looked exactly like his picture and truly did love the outdoors. That would be wonderful. She would love to have someone to take with her whenever she, Travis, Sandra, and Liam went on their adventures.

They often went exploring, climbing, hiking, camping, and anything else you could think of that would bring them closer to nature. Since Liam traveled for work frequently, the company he owned had a private jet that they often used to travel to the vast beauties of the world.

Amarah admired the love her brother and sister-in-law shared. Travis and Sandra were high school sweethearts and married right after graduation. Sandra had supported his desire to serve in the Navy and stuck by his side through all the deployments and missions he went on, waiting with open arms and an understanding mindset that he might come back a little different than when he left.

But their love never wavered once. Thirteen years and three kids later, they were still best friends and lovers. Seeing them together, sharing a life filled with love and devotion made her heart ache. Amarah wanted a love like that, and she wasn't going to settle for less.

Despite the butterflies fluttering around in her stomach and her head screaming at her to stop, she clicked "accept" and a private message chat was created. She took a deep breath, sent a simple "Hello," then quickly closed the app and set her phone down before she could talk herself out of it. It was done. She released a nervous breath because if you rip it off like a Band-Aid, it's supposed to get easier. Or so she'd heard.

She welcomed the distraction from her overthinking and lost herself in her spreadsheets, only to be pulled back to reality ten minutes later when her phone dinged again. This time, it was a private message. Derick, or at least whoever was claiming to be Derick, had responded. With her terrible luck, it was probably some middle-aged man who still lived in his mom's basement.

Derick: Hello, how are you?

Amarah: I'm doing pretty good. How about yourself?

Derick: I woke up this morning so I can't complain. Haha! Are you actually the woman in your profile photo or are you just some forty year old man who lives in his mom's basement?

Amarah couldn't help but laugh, the sound bouncing off her office walls. He had a good sense of humor and that was a point in his favor.

Amarah: Hmm skeptical, are we? I could ask you the same thing.

Derick: Touché. Well, the only way to find out would be to meet in person. Are you free for dinner tonight?

Amarah: Wow! You don't like to waste any time, do you? Lol

Derick: Well, tomorrow is never guaranteed. The way I see it, we can do what would take us days of texting off and on in one sit-down meal. Good food, drinks, great conversation, what do you say?

Amarah: You've got a good point. How can I say no to that? Name the place and time. I'm good with any kind of food.

Derick: How about Saltgrass Steak House around 5:30?

Amarah: Sounds great.

Derick: Awesome! I'm really looking forward to meeting you, Amarah.

Amarah: Me too! Bye for now.

She closed her phone and set it aside, letting out a deep breath that she didn't realize she had been holding. *That went better than I thought it would,* she thought. Despite her reservations about online dating, she surprised herself when she realized she was actually looking forward to meeting this man. So far, Derick was passing the "Liam" test.

CHAPTER 2

As Amarah's workday progressed, she found herself growing both more nervous and excited about her date. She silently prayed that he somewhat resembled his photo. She didn't want to have to try to find a way out of an awkward situation. Though she was beyond blessed that there were people she could call if she needed an exit strategy.

Sandra would come up with some juicy emergency that would grant Amarah the opportunity to leave right then and there, no questions asked. Travis would storm into the place, most likely punch Derick in the face for even daring to breathe the same air as his little sister, and escort her safely home. Liam would... She stopped herself from that line of thought, even as butterflies erupted in her stomach as they did anytime that man crossed her mind.

Amarah signed out of her computer, turned off the lights, and closed her office door as she left for the day. She jumped in her gunmetal grey Chevy Tahoe and drove straight to the restaurant, thankful that she was already dressed up and didn't have to go home and change. She wore a blue form-fitting V-neck tank top that was tucked into her black pencil skirt, and her favorite pair of black stiletto heels that accentuated her legs and ass.

Before she knew it, she was pulling into the restaurant. After parking, she quickly checked her makeup in the visor mirror, grabbed her purse, and walked inside. Unsure if her date was here yet or not, she took a seat on one of the faux leather benches in the waiting area and pulled out her phone.

Amarah: I'm here.

Derick: Me too. I grabbed us a table in the bar area.

As she stood, Amarah straightened her clothes, took a calming breath, and tried to will the nervous butterflies in her stomach to calm down. He was punctual. That was a good sign, one that gained him another point in his favor. Rounding a corner, she turned into the bar area where booths lined the walls and high-top tables were scattered around the room.

There was a long L-shaped bar with multiple stools along it, and a mirrored wall behind the bar housed shelves that displayed an assortment of liquor bottles. The walls contained mounted animal skulls, horns, and antlers as well as an abundance of western photos and artwork. Turn of the century country music played softly throughout the restaurant.

As she peered around, her gaze stopped on a certain blond-haired blue-eyed man. Her jaw practically hit the floor because holy crap, was that man hot. But it didn't matter how beautiful he was. She needed to not lose her head. Hot guys were a dime a dozen. It would be his personality and his qualities she needed to discover before she let her hormones make any decisions. She did, however, send up a silent thank you that Derick was in fact real and resembled his photos perfectly.

Finding herself a little nervous, she smiled sheepishly and walked over to the table he was sitting at. As she approached, he stood and picked up a small bouquet of carnations, daisies, and roses. They were surrounded by greenery and varied in shades of yellow and orange, making the flowers look like a beautiful sunrise.

She gasped as she accepted the bouquet. "These are heavenly." Amarah beamed and took a whiff of the flowers, letting their sweet aroma relax her.

Gardening was a huge hobby of hers. She'd rather spend her evenings and weekends kneeling in the dirt, picking weeds, tending to her array of flowers, than at some club getting drunk and dancing with friends.

"They pale in comparison to you." His voice rolled over her, causing goosebumps to rise along her arms in excitement.

She reluctantly tore her gaze from the flowers to observe his appearance more closely. He wore a tight-fitting dark green T-shirt, a pair of nice dark blue jeans, and black and white Converse. *A Converse man. That gains him yet another point in my book.* She liked his height too. Not too tall, just shy of six feet but still taller than her when she had heels on. The green of his shirt played well with his tanned skin and his arms were defined with lean muscles. He looked mouthwatering.

"I'm Derick," he said as his eyes scanned her. "Wow, you look…" He paused, searching for the right words and she found herself holding her breath in anticipation. "breathtaking." His deep voice was like honey, so smooth and sweet. Motioning a hand toward the chair that sat across from him, he spoke again. "Please, have a seat."

She pulled out her chair and sat, setting her purse in one of the other chairs and her flowers atop their table.

"Thank you. I'm Amarah. It's nice to meet you," she said with a smile.

Their server came by, greeted them, and took their drink and food orders.

"Tell me about yourself. What do you do for work?" Derick inquired.

"I'm a credit analyst. Numbers are like a second language to me," Amarah said nervously. She omitted where she worked, though. Call her guarded, but she had only just met the man, after all.

"And what does a beautiful and intelligent woman like yourself like to do for fun?" Derick asked with a dashing smile.

She could feel a blush heating her cheeks at his blatant compliment. "I love being outdoors; hiking, camping, climbing, things like that."

His eyes lit up in surprise as their server dropped off their beers before disappearing into the kitchen again. "So, you're a unicorn." Derick laughed, the sound melodic to her ears.

Amarah pinched her brows together in confusion. "A unicorn?"

Derick took a sip from his beer before he said, "Yeah, you know, someone who's the complete package of what you want in a partner. A perfect person that only exists on the pages of a story."

"Oh, that makes sense." She laughed in understanding, taking a drink from her own beer, needing something to do with her hands so she didn't appear as nervous as she felt.

"It's a compliment, trust me." He winked, sending the butterflies in Amarah's stomach soaring erratically.

"What do you do for work?" she asked.

"I work in construction for a company that flips houses."

"That sounds fun. Do you like it?"

"Yeah. I enjoy working with my hands and the pay is great, so no complaints here." He laughed.

"What are you usually up to when you are not working?"

"I'm always outdoors doing something. Do you snowboard?"

"As much as I can!" She couldn't contain the smile that touched her eyes. "My friends and I usually buy the "ultimate all resort" passes each season and try to hit a new mountain a few times a month."

"I do the same thing. I would love to take you along with me, see if you can keep up," he teased as their server delivered their food.

"I'm pretty competitive and know my way down a mountain. I might hold you to that." She cut into her juicy pink steak, the knife slicing through it like butter.

Amarah liked how he took charge of the conversation and listened to her answers as if he genuinely cared about what she had to say. It was a breath of relief from other guys she'd dated. They continued picking each other's brains about their favorite places to go, places they wanted to visit, and favorite hiking spots.

"Let me ask you something," she said, wanting to get some of the focus off her for a moment.

"Sure," he answered. "Go ahead."

"Can you tell me something about you that isn't in your profile? Tell me something meaningful about who you are." She started the question playfully but by the end, the mood had become more serious.

Derick stared at her as the silence stretched between them. Finally, he nodded. "Very well," he said. "I served in the US Army, two combat tours. I don't like to talk about it though." His eyes shifted to a sterling silver ring he wore on his right ring finger.

Amarah followed his gaze. She wasn't able to see the finer details, but she saw an eagle with stretched wings behind a shield with a star on it. There was writing around the edge, but she couldn't make out what it said.

"Does that tell you what you want to know?" he asked. His eyes appeared haunted by something.

She touched his hand gently. "It does," she said in earnest. "My brother served." *And Liam.* She pushed the thought of Liam away and focused on Derick. "Thank you," she continued, still touching his hand.

He smiled and his eyes softened. Just then, he looked up as the waiter arrived to drop off the bill. She started to reach for her wallet, but he stopped her.

"I was the one who asked you out. I can't allow you to pay. Besides, my mother would beat me if I did." He grinned.

She laughed. "Thank you."

After paying, he escorted her to her SUV. They stood around, talking for a little while longer before Amarah checked the time and winced. Hours had passed by like minutes. That was another good sign. She truly found herself enjoying his company and conversation.

"Unfortunately, it's getting late." She was surprised to hear some regret in her voice.

She had been hesitant about this online dating thing from the beginning, having it in her mind that it was going to implode on her horribly but to her surprise, it was the opposite.

"Yeah, I can't believe how fast this evening went by. I enjoyed your company, Amarah." He opened her car door, smiling at her.

Chivalry had just gained him another point. "I enjoyed your company as well, Derick."

"I like the sound of my name on those lips of yours." He closed the little distance there was between them, cupped her chin, and kissed her.

She closed her eyes and leaned into him. His lips were full and strong, yet surprisingly soft at the same time. He didn't try to take the kiss deeper. He just held his lips against hers, luxuriating in the feel of hers pressed against his. It was just a simple kiss that surprisingly still had her stomach doing somersaults and heat rising in her core. After a moment, he pulled back.

"Wow," Derick said softly.

"Wow," she agreed, her voice barely above a whisper.

"I'd really like to see you again."

"I'd like that too."

"I'll call you." He handed her his iPhone.

Despite her shaky fingers, she put in her number. Amarah didn't bother trying to keep the grin off her face as she climbed in. With a quick wave, Derick shut the door. Curiosity won out, wondering what kind of vehicle he drove. Her vision followed as he made his way through the parking lot, weaving through the cars before climbing into a newer, deep red Dodge Ram.

He was a truck man and that was yet another point in his favor as far as she was concerned. In all her dating life, she would rank this as one of her best first dates. And she'd had a lot of those. Second and third dates, however? That was a whole other story. All she could do was hope that, if there were more with Derick, each one would only get better from here on out.

CHAPTER 3

Derick and Amarah texted off and on over the course of the next week. They met up for a quick lunch date one day and dinner one evening. She found that both dates were just as amazing as the first—great conversation followed by a steamy kiss when it was time to say goodbye. A kiss that he never tried to push further. To say it was a breath of relief would have been an understatement.

This weekend would be their fourth date. Amarah felt a growing sense of anticipation as the time to meet approached. In their previous conversations, they found that they both loved horror movies, so they decided to go see one together. Her pulse quickened at the sight of the hunk standing before her as she made her way to Derick, who waited in front of the ticket booth.

He wore a dark purple Polo shirt that clung to his lean muscled torso in all the right ways and was tucked into a pair of form-fitting blue jeans. His signature Converse shoes completed his outfit. It was a simple configuration, but the way it hugged his fit body had her imagination trying to picture what he looked like without those clothes on. And with his active lifestyle and his profile picture on Desire, she already knew she'd love his body. She could feel heat painting her cheeks at the inappropriate thought.

He smiled brightly when he saw her, pulled her into a tight hug, and kissed her cheek sweetly. His sexy smile instantly awakened the butterflies that swarmed in her stomach. Pulling back slightly, she watched as his gaze slid down her body, taking in her simple blue sundress that exposed her long, tanned legs and a pair of black ballet flats. His eyes slowly worked their way back up, hesitating briefly at the hint of exposed cleavage the dress teased before his eyes met hers again.

"Wow, I don't think I'll ever get used to how beautiful you are." His confession stole the very breath from her lungs. "Though, wearing a dress like that will have every man's gaze on you."

That statement struck her as a bit odd. Did he not like it? By the heated look in his eyes, she believed he loved the dress. Maybe he just didn't want other men looking. She decided to shrug it off. She could control men's eyes about as much as she could control the weather.

"Thank you." Amarah blushed. "You're not so bad yourself," she said as she entered the theater through the door he held open for her.

After getting their tickets, popcorn, and drinks, they made their way to the auditorium. They agreed that the only place worth sitting for maximum movie enjoyment was directly in the middle of the furthest row back. Since the movie they were seeing had been out for almost two weeks already, they had the whole place to themselves, except for one other couple who sat down in the front row.

"If you get too scared, you can sit on my lap. I'll protect you," Derick teased as they started to settle into their seats.

"Ditto!" she threw back at him with an arched eyebrow.

"Ouch!" he mouthed dramatically and clutched a hand to his heart. She just rolled her eyes and laughed as they arranged their drinks and popcorn and got comfortable.

"This will tell me a lot about you, so answer wisely." She shifted toward him with a serious face. "What's your favorite scary movie?" she asked, unable to stop the grin that pulled at her full lips.

"I see what you did there," Derick said with what appeared to be both surprise and pride in his voice after catching the iconic quote. "That's such a hard question, because you have different genres in horror. You've got slashers, suspense, supernatural, paranormal, and many more with each one bringing its own twist to horror. But if I had to choose one..." He paused for a moment as he thought about it. "I would have to say *Cape Fear*."

"Oh, good choice. That's more of a thriller, but since you're cute, I'll let it slide." She gave him a sensual grin.

"What's yours?" he asked with an eyebrow raised in question.

"Easy. *Halloween*." Amarah smiled at him. "I've watched it so many times in my life, I could watch it blindfolded and be able to picture the entire movie in my head."

"A Myers girl. I like it," he said with a wink that sent the butterflies in her stomach into overdrive.

As the lights dimmed and the previews started, he would lean over occasionally and tell her which ones looked good and which ones he wanted to take her to see. Making plans for future dates was always a good sign. It had her smiling to herself.

During one of the movie's particularly intense sequences, Amarah glanced over at Derick and found him hunched over his popcorn bucket, eyes glued to the screen while shoveling handfuls into his mouth. Clearly, he was deep into the movie. All she could do was shake her head and laugh to herself. Once it was over, they gathered up all their stuff and made their way out of the theater, throwing away their trash.

"How did you like the movie?" he asked as he escorted her to her car, his fingers laced through hers.

"It was good. A few unpredictable jump scares got me. What did you think of it?" she asked as they reached her vehicle.

"I thought it was great. I couldn't take my eyes off the screen." He laughed lightly.

"I noticed." Amarah chuckled.

When it came time to say goodbye, Derick stepped closer and pressed his lips to hers. She leaned into it and wrapped her arms around his neck. She liked the fact that she was getting more comfortable with him. He nibbled her bottom lip, and she subconsciously let out a small moan. Derick responded by pressing her against her vehicle, his body molding to hers.

His boldness took her breath away. He felt strong and masculine, and she felt her femininity respond. Her heart hammered as his tongue slid along her lips, demanding entrance. She surrendered and entangled her tongue with his.

His arms were wrapped around her waist and his hands caressed the small of her back. He slid his right hand down, spread his fingers wide, and slowly grabbed a handful of her ass through the light fabric of her dress. Amarah gasped and her eyes popped open in surprise.

Derick must've felt her tense beneath him because he stopped and pulled back. "I'm so sorry. It's just... You're so damned sexy and I got carried away in the moment."

"No, it's ok. You just surprised me, that's all. It felt... nice." She hesitated before continuing, "There's one thing I need to tell you though."

Amarah was reluctant because she knew from experience that this was the moment that sent most men running away from her as fast as they could go. The thought of Derick leaving had an uneasy feeling sitting heavy in the pit of her stomach. The feeling both surprised and scared her. She was hesitant from the start with the whole online dating thing, but the past week had been some of the happiest days she'd had in a long time. Each day she felt herself falling a bit more for him, so the thought of him not accepting her confession and leaving had fear trying to tarnish her good mood.

"You're a wanted woman and on the lam? No wait, you're a spy and on a mission right now? No, no, wait... You're not actually a man, are you?" He scrunched his face in a teasing manner.

"No! Nothing like that." She laughed and then went on more seriously, "It's just that I'm not comfortable doing anything... physical at the moment." She rushed on. "Hugs and kisses are fine. Welcomed, in fact. I'm even ok with the occasional roaming hand, but nothing further than that. Just until I get more comfortable with you. Is that something you can live with for a little while?"

Derick released his hold on her and took a small step back as a look of shock crossed his chiseled features. She watched with bated breath as his blue gaze skimmed over her angular features, dipped down her front, and back up. An unspoken emotion flashed through his vision.

"Are you a virgin?" His head cocked to the side with genuine curiosity.

"Yes." Amarah wrung her hands together nervously before adding, "Is that a deal breaker for you?"

Derick cupped her chin gently in his strong calloused hand, which surprisingly was still comforting, and tilted her face up a bit, forcing her eyes to meet his.

"Of course not." A grin spread wide across his full lips. "The last thing I want is for you to feel pressured into doing something you don't want to do. You set the pace and I'll gladly follow."

That sounded familiar. She had heard other men say the same words before only to find that they had no intention of going at "her pace." A part of her remained wary, but she truly hoped that Derick was going to be different from the other men she had dated.

"That means a lot, Derick. Thank you," she said, gazing into the sea in his eyes and forcing a smile despite her wariness. She knew that only time would tell if he truly meant what he said or not.

Amarah leaned back in to continue their kiss and Derick wrapped one hand around her waist, replaced the other on her ass, and pressed his fingers into the supple flesh he found there. With their mouths and bodies pressed together, they stayed like that for a bit, enjoying the connection and sparks that flew between them, only stopping when they both needed to come up for air. It was with reluctance that they finally bid each other good night.

CHAPTER 4

The next day, Amarah woke up in a rather good mood. She had a big smile on her face as she stretched in bed before she rolled over and grabbed her phone off the dark wood nightstand. The time on her screen showed that it was just after 10 a.m. She had to be at her brother and sister-in-law's house by noon for their biweekly family cookout.

Her eyes caught on the text notification and butterflies fluttered as she read it.

Derick: Good morning, beautiful!

Amarah: Good morning to you, handsome.

Derick: Do you get to relax at home today?

Amarah: Not quite. I have a cookout with my family at my brother's house. What about you? Any plans today?

Derick: I have to work, unfortunately.

Amarah: Well, I hope your day goes by quickly.

Derick: Have fun with the family.

Amarah: I always do. Miss you!

Derick: Miss you more!

She loved good morning texts, and even more so when the man texted first. It showed that they were thinking of you when they woke up and the thought made her swoon. She threw the covers off, made her bed, and walked to her bathroom with a little pep in her step. She hummed to herself as she brushed her golden hair out and braided it back into a single French braid. The summers in Oklahoma were brutal and she didn't want the humidity making her hair stick to her skin.

After brushing her teeth, she started on her makeup. She never wore a lot—just eye makeup and maybe some lip gloss or lipstick if it were a special occasion. Her mother always told her that natural beauty was the best and it helped instill a bold confidence in her to be comfortable and happy in her own skin.

Amarah threw on a light blue tank top and a pair of jean shorts that stopped mid-thigh, showing off a good amount of her legs. She checked the time on her phone again and smiled as she slipped her feet into her favorite pair of black Converse, grabbed her purse and keys, and left her house, making sure to lock the door behind her.

She rolled both windows down in her Tahoe and cranked the radio up as she drove the twenty minutes to her brother's house, singing loudly. Travis and Sandra lived in a quiet suburb on the outskirts of the city. They wanted a quieter life when Travis got out of the military, so they bought a house and moved back home to Oklahoma. Just about every other Saturday, for the last two years or so, they've had cookouts there, rain or shine. It was a wonderful way for everyone to visit and stay close to each other.

As she pulled into the neighborhood, she saw kids playing in the yards—some jumping on trampolines, some running through sprinklers, and others playing with chalk or riding bikes. The streets were lined with beautiful, large, single and two-story homes, all with a mixture of wood, brick, or rock exteriors.

The houses all sat on well-manicured one-acre plots, so they weren't on top of their neighbors. She wanted to live in this neighborhood one day. There was a prestigious school nearby that had a waiting list unless you lived in the neighborhood. Whenever she finally got married and had kids, this was her dream.

She pulled into the long, paved driveway of a single-story rock home with an attached three-car garage. A large garden lined the front of the home that was filled with different shrubs and a variety of bright, colorful flowers that she helped Sandra plant when they first moved in. She parked behind her parent's vehicle and walked inside.

"Knock, knock!" Amarah shouted through the home.

The sounds of sportscasters discussing replays of an old game flowed from the mounted flatscreen in the living room, filling the open concept house. She found no one inside as she made her way across the hardwood floors through to the back wall of floor-to-ceiling glass windows that flooded the space with natural light. The French doors were open to the covered patio and a smile crossed her lips when the sounds of conversation and kids laughing reached her ears.

"Aunt Amarah!" Three children screamed in unison as she turned her head and saw her two nieces, each with long fiery hair, and her nephew, a small blond-haired boy, climbing off the trampoline and rushing toward her. They threw their arms around her, nearly tackling her in a tight hug.

"Hey, kiddos!" she greeted as she hugged them back.

They let go and took off back toward the playground that sat next to the trampoline, giggling the entire way. Amarah walked over to where her brother and father stood, each with a beer in their hands as Travis manned the grill sporting the apron that she got him for Christmas a few years back that said, *my wife loves my meat.*

Travis got most of the height in the family. Although Amarah was tall for a woman, standing at five-foot-seven, Travis had reached six feet by the time he hit junior high. He had broad shoulders and was packed with muscles. They shared the same deep blue eyes and blond hair, though his was shorter than hers, the summer breeze causing it to brush the tops of his shoulders.

"Hey, sis," Travis said as he pulled her into a single-armed hug.

"What's up, Trav?" She smiled then turned to her dad.

"Hey, sweetie," Oscar said as he pulled his daughter into a hug and kissed the top of her head.

Her father was just as tall as Travis, but he was leaner and had rocked the bald look since his early thirties. He kept his face clean-shaven, and his deep blue eyes were framed with laugh lines.

"Hey, Dad." She smiled lovingly at him.

Not every kid got the blessing of growing up in a household with both parental figures not only present but actively involved in their kids' lives. Not to mention that both parental figures had a healthy and loving relationship with each other. Even now, her parents could barely keep their hands to themselves. It was as if they were still teenagers in the early stages of dating. To her, family was everything, and she counted her blessings with the family she was born into and each new addition that joined later in life.

There was a sitting area on the other side of the covered patio that held a large sectional sofa and an outdoor fireplace. Her mother and Sandra were sitting there relaxing as they watched the kids play in the backyard.

Sandra smiled and held up a wine cooler for Amarah, raising her eyebrows mischievously. She had her long, fiery hair pulled up into a messy bun, allowing her slim face and cheekbones that were peppered with freckles to be unobstructed. By looking at her, you would never know her body ever bore children, let alone three. She prided herself on working out and staying active.

Amarah joined the ladies on the sofa, greeting them as she graciously accepted the chilled wine cooler from her sister-in-law. Perfect weather, clear blue skies, surrounded by laughter and family, great food and drinks, she cherished days like these.

Amarah got lost in conversation, only to be pulled out of it when the sounds of a familiar voice reached her ears. She shifted her eyes over her mother's shoulder, and her heart practically skipped a beat as Liam Godrik strode through the back door. He embraced Travis, each man slapping the back of the other, and then shook her father's hand before accepting a beer.

Liam—her brother's best friend, her childhood crush. The man she had dreamed would father her unborn children one day, much to her dismay, was the same man who would never love her the way she wanted him to. Their relationship had never pushed past the boundaries of friendship, no matter how desperately she wished they would shift to something more intimate.

Because her brain likes to torment her, she couldn't stop her eyes from traveling down the god of a man's frame. Even in simple everyday clothing, he looked devilishly wicked. The plain black T-shirt he wore clung to him, temptingly forming around all his muscles. His blue jeans were tight around his thick, long legs and the cuffs were pulled over a pair of brown square-toed boots. The shaded tattoos that painted both arms were on full display, and she instantly felt her core clench with need.

She cursed inwardly to herself. Her body always reacted to him that way, coming alive whenever she sensed him close by, no matter how many times she scolded and preached to herself that he would never look at her or want her the way she wished he would.

As if sensing her gaze, Liam's green eyes crossed the space and locked onto hers. A grin pulled at one side of his neatly trimmed black beard as he raised his beer slightly to her, tipped his head in a silent greeting, and took a sip before returning to his conversation with her dad and brother.

Once the burgers and hot dogs were done on the grill, everyone filed inside as the women prepped the toppings and side dishes. Sandra fixed plates for the kids first and got them situated at the table before everyone else made their plates and joined the whitewashed wooden family table that was large enough to seat fifteen people comfortably.

Out of all the places, Liam always chose to sit next to Amarah. She was positive he did it to get a rise out of her. He'd told her, on more than one occasion, that he loved messing with her and getting on her last nerve. That it gave his life meaning to be a nuisance in hers. It was a game the two always played anytime they were around each other.

"So, Cupcake, what's new since the last time we talked?" Liam asked as he took a bite of his burger. His deep voice washed through her like expensive, smooth whisky.

"Nothing much, just work." She shrugged casually.

Amarah deliberately left out the fact that she had started dating someone. Maybe she was superstitious, but she didn't want to jinx anything by bragging about her new relationship, especially to Sandra, even though they were as close as blood sisters. Keeping her in the dark was difficult, but Amarah wanted to make sure the budding relationship was rock solid first.

She knew that when Travis eventually found out, his protectiveness would kick in and he would want to know every little detail about Derick. She pursed her lips in thought. If she brought Derick around, how would Liam react? How did she *want* Liam to react? This was the real issue weighing on her mind.

For a moment, she envisioned Liam overcome with jealousy and suddenly realizing that he had wanted her all along. Her pulse quickened at the thought of Liam confessing his love and desire for her, subconsciously crossing her legs as heat rose deep within. She quickly shook the feeling away. Liam didn't think of her like that. He was protective of her in the same way as her older brother was. Hell, the man could be *more* protective than Travis sometimes.

"Something's different," Liam said, pulling her from her thoughts as his bright green eyes raked over her pointed features. "You seem," he paused, observing her, "more happy than usual."

She would be shocked if he were an average man, but nothing about Liam was average. Especially since he and Travis joined the Navy and became SEALs, his eyes were like a hawk and his mind was sharp when it came to observation. Which, in his former line of work, would have been drilled into him from rigorous training. Traits like that don't just go away.

He flashed her a breathtaking smile. "It's because I'm here, isn't it?"

Amarah shifted in her seat, squeezing her crossed legs together even tighter to try and alleviate the ache pulsing between them. His gaze dropped, tracking the movement, and his grin turned wicked as he slowly reached his large hand over and placed it atop her bare thigh.

"Stop that!" Amarah shouted no louder than a whisper as she smacked his hand away, her cheeks almost as red as Sandra's hair. He was always saying and doing things like that with her. She knew he did it just to get under her skin.

"Don't pretend you don't like it." He chuckled as he removed his hand. Liam leaned in closer, and Amarah froze, holding her breath. "I can spot a lie from a mile away," he said low enough for only her to hear, the sound sending a delicious shiver to roll down her spine.

She quietly cleared her throat, hoping her voice wouldn't betray her emotions. "Nothing's different. I'm the same old me." She averted her eyes and took another bite of her food, desperately wanting to change the subject and get the attention off herself. "What's new with you?"

His eyes narrowed ever so slightly, but then his face was schooled into a calm, carefree demeanor. "Nothing new to report here, either," he said with a kind smile.

CHAPTER 5

Amarah managed to get through dinner without being interrogated or revealing the fact that she was seeing someone. It was another relaxing and successful day filled with the wonderful company of family.

"How's your summer going?" Amarah asked Sandra as she helped her and her mother clean up the kitchen after dinner.

"It's been great! The kids are keeping me busy since school ended, but luckily the weather's been nice enough to let them run wild outside and get all that energy out." Sandra laughed as she rinsed off a plate before handing it to Amarah to dry.

"They get it from their father. He always had too much energy as a child. I used to call him my Energizer Bunny." Charlette said as she wiped down the countertops. A smile spread across her face as she heard the kids' laughter flutter out from the playroom.

"Used to? Mom, he still has too much energy. The man can't sit still for longer than ten minutes." Amarah laughed while Sandra nodded her head and smiled.

"That's true. He makes me tired just watching him," Charlette joked. "How have you been, dear?"

"I've been good." She couldn't contain the smile that spread across her face at the reminder of her budding relationship with Derick.

"Well, be better and find yourself a man already. I need more grandbabies to spoil and love on," Charlette teased.

"Mom!" Amarah's cheeks started to color.

Charlette laughed. "What? I'm not getting any younger dear, and I want to play and keep up with my grandbabies while I'm still relatively young."

Sandra joined in on the teasing, giving her sister-in-law a playful nudge on the shoulder. "Think of how beautiful the babies would be if she and Liam made them."

Amarah's cheeks were on fire now.

"Oh, they would be absolutely gorgeous!" Charlette swooned, ignoring the look of embarrassment on her daughter's face.

"Ok, y'all need to stop. That's never going to happen," Amarah finally said, trying to squash this conversation before the boys overheard from their spot in the living room.

Liam, Travis, and Oscar sat on the sectional sofa in front of the mounted flat-screen, deep in conversation about whatever they were watching on Sports Center.

"Honey, with the way that man looks at you, I'm surprised nothing has happened between the two of y'all yet." Charlette's tone was gentle. Sandra nodded her head in agreement.

"He doesn't see me as anything but a little sister and y'all know it." Amarah said, unable to stop her gaze from flicking through the room and landing on the topic of discussion.

The way Liam was positioned on the couch gave her a great view of his side profile. She was mesmerized by the slight flex of his arm as he took a drink from the beer he held. Her body screamed at her, craving his full attention and to be touched by him in all her most private and sensitive areas.

His attention was on Oscar, who was deep in a rant about some athlete. Again, as if sensing her deep blue gaze, he shifted his vision, looking past her father and meeting her eyes. His bright green irises sparkled with mischief and amusement as he took in the flushed color of her cheeks. Amarah quickly averted her eyes, dropping them to the counter in front of her.

"Anyway," Amarah wanted to change the subject desperately, "are you and Dad excited about your cruise?" She turned her back to the living room so her will wouldn't break again, and she wouldn't be tempted and get caught gawking at a certain someone.

The women got lost in another conversation about what her parents should do while on their vacation. After they finished cleaning the kitchen, everyone said their goodbyes and left.

Three weeks went by, and they were nothing short of wonderful. Amarah found herself thinking about Derick all the time. She wanted to talk to him, see him, kiss him, and run her hands over that firm body of his. She realized she was starting to fall for him. She liked a lot of his qualities—how caring he could be, how chivalrous he was, how he listened to her.

He would always ask her about her day and seemed genuinely interested in her responses. They texted all the time and talked on the phone almost every night while lying in bed, sometimes until one of them fell asleep on the other. They had a lot more in common than she ever believed possible, especially their shared love of the outdoors.

He'd even talked about taking her away for a weekend to his family's cabin a few hours away in Arkansas. He talked about the many trails they would hike together and the large, clear blue lake there that was perfect for boating and swimming. Derick spoke of the beautiful night sky and the tapestry of stars visible away from the lights of civilization that they would enjoy while snuggling under a blanket next to the fire pit on the cabin's back porch.

To her surprise, she found herself considering it. The way this first month had gone, and how close they had gotten, she thought that would be a great place to take their relationship to the next level. More and more, she felt that she had finally found a man worthy of giving her virginity to and imagining the things he could do to her made her core heat in agreement.

She had noticed, however, a few instances where he came across as jealous or slightly controlling in a way. It was only a moment here or there thrown casually in a conversation about her clothing choices in public or people she hung out with outside of work, but she chalked it up to misreading things, or kinks in their new relationship that still needed to be worked out and fine-tuned. They weren't that big of a deal or frequent enough to be red flags yet, so she pushed it to the back of her mind.

Amarah thought more about inviting him to the family cookouts. That thought scared her a little though. Neither Amarah nor Liam had ever brought a date. It would be a pretty big deal.

She also had never introduced a boyfriend to her family before, not even while she was growing up, so finding herself wanting to with Derick was nerve-wracking, but exciting.

She would give it another month or so before deciding on introducing him, but things were looking promising. She tried hard to find something negative about him, but there just wasn't. Maybe time would reveal something, but fingers crossed he was one of the good ones.

As the workweek drew to a close on Friday afternoon, her anticipation grew with each passing hour until she could see Derick again. Her gaze repeatedly wandered to the time displayed in the corner of her computer screen where each minute that passed felt like an eternity. They planned to meet at a charming local bar to go dancing. She loved to dance, and when Derick told her he would take her, she was over the moon excited.

When work finally ended, Amarah rushed home to get ready. Her house was small, but she never really needed that much space. She stumbled upon the listing a few years ago of a newer one-bedroom, one-bathroom duplex in a nice, quiet neighborhood.

The previous renters had built a beautiful garden out front that contained a small rose bush along with a handful of tulips and hydrangeas. Over the years, Amarah continued tending to the garden, giving it lots of love and attention, causing the rose bush to triple in size and the flowers to produce breathtaking blossoms each year.

The living room was carpeted and big enough to fit a small grey sectional sofa, a low, dark wooden coffee table that housed a beautiful decorative glass plate she picked up a few years ago on a trip she took to Mexico, and a small entertainment center.

The entertainment center was framed by tall bookshelves made of the same dark wood on each end and was filled with a variety of books and souvenirs from her travels. The kitchen was open to the living room, separated by a large island that housed three dark wooden barstools and was tiled with ceramic that looked like dark hardwood floors.

A small T-shaped hallway off the right side between the kitchen and living room led to the rest of the home. Straight ahead was her bathroom, to the left was her cozy bedroom, and to the right was her small laundry room.

Making her way to her bedroom, she changed out of her work attire and put on a billowing purple tank top that hung low to show off just the right amount of cleavage and slipped on her favorite pair of Wrangler jeans. She knew those jeans hugged her ass so good it should be illegal. She lightly touched up her hair and makeup, allowing the golden strands to hang freely down her back, then lined her lips with a shimmery clear lip gloss. After pulling on a pair of brown square-toed boots, she was out the door again.

CHAPTER 6

Amarah's Uber dropped her off at the Open Range bar. She checked the time, realizing she was a little early as she walked through the front door. The sound of muffled music filled her ears and she made her way to a bouncer who looked as if he ran a prison gang. He was at least six-foot-five, and over 250 pounds of beefy muscle with colorful tattoos completely covering the exposed skin of his neck and arms. The permanent scowl on his meaty face made him look quite intimidating.

She dug out her ID and handed it to the brick wall of a man in front of her. He checked it, gave her a once over, and checked it again. She was used to people thinking she was younger than she truly was, so she waited patiently. He likely thought she was some high schooler trying to have a good night. Once he verified the ID wasn't fake, he smiled and handed it back to her with a nod of his head.

"You should smile more. It makes you look even more intimidating," she joked.

The man's large shoulders moved slightly as he chuckled lightly to himself and shook his bald head at her. She pushed her way through the double doors where the atmosphere enveloped her completely. Thankfully it was early enough that the bar wasn't crowded yet. It would be this way until the usual Friday night crowd came spilling in around 10 p.m.

Being a bar in Oklahoma, it was heavily decorated in Western adornments. A large horseshoe-shaped bar protruded off the left wall with at least twenty or more barstools placed around it. A stage was centered along the back wall that was set up for the live bands that performed each weekend.

On the right wall was another large bar, mirroring the other. A large wooden dance floor filled the middle of the space, giving plenty of room for people to dance around without it getting overly crowded. Ranch equipment and tools, horseshoes, saddles and bridals, and photos from the Old West decorated the walls.

Amarah walked over to the bar closest to her, pulled out a stool, and sat down. The bartender, who was in the middle of mixing a drink, glanced over at her as she sat.

With a smile on his face, he shouted, "I'll be right there, sweetheart!"

She smiled back and gave him a nod. Waiting didn't bother her. She took that time to peer around and people-watch. A group of friends took shots together, people swung and spun partners around the dance floor, and others sat at tables scattered around, casually drinking and chatting.

"What can I get you, hun?" the bartender said, pulling her from her thoughts as she turned back to face him.

"I'll have a margarita, please."

"Classic or flavored?"

"Classic."

"You got it, hun," the bartender responded, never once letting his smile falter.

"Can I have it with sugar on the rim instead of salt please?"

"Sure can!" He beamed as he turned to start on her drink. He handed it to her a few moments later. "Do you want to start a tab?"

"No, it's ok." She passed him a ten-dollar bill. "Keep the change," she said with a smile. He tipped his hat, thanking her, and moved away to check on his other customers.

Amarah closed her eyes as she took the first sip of her cold margarita, letting the alcohol touch her soul. It had been a long day at work, and she was glad to be out of there.

"Hey there, Cupcake."

A chill ran down her body straight to her sex. She knew that deep, sultry voice anywhere. Her eyes popped open to see that Liam now occupied the barstool next to her.

"Liam." Her heart rate spiked. She grew annoyed at the way her body reacted to him. *Why did he have to be so damned attractive?*

Almost against her will, her eyes traveled over his tall frame. He must've just gotten off work, because he looked sinfully delicious dressed in a dark grey business suit tailored perfectly to fit his tall, muscular body. His black hair was short on top and cut into a medium fade on the sides. His beard was trimmed to an artful black scruff that made you want to feel it against your skin. She imagined how it would feel against her inner thighs, then angrily shook her head to clear those thoughts and glared at him.

His green eyes twinkled with amusement as he gazed at her. It always amazed her how professional he looked. You'd never know the man was covered in tattoos down both arms and across his chest and back. She hated how perfect he looked all the time. She would pay good money to see him look disheveled. Just once.

"What are you up to, sitting here all alone?" Liam asked as he glanced around, as if checking to make sure he didn't overlook her companion.

"What? I can't come out for a drink by myself after a long day at work?" she asked with a raised brow, still casually sipping from her drink.

"Well, you can, but it's not exactly safe. Especially for a small woman like yourself," he said half-laughing.

She pinned him with a look, knowing he only said that to get under her skin. It always rattled her when people thought she couldn't take care of herself. Both her brother and Liam had shown her a few fighting techniques over the years, in case she ever needed them for self-defense. She wasn't completely helpless, nor that small, but next to this tower of a man, most people would look small.

"I'm going to ignore that last statement." Amarah rolled her eyes and took another sip from her margarita. "I happen to be meeting someone here."

"Who's the poor bastard?"

"My private life is none of your concern. And what makes you think I'm meeting a guy? I could be meeting Sandra or other friends of mine for a girl's night."

Liam raised a thick dark eyebrow at her before he slowly ran his gaze down her body and back up, pausing briefly at her exposed cleavage and finally meeting her gaze. "Because your tits are on display, which means you are trying to impress a man. Either you're meeting one here for a date, or while out on your 'girl's night' you plan to snare a poor unsuspecting victim and take him home."

She rolled her eyes again, purposefully ignoring the fact that not only did Liam look at her breasts, but he openly talked about them. "You know me better than that."

"Ok, ok, fine, you don't have to twist my arm. I'll grace you with my company until they show up." He raised one hand to get the bartender's attention. "A whisky and Coke." The bartender nodded and got to work.

Amarah just shook her head, knowing it was futile to argue with Liam. She could waste her breath telling him to leave, that she would be fine on her own, but the stubborn man never listened. Instead, she turned back forward on the wooden stool and sipped some more. After Liam was handed his drink, they talked for a while, catching up.

"Hey there, handsome. Do you want to buy me a drink?" A red-headed woman approached Liam with a sensual smile and started rubbing his bicep seductively.

This woman was drop-dead gorgeous. There was no way she wasn't a model with her tall, slim figure and curves that would make any man's—and quite a few women's—mouth water. She wore a tight black dress that barely covered her ass and showed off an unseemly amount of cleavage that had to cost quite a few grand. She acted as if Amarah wasn't even there. Typical.

"No, thanks. I'm in the middle of a conversation," he said while peeling the woman's well-manicured hand from his arm, not even sparing her a glance.

The woman's face contorted into a look of disgust. Clearly, she wasn't used to being turned down. She turned to Amarah, looked her up and down, rolled her eyes, and shifted her gaze back to Liam.

"Oh, I promise you, baby, I am way better company than this… thing over here," she purred while cutting her eyes at Amarah.

Still not turning to look at her, Liam took a sip of his drink and said, "I doubt that. Now get lost."

Oh, the look of anger she displayed. Her face was almost as red as her hair. Turning on her stiletto heel, she stalked off through the growing crowd of people to find her next unsuspecting victim. Amarah snickered as she watched her fade into the crowd.

"You don't have to keep me company. I wouldn't want to stand in the way of you having a fun night," she said as she took another drink.

She tried hard to ignore the pang of hurt and jealousy that stabbed her heart at the thought of Liam with a woman who wasn't her. She quickly forced the image that tried to conjure itself in her mind away.

"Nah, not my type," Liam said, shrugging his shoulders.

"Oh? And what is your type?"

With his elbows resting atop the bar and the crystal glass clutched in his hand, Liam turned his gaze toward her. Intensity burned in the greens of his irises as he studied her face before dropping lower, taking in her appearance again.

Amarah's lungs refused to breathe as she sat frozen on her stool, feeling the caress of his gaze as if it were a physical touch. Hope blossomed in her chest. A dangerous emotion that would only lead to trouble and heartbreak. But before he could answer, someone tapped on her shoulder. She twisted, and it took her far too long to snap back to reality to realize Derick was standing there.

A deep blush heated her cheeks, and she was thankful for the dim lighting of the bar so her embarrassment wasn't so obvious. For a moment, she'd forgotten all about the fact that she was there to meet up with Derick. That's just what Liam has always done to her, muddled her mind and made it feel as if they were the only people in the world when he spoke to her.

Amarah quickly greeted Derick with a smile, purposefully ignoring the feeling of eyes on her. Eyes that were burning a hole in her back. Eyes, she knew with every fiber of her being, belonged to her childhood crush.

"Are you going to introduce me to your... friend over here?" Derick said through gritted teeth and a smile that appeared forced.

"Oh, sorry. Derick, this is Liam. We grew up together. Liam, this is Derick." She motioned a hand between the two.

Nerves had her fiddling with her hands. That wasn't how she wanted to tell everyone about Derick. She still wanted to wait a while longer, just to make sure what she had with him was real and had the potential to grow into a deep, meaningful, intimate adult relationship. But there was no going back now. She could try to lie, tell him that Derick was just a friend from work, but with his observation skills, she knew Liam would see right through her deception.

Liam didn't speak, didn't stand to shake the man's hand. Hell, he barely even blinked. He just sat there, his drink clutched in his hand as he took a casual sip as if bored with the interaction. Numerous questions flew through her mind. Would Liam keep her secret? Would he tell Travis about the interaction tonight, that she was now involved with someone?

She really didn't want to wake up tomorrow to her brother grilling her about her love life. Not that there has ever been much to tell in the first place. However, Liam wasn't the kind of man to gossip. He was someone who'd take your secrets to the grave. Who knew just how many secrets related to national security were buried in the recesses of his mind? If she were lucky, he would keep this bit of information to himself until she came out and told everyone herself. A girl can only hope.

Derick turned to her, pulled her into his arms, and gave her a long kiss, sliding one hand down and giving her ass a full squeeze. It yanked her from her thoughts and took her by surprise. She wasn't against PDA, but she had only known the man for a short while. She wasn't comfortable acting like that around someone she knew just yet, but *especially* in front of Liam.

Once Derick pulled away, she watched as he glanced over at Liam. Was that disappointment that flashed through his eyes? Did he not enjoy the kiss? Did he have a problem with Liam? The last thing she needed was the men in her life not getting along. They didn't have to be best friends, but if they couldn't at least be cordial with one another, it would make things very awkward at gatherings and would most likely put a strain on their new relationship.

Amarah followed Derick's line of sight, observing Liam still sitting on the barstool, sipping from his whiskey and coke with the same bored expression across his stupidly handsome face. Before she could fill the awkward silence with nervous rambling, Derick took hold of her hand. His rough calluses were a contrast to her smooth, delicate skin.

"Come on, love. I have a fun night planned for us."

Amarah tried to say goodbye to Liam, but Derick pulled her away too fast, maneuvering his way through the growing crowd. He was moving rather quickly, forcing her to speedwalk just to keep up. She also noticed that his grip was unusually tight.

She tried to tell him, but either he ignored her or couldn't hear her over the music. She prayed for the latter. When she tried to pull her hand free, his grip only grew tighter. It was becoming painful, and she was forced to stifle a wince. This wasn't right. Why was he doing this?

CHAPTER 7

Once they got to a quiet spot in the back of the bar by the restrooms, Amarah finally managed to yank her hand free. Derick rounded on her with a look she'd never seen before. Pure fury poured from him in waves. Amarah stood there, looking at him while rubbing soothing circles over her hurt hand.

"What the hell, Derick? Did you not hear me telling you that you were hurting my hand?" she demanded, upset with him for the first time since meeting him.

"Why the fuck were you drinking with that man?" he seethed in a tone she'd never heard from him before. A tone so low and laced with danger that it caused the hairs on her arms and the back of her neck to rise.

She nearly stumbled backward, but she steeled her spine. In the entire time she'd known him, not once had she ever heard him curse or speak to her in such a manner. *Am I in The Twilight Zone or something?* She couldn't figure out why he was so mad or why he was acting this way.

"He saw me waiting for you and kept me company till you got there. Why? Is that a problem?"

This was not like him. There were a few instances in which he came across as jealous when she would go to lunch with work friends, some of whom happened to be guys. She never went alone with them, always with a group of people, but he still got upset. Other than those rare occasions, he was laid back and mellow. One of the qualities she liked so much about him.

"Yes. I saw the way he was looking at you. He has more than just friendship on his mind. I don't want you to ever see or talk to that man again," Derick demanded.

She was more confused than ever. Like hell if she was going to let a man tell her who she could talk to or hang out with. Within reason, of course.

"I told you, we grew up together. He's my brother's best friend. We've known each other since I was in grade school. There's never been anything romantic between us. He sees me as a little sister," Amarah stated.

She was not about to tell him that Liam had been her first crush growing up, but she didn't lie. She always knew deep down that Liam would never see her as anything more than a little sister. It had forced her to give up hope long ago that he may one day realize he loved her.

"And I'm sorry Derick, but you have no right to tell me who I can and can't be friends with."

He did not like that one bit. Derick closed the space between them in one big step before he leaned his head down to glare into her eyes. "Yes, I do, love. Being with me means you belong to me. I hoped that you would stop hanging out with other men after I mentioned I didn't like it but here you are. You've forced my hand, so I have to put my foot down. You *will* obey or there will be consequences." His tone was menacing.

"I forced your hand?" She repeated his words in disbelief. "Derick, I've never done anything remotely inappropriate with those men I work with. A group of us grabbed lunch a few times. It was completely platonic and innocent."

"I am the only man you're allowed to be with." Derick straightened and crossed his muscular arms across his chest.

The action stated there was no changing his mind on the subject, but Amarah wasn't about to submit to that.

"So, I can't have any friends?" Her brows furrowed together tightly with anger as her voice began to rise in frustration.

"Not male ones, no," he stated simply, like there was nothing wrong with his way of thinking.

She looked him dead into his eyes, trying to process what she'd just heard. To her horrification, she realized that Derick wasn't joking.

Was it all a lie? A front to get her to drop her guard and fall for him and now that she had, he was letting his true colors shine? Her survival instinct finally kicked in. She knew she needed to get out of this. Now.

"Unbelievable. Derick, that's ludicrous. I would never tell you that you couldn't have friends that were girls. That's where trust comes in."

"This isn't about me. This is about your wrongdoing and us needing to fix it. You'll never see him again."

"No," Amarah rebuked, hesitating briefly at the rage that flared in Derick's eyes. His jaw ticked as she continued. "He means too much to me. He's family."

"Does he mean more to you than I do?" he asked in a dangerously low voice.

Was he seriously going to make her choose? It wasn't even a struggle for her to make that decision. Yes, things with Derick were nothing short of wonderful and she liked a lot about him, but she would choose Liam. Every time. They had too much history; a past that meant the world to her.

"Yes," she said, her voice a bit shaky.

"Huh." Derick sighed, shaking his head in disappointment. "That was the wrong answer."

"Okay, I have no idea what happened to the sweet, caring guy I was talking to this whole time, but I'll not be a part of this. Whatever 'this' is," Amarah said, motioning between them with her hand. "I won't be controlled by anyone. Ever. If that's what you want, that's fine, but it won't be with me." She took a deep breath, mentally preparing herself to speak the next words she knew would hurt to say. "Lose my number, Derick. We're done here." Her voice cracked as devastation marred her features.

This is why she didn't date. Somehow, she always attracted the crazies. Amarah turned to walk away, but Derick gripped her bicep and yanked her back to his side. This time she was unable to hide her wince as his large hand constricted around her arm.

He slowly bent his head down till his lips brushed the shell of her ear. "You think you can get rid of me? That's cute. I told you that was the wrong answer. But don't worry, we'll correct your mistakes and things will go back to the way they were between us." He chuckled lightly, the sound sending her stomach churning.

When Amarah turned her head to look at Derick's face, he wore a smile that sent chills down her body. At that moment, she realized how completely nuts the man truly was. How had she not discovered that until now? This time, he let her yank her arm out of his grip.

She backed away slowly, holding his gaze as she warned, "Stay the hell away from me, you psychopath!"

She turned on her heel and walked back into the growing crowd of people. Amarah glanced back a few times, making sure he wasn't following her. Thankfully, he wasn't. Derick just stood there, not moving, watching her with that uneasy, creepy smile on his face. She made it back to the bar and looked back in his direction one last time, but he was gone. Her gaze frantically searched around, but he was nowhere to be found.

Ok, calm down, Amarah. You're fine. Deep breaths. You're in a public place, with people all around you. He won't try anything here. She prayed he left. Her head was spinning so fast, trying to comprehend exactly what happened back there. She needed some time to process everything fully and clearly, but she knew she wouldn't be able to do that until she got back home and calmed down. Amarah just wanted to get the hell out of there.

She could call an Uber, but that would mean she would need to leave the building alone and go out into the dimly lit parking lot to find her ride. Leaving the safety of the crowded bar would be beyond idiotic, so that option was a no-go. She thought for a moment longer as another idea struck her. She tried looking around for Liam to see if he was still there. She could get a ride home from him, knowing she'd be safe.

Amarah scanned the crowd and finally found him on her second pass. He was leaning against a post by the dance floor talking to a short, raven-haired girl. She could go over there and ask for a ride, but she didn't want to interrupt. Instead, she leaned against the bar and released a heavy sigh, feeling the need for a stiff drink after what had just transpired. Without hesitation, she took out a ten-dollar bill and flagged down the bartender.

"How many tequila shots can I get with this?" she asked the man, trying hard to keep her hands from trembling.

He scrunched his thick, dark, bushy eyebrows together, his answer hesitant. "Five."

"Sounds good to me," Amarah said, sliding him the money.

He stood there for a second but didn't question her. He placed the shot glasses in front of her and filled them to the rim. She looked at them for a moment, knowing she'd regret this tomorrow, but right then she didn't care. She just needed something that would take the edge off—fast—and what better way than with straight shots?

Amarah drank the first one, scrunching up her face as the clear liquid burned a path down her throat. She let it settle deep in her chest before she took a few breaths, psyching herself up for the next one. She downed the second one in a swift motion. She groaned and shook her head, finding that one had more burn to it. She prepared herself for the third shot, then threw it back and set the empty glass next to the others.

A loud groan slipped past her lips, quickly drowned out by the music. Then, a welcoming warmth began to spread through her chest, already working to relax her frantic nerves. She was about to reach for another when a pair of hands grabbed the last two shots.

"Hey!" Amarah called out, scowling. "Those are mine!"

Liam looked down at her with one thick brow perched high upon his head and an amused smile tugging at one side of his full lips.

"What are you doing?" he asked flatly.

"Folding laundry," she said sarcastically, rolling her eyes. "What does it look like I'm doing, Liam?"

"Making a bad decision."

"Since when did you become my father?"

"When you thought it was a good idea to take five shots back-to-back." Liam threw back one of the shots, acting as if it were water, and then added, "Why are you doing that anyway? Trouble in paradise?"

"Again, my private life is none of your concern. Can I have that last one back, or do you plan on drinking that one too?" Amarah stood there with her arms crossed over her chest defiantly. Liam grinned at her and then swallowed the tequila. "You're an asshole, you know that?"

"Oh, come on. You're mad because you know I'm right. If you're by yourself again, which right now that's what it seems like," he said, looking around the bar, presumably searching for Derick, "then drinking erratically like this is only going to get you into trouble." Liam set the two empty shot glasses back on the bar with the others. He turned back towards her, but his vision dipped to her arm, and his voice turned serious. "What's that?"

CHAPTER 8

Amarah pulled her brows together in confusion as she followed Liam's gaze. Sure enough, there was a mark forming on her arm. Had Derick squeezed her that hard? Enough to leave a mark?

Shit, she thought as she tried to figure out how to explain it. If she told him the truth, Liam would murder Derick. Not in a figurative way, no, the kind of murder that would leave no evidence and no body. Only a missing person's cold case file for the rest of eternity.

"Some girl—who clearly had one too many—tripped in her heels and grabbed my arm to stop herself from falling to the floor," Amarah said, shrugging it off like it was no big deal.

She hated lying and she wasn't very good at it either. She especially hated lying to Liam, but this was her mess to clean up, not his.

"Now, stop changing the subject. I hate how you and my brother don't think I can handle myself. Just because I'm a woman doesn't mean I don't know how to fight or take care of myself if need be."

"Ok then, prove it," Liam said, shrugging casually.

"How exactly—" Before she could finish her sentence, he had lifted her by her hips and sat her down on a barstool next to them. "Liam, what are you doing?!"

He didn't answer her, instead maneuvering both of her arms behind her back and trapping her small hands in just one of his. He then proceeded to push her legs apart with his other hand and moved to stand right between them. His body leaned toward her, causing her to tilt back until her shoulders hit the edge of the bar. Amarah was speechless, in complete shock.

Holding her there, he looked at her. "I have you trapped. What are you going to do?"

She couldn't form words yet, still trying to wrap her head around how fast he got her where he wanted her, and so easily too, as if she weighed nothing to him.

"What... How... I..." She couldn't think, couldn't breathe, as if he stole all the air from her lungs.

"Come on, Cupcake. You said you could handle yourself," Liam's voice was teasing and low as he moved in closer, nearly causing her toes to curl from desire.

He lowered his head till the tip of his nose trailed across her skin, starting at the top of her cleavage and moving up over her collarbone and the side of her neck till he whispered in a husky voice in her ear, "I could take you on this barstool right now. Fuck you in front of all these people, and there wouldn't be a damn thing you could do to stop me."

He was right though. Especially after having a few drinks, there was no way she could fend off a full-grown man on top of her like this. Amarah couldn't admit that now, could she? He would never let her live it down.

From the moment Liam spread her legs, stepped between them, and pinned her down against the bar, she'd found it difficult to breathe. Not because of his weight on her, but because he was so close to her. So intimately close. She could smell the hint of alcohol on his breath and the woodsy scent of his body wash, feel the tingles and goosebumps everywhere his nose touched her bare skin, and—Lord have mercy— what he whispered in her ear had her body wet and ready for him.

She realized she would let him do it too, as scary as that sounded. Despite her better judgment, she'd let him fuck her in front of so many strangers if that's what he wanted. A part of her secretly wanted that too. Anything to get a taste of him, have a part of him. He had that much effect on her, but she had to force all that down. Liam would never look at her the way she wanted him to. She'd never see his eyes filled with lust and hunger for her.

She took a deep breath to steady her voice. "I don't know, probably head butt you, grab one of these beer bottles, break it upside your head, and kick you off of me?"

Pride blossomed in her chest at her quick and creative thinking. Something she had Travis and Liam to thank. They taught her how anything can be used as a weapon if wielded properly.

Still leaning against her, Liam spoke in an amused tone. "Hmm, using your surroundings as weapons. I like it. That could work if you didn't hurt yourself in the process with the head butt. Those can be pretty tricky to execute properly."

She had to get this man off of her before she said something she could never take back. Was it her imagination or had his breathing shifted too? All she could do was squirm underneath his frame. That caused Liam to fully push himself down on her, halting her completely.

That's when she felt it—the hard bulge now pressed against her lower stomach. *Oh, sweet heavens*, she thought. Her eyes frantically shot up to his, feeling her face heat, and he smiled knowingly. She was trapped in his gaze, his green eyes holding her hostage. Was there a hint of want in his eyes? No, she had to be making that up. Her hormones were messing with her, making her misinterpret things.

"You've proven your point. You can get off me now," Amarah finally found the courage to say, even if it came out a bit breathless.

After a brief pause, as if Liam wanted to make this moment last as long as he could, he chuckled and finally stood upright again, releasing her arms. She pushed him back and quickly jumped off the barstool.

"Stay here. I need to close my tab and then I'll take you home," he said as he flagged down the bartender so he could pay.

Being confined in such close quarters with him after what had just happened, that was the last thing Amarah needed. Without thinking and with his back toward her, she made a beeline for the exit.

CHAPTER 9

Amarah desperately needed some air, air that was not being occupied by Liam. She paced back and forth outside, fanning herself with her hand and allowing the night breeze to clear her mind. Images of Liam pressing her against the bar kept flashing through her mind, as well as the feeling of his erection against her stomach.

She only felt it for a few seconds, but Lord, her imagination was running wild with what it would look like if she had a full, unobstructed view. After a few minutes, she pulled out her phone and opened her Uber app. She was in the middle of arranging a ride home when a guy approached her.

"Hey, me and some friends are going back to my place to keep the party going. Do you want to come with?" he asked, pointing to a group of friends, both girls and guys, half of whom appeared drunker than a skunk. What they needed was a cold shower and sleep, not more alcohol.

"No thanks, it's been a long day. I'm going to call it a night." Amarah said, pointing to her phone.

"Oh, come on. A beautiful young woman like yourself needs to let loose and have some fun. I promise it'll be a blast."

Before she could refuse again, Liam came casually striding up. His suit jacket was rebuttoned and not a stitch of clothing was wrinkled or out of place. It further infuriated her with how collected he appeared all the time. She, on the other hand, was glad there was no mirror present. She was positive her face and neck bore a blush that had nothing to do with the alcohol she'd consumed.

"There you are, Cupcake. Sorry man, but she's with me." Liam kept his voice light, but Amarah saw the unspoken threat he held in his gaze. The stranger took one look at Liam, gave him a curt nod, and walked away. "Come on, let's get you home."

"No thanks, I'll pass. I'm calling an Uber. And stop calling me that!" she said, completely avoiding eye contact.

Amarah couldn't look at him. Every time she tried, all she could picture was him on top of her, the feeling of his hard cock against her stomach still fresh in her mind. She could feel her cheeks heating again. *Stupid hormones!*

"Getting into a random car—intoxicated—with a stranger, and having them take you to your house? I'll never understand why people are so trusting." He finished with a heavy sigh and a disappointed shake of his head.

"What is it with you and safety?" Amarah questioned, throwing her hands up in frustration and finally looking up at him.

"Because in my line of work, I've seen a lot of evil in this world. You have no idea how truly dark the world we live in is. And if I seem overbearing or controlling or overprotective to you by pointing it out when I see it, then so be it. But I'll keep you and everyone I care about from harm every chance I can."

Sighing internally, she knew he was right. Her brother was the exact same way. She couldn't even begin to imagine the amount of darkness they'd borne witness to from being a Navy SEAL. So, she didn't push him.

"Ok," was all Amarah said, and she started walking toward the parking lot. Liam fell into step beside her. When they reached his black Chevy truck, he opened the door for her, and she climbed in.

The ride home was pretty quiet. Not the awkward type Amarah feared it would be, but a comfortable silence. She made it a point to look out her window the whole time though, avoiding eye contact at all costs. Before she knew it, they were pulling up to her house.

Liam shut the engine off and walked her to her front door. She'd never admit this out loud, but she was glad she didn't take those last two shots. They were hitting her, and she had to concentrate extra hard as she dug out her keys and examined them closely. After finally finding her house key, she tried to put it into the lock, but her swaying vision caused her to miss.

A large, warm hand wrapped around hers, guided the key into the lock, turned it, and then the contact was gone. Before she opened the door, she turned to look at him.

"Thank you."

She didn't elaborate. She knew Liam would grasp the full meaning of her words. *Thank you for always keeping me safe.*

He just smiled and said, "Always. Good night, Cupcake."

Liam shocked her for the second time that night by placing a soft kiss on her forehead. Amarah froze in place. Even though he kissed her forehead, it still sent sparks straight to her toes and back up again, causing arousal to flood her body. She opened her mouth to invite him in, but nothing came out.

Even with liquid courage flowing through her body, Amarah was still too scared to ask or make a move. With a sigh, she opened the door, walked in, and shut it. A smile tugged her lips up because she knew Liam hadn't left yet. He was still standing on her porch, and he would stay there until he heard the locks on her door click into place. One of the many, many reasons she loved the man.

After making sure she was secure for the night, Amarah made her way to her bathroom to get cleaned up. The very cold shower she suffered through didn't help as it usually did. She was still all worked up, more so now that the alcohol coursing through her was an added factor.

After brushing her teeth and braiding her hair back, she checked her phone before crawling into bed. There was a text from Derick. *Shit.* With what happened with Liam, she'd forgotten all about him.

> **Derick:** I'm sorry you had to see me that way. I hated putting my hands on you. Please meet me for coffee. I'll prove that you chose wrong. We'll work this out.

She didn't respond. She simply stared at it for what felt like hours. Amarah closed out of it without a response. Derick didn't deserve one, and even if he did, she didn't know what she would say. He made his intentions rather clear, and she wanted no part of that. She spoke her piece, and that was it. Anything more would be her repeating herself.

"Actually, I believe this further proves that I made the right choice," Amarah said out loud as if the shadows in her bedroom would respond. She didn't miss that he said he hated putting his hands on her but not that he was sorry. "Well, I hate to disappoint, but no way in hell, dude." She rolled her eyes as she plugged her phone into the charger, turned off her lamp, and snuggled into her comforter.

She gaped at her ceiling, wishing for sleep to overtake her but her mind wouldn't shut off. It kept reverting to her on that barstool, with Liam's body on top of hers, those unholy words he spoke to her on repeat. Beyond frustrated, she finally gave in to her needs.

Amarah opened the bottom drawer of her nightstand and pulled out her trusty friend. She'd made a pact with herself to wait for the right man before sex, and she'd made it twenty-two years so far. That didn't mean she couldn't play with herself. To hold herself over until that day finally arrived.

She pulled her nightgown up to her waist and slipped off her thong. She slipped her index finger through the rubber ring of her black finger vibrator and turned it on. She placed it between her parted legs, rubbing small, slow circles against her bundle of nerves. Her eyes fluttered closed as she pictured Liam's wicked words coming true, him taking her on that barstool.

Once her body reached a delicious hum, she applied more pressure to her swollen clit, rubbing faster circles against it, and used her other hand to massage one of her full breasts. She imagined Liam's large hands on them, squeezing them, rolling, and pinching her perky hard nipples. She wondered what his mouth would feel like—the heat of his breath against her sensitive flesh, the feel of his tongue across her hardened nipples.

Would he be delicate with her, keeping his movements slow and deliberate? Would he act like a predatory beast and ravish her? Amarah was no fool. She knew Liam had most likely been with a fair share of women over the years, so she knew he'd be experienced and knowledgeable in the art of pleasing his partner. The intensity of her imagination had an orgasm starting to build in the pit of her stomach.

Her illusions went wild as she pictured Liam's chiseled body looming over her as she sat naked and helpless beneath him atop the stool, her torso pressed back against the bar. She pictured him withdrawing his dick out of her tightened core to the tip and slowly thrusting it back in, burying himself deep inside of her center. The tightening in her stomach grew until she went over the edge and moaned his name as her body convulsed, her release coating her inner thighs.

Amarah's body felt like Jello after her finish rocked through her. With her eyes still closed, she lay there for a minute, only half-sated, until her breathing became normal again. She cleaned off and put her vibrator back in its drawer, slid her underwear back on, snuggled into her body pillow, and allowed herself to drift off to sleep with a smile on her face, still riding the high from her finish.

CHAPTER 10

The weekend was over too fast, and it was back to work for Amarah. She'd spent the last two days mourning the loss of her relationship with Derick. She cried… a lot, ate her weight in ice cream and greasy takeout, and watched sappy romance movies until there wasn't a tear left in her. She didn't know why it was hurting her so much. They'd only been dating for a month.

During that month, however, she'd devoted her entire heart to their relationship, making sure she was committed to the fullest. For Derick to reveal the ugly truth of his nature the way he did, it stung, no matter the length of their time together.

She'd developed strong feelings for the man, so much so that she'd considered giving her virginity to him. However, she was thankful that he did this early on before their lives got too intertwined. That would've caused a messy separation with more emotional damage.

Besides the text Friday night about wanting to meet up for coffee to talk, she hadn't heard anything else from Derick. She hoped that he'd get the hint, but that would be too easy, and unfortunately, she was never that lucky.

He also didn't strike her as the kind of person to give up easily. This could be a long and ugly road, but Amarah would remain strong and not waver.

No matter how sweet or caring he might appear to be, no matter how attractive he was, those things aren't worth the pain of being controlled like that. She knew what she wanted in a partner, and that damn sure wasn't it.

Being submissive is one thing. It's okay in the bedroom and some people get off on being told what they can and cannot do, but his version of control—his vision for his partner was more about possession over an object.

Amarah woke up to a text Monday morning that had her sighing heavily.

Derick: Love, you can't avoid me. I'm not going anywhere.

Oh Lord, this man was all sorts of crazy, she groaned inwardly, choosing to ignore him again. Surely, he'd get the hint… Right?

Amarah rolled out of bed, got ready, and padded across her bedroom to her closet. She sifted through her dresses, the hangers scraping against the metal rod with each pass. Two lines formed between her brows after not finding the pastel pink dress she was looking for.

She started a second look, to no avail. Amarah let out a frustrated breath as she exited her bedroom and entered her laundry room. She didn't remember wearing the dress recently, but she'd look anyway. Unfortunately, it was nowhere to be found.

She decided to push it from her mind and do a more thorough search later. She knew it was around there somewhere. Amarah quickly plucked another dress from a hanger, slipped into it, and left for work.

Tuesday rolled around and Amarah was in the break room alone eating her lunch while reading her current romance book. She was lost in a fantasy world, the words on the pages forming into a movie playing out all around her. As her phone began to ring, she was jolted back to reality. She bookmarked her current page with a frustrated sigh and set it aside on the table. When she picked up her phone, her stomach sank instantly.

It was him. Derick. She wasn't about to answer, but she wasn't about to decline it and confirm that she was actively avoiding him. She let it ring until it eventually sent her unwelcome caller to voicemail.

Once the call ended, she let out a breath she didn't realize she was holding. She dropped her shoulders and relaxed again as she went back to eating her lunch and continued where she left off in her book. A minute later, she got a voicemail notification. She took a deep breath, punched in her voicemail code, and listened to it.

"You can't avoid me forever. I'll find you and we'll talk. Now, whether that be on your terms or mine is up to you. I suggest you reach out."

What. The. Hell. Her food was suddenly in the back of her throat. Amarah ran to the bathroom and saw her lunch again in a less appealing manner. He had just threatened her. Surely, he wouldn't physically act on it, right? She remembered back to that night at the bar, how he hurt her hand and grabbed her arm so hard it left a mark. Evidently, he was comfortable putting his hands on a woman. This had to be a ploy to get her to cave and speak with him. Derick was proving to be more creative than she gave him credit for.

She left the stall, grabbed a paper towel, and dampened it in the sink before she began lightly dabbing it across her clammy forehead and the back of her neck. She stared aimlessly at her reflection as she considered all her options.

Should she call his bluff? Should she talk to him and stress that she wants out? Should she possibly threaten him in return or threaten to get the cops involved? She didn't want to play games with him, so she chose a different option. She chose to keep ignoring him.

Unfortunately, by the time Wednesday rolled around, Amarah was on edge, jumping at every sound she heard, thinking Derick had inevitably found her. She was constantly looking over her shoulder anytime she was in public and caught herself checking her phone multiple times a minute, waiting for some kind of message.

All day she checked, and every time she did, there was nothing. She didn't know whether to be relieved or worried. By the time bedtime arose, she'd convinced herself she wasn't going to hear from him. You'd be surprised what your brain will convince itself of when it's desperate enough.

She forced herself to take a deep breath as she crawled into bed for the night and snuggled into her covers. As Amarah was on the verge of sleep, her phone started ringing, the sound echoing through the deafening silence.

She gasped and practically jumped a foot off her bed, sending her hand to clutch at her chest as she tried to take deep breaths to calm her racing heart. With a shaky hand, she reached over and grabbed her phone that was vibrating against her nightstand.

Amarah nervously flipped it over and saw Derick's name on the caller ID. All the color drained from her face. Frozen in fear, all she could do was watch it, letting it ring and ring, the seconds passing by like minutes.

Once it stopped, she waited for the voicemail she knew would inevitably follow. A moment later, there it was, acting like a beacon of pure agony and doom. She took a deep breath, closed her eyes, and listened to it.

"I WARNED YOU, AMARAH! I'M DONE BEING NICE! YOU HAD MULTIPLE CHANCES TO REACH OUT BUT YOU CHOSE TO IGNORE ME TIME AND TIME AGAIN! I WILL FIND YOU AND YOU'LL BE FORCED TO TALK TO ME! YOU CHOSE WRONG AND NOW IT'S MY RESPONSIBILITY TO CORRECT YOUR MISTAKE AND FIX OUR RELATIONSHIP. I'M COMING FOR WHAT'S MINE... YOU!"

Derick was so loud and pissed off that he screamed the whole time, forcing Amarah to hold the phone away from her ear. The rage that came from him, the threats he stated, sent pure fear and adrenaline coursing through her bloodstream. *No, that's impossible. He doesn't know where I live or work. It's just empty threats.* She coached herself through slow, deep breaths.

She reminded herself that she'd been smart, always meeting wherever the date took place. She never allowed anyone to pick her up from her work or home. Her father made sure to drill that into her brain. She sent up a silent thank you to him that she listened and followed that rule.

Not wanting to take any chances though, she got up out of bed and made sure her doors were locked, clearing her house to make sure no one was hiding anywhere. On her way back to her bedroom, something caught her attention, drawing her eyes to a bookshelf that framed the left side of her entertainment center.

Amarah walked over and noticed a few of her books were out of order, only noticing the change because the colorful spines of a fantasy series were a shelf higher than where she originally had them. Or had they always been there? She groaned out loud in frustration, cursing Derick for adding extra stress in her life that she felt was starting to make her lose her mind.

Shaking her head and rolling her eyes, she was too tired to deal with anything. She reluctantly crawled back into bed.

Another rule she thanked her father for was to know how to shoot and to always have a gun around. He would always say, "Rather have it and not need it, than need it and not have it." She reached over, opened the top drawer of her nightstand, punched in the four-digit code to her small gun safe, and pulled out her pistol.

Amarah always kept it chambered and ready to go. She tucked it under the pillow next to her for easier access and tried to force herself to sleep. The knowledge that it was right there, in case she needed it, did help ease her worry. It was still a fight to shut her paranoia off and allow her brain to power down.

She got crap sleep that night, her brain never allowing her to fall into a full, deep sleep. Her mind wanted to remain alert, causing her to jump at every creaking sound her house made, making her think Derick had found her and was trying to get inside.

CHAPTER 11

Thursday came and went, and Amarah was on edge, even worse than before. She hardly got any work done, had no appetite, and her brain was overthinking everything. But no text, no call, no voicemail. Again, she didn't know whether to be thankful or worried about that. Did his threats hold promise, or were they just empty words to scare her into submission?

Amarah woke up feeling a little better on Friday. It had been more than twenty-four hours with no contact from Derick. She was hoping for another day of nothing. She told herself that she just had to make it through today and she could stay home all weekend and treat herself to some much-needed self-care.

Well, aside from going to the cookout at Travis and Sandra's house tomorrow. She knew, though, that without a shadow of a doubt, she'd be safe, and it would be suicide for Derick if he chose to confront her there. She found herself looking forward to it. What she wouldn't give to have a few hours of peace of mind and to not feel the need to fear for her safety.

Amarah coached herself to keep a positive attitude, that this would be over soon. She made it a habit that anytime she felt the need to check her phone, she'd pinch herself on the hand. She was not going to let this man rule her into living her life in fear. She got through all morning with no contact and no obsessive checking of the phone. She counted that as a win and treated herself and a few of her coworkers to lunch.

They all met up at a small diner by their office building. It was therapeutic in a way. She felt herself starting to come out of her shell again. She was laughing, joking, and having a good time. Her friends were a welcome distraction, and she'd truly forgotten all about Derick for just a little while.

It was a welcome relief. Once they all got back, she knew that she only had a few more hours until quitting time. She had some reports to work through that would easily fill that time and keep her busy.

With an hour left in her workday, she was leaning over her desk, squinting and pointing at her computer screen, deep in thought going over a budget spreadsheet, when she jumped at the sound of someone rapping on her office door.

"Oh, shit!" Amarah gasped. "You scared the crap out of..." She trailed off, hand clutched to her chest when she looked and realized who was standing at her door.

Derick. How... How was he there? Her heart rate spiked, and her stomach turned over. Amarah's lunch was suddenly in her throat, threatening to reappear, but she clamped her mouth shut, forcing herself to keep it down.

He strolled into her office and gently closed the door with a soft click that had her flinching. "Hello, love," he said with a cynical smile on his face.

He was dressed casually today, wearing a plain black V-neck T-shirt, blue jeans, and black sneakers. A sight that not so long ago would have had her mouth watering now repulsed her and made her skin crawl as if hundreds of spiders covered it.

She forced herself to not visibly shudder as she began to take slow calming breaths. Her building had security that would be there in a minute if she needed it.

Amarah had no idea what gave her this idea but suddenly it popped into her head to record their conversation. She nonchalantly grabbed her phone, swiped over to the camera, clicked the video, and started recording. Her phone was on silent so Derick wouldn't have heard the noise that signaled a recording had started. She then turned her phone over and calmly placed it on her desk with the screen facing down.

"What are you doing here?" she asked, cursing inwardly as her voice came out slightly shaky. She didn't want to give this man any notion that his presence had any effect on her.

"I told you that I'd find you. We need to talk."

Derick strolled over and sat in one of the armchairs she had in front of her desk as if he owned the place. He crossed an ankle over his knee, leaned back in the chair, and made himself comfortable.

"How do you know where I work?" Her voice was a little stronger this time.

"I have my ways," he said with a shrug.

"So, you're stalking me now? I don't want you here. Please leave."

"You look beautiful today, as always. Although I've told you before, you can't be wearing clothing like that." His eyes darkened slightly as he took in the little black form-fitting dress that stopped just above her knees and showed off a little bit of cleavage.

"What's wrong with this dress?" She gazed down at herself briefly before looking back at him.

"It's showing off too much of those pretty tits of yours." Derick's eyes dipped hungrily into the curves of her breasts that were unobstructed by the fabric. "I happen to love it. However, so does every other man in this place." A little of his jealousy showed through as a look of possession flashed across his face, but it was gone just as fast.

"As I've said before, you can't tell me what I can and can't wear. Every bit of clothing I own is publicly acceptable."

He narrowed his eyes and cocked his head to the side. "Also, I thought I told you that I was the only guy you were allowed to hang out with."

"What are you talking about?" she questioned, creases forming between her brows.

"Your lunch dates today," he stated as he gazed around, taking in her office.

"So, you are following me! Unbelievable. Derick, that's beyond wrong on so many levels and I told you before, you're not allowed to dictate who I hang out with. I never once gave you a reason to suspect that I was unfaithful." A part of her felt like it was futile to defend her actions.

Derick's tone dropped an octave. "I don't like it when you disobey me."

That sent the hairs on her arms and the back of her neck standing up.

Amarah steeled her spine. "You have no say in my life anymore, Derick."

"Must I always repeat myself?" He sighed as he ran a hand through the top of his golden hair. "I told you that you chose wrong."

"I disagree. Yeah, when we first met, you were great, caring, kind, and compassionate. You always asked questions as if you genuinely took an interest in what I was saying, and you were a wonderful listener. Over the last month, I did start to develop feelings for you, but you started to let your true colors shine when you occasionally showed signs of control, jealousy, and possession. Then you put your hands on me and hurt me in anger, Derick." She had to take a breath, her voice becoming shaky again. That was hard for her to relive and talk about. "I will not be controlled or forced to do anything I don't want to do. I believe I chose rather wisely." Amarah ended with her chin held high.

Derick chuckled. He actually chuckled a little bit. The audacity of that man.

"That's cute that you thought you had a choice," he said menacingly as he stood, placed his closed fists on the desk, and leaned over to be closer to her. He was so close that she felt like he was stealing the air right from her lungs. She leaned further back in her chair. "I'll correct your mistake. I'm in your life now, love."

CHAPTER 12

Amarah couldn't take it anymore. For some reason, it was like Derick was taking up all the air in her office and she couldn't breathe, couldn't fill her lungs with enough oxygen, no matter how hard she tried or how deep a breath she took.

She had to get out of that room and get away from him. Abruptly, she got up and made a break for the door. Derick was ready for her and beat her to it, blocking her from opening it. He pushed her back flat against the solid wood, placing one of his legs between hers, pinning her in place.

"Shh," he cooed in a sweet, low seductive voice as he used one hand to caress her cheek, his face mere inches from hers. "I promise you this: I'll treat you like a queen, and you'll never want for anything. I must warn you though, I won't hesitate to correct your mistakes now and in the future. Be a good girl and tell me what I know to be true. Tell me that you're mine and mine alone."

He was off his meds if he thought there was ever a possibility that she'd agree to be his. Amarah closed her eyes as she forced herself to take a deep breath.

"I can't, Derick," she pleaded with him. "Please, get off of me."

"I can't do that. Tell me what I need to do to change your mind." He dipped his head and started placing soft, gentle kisses along her neck. At one time, her body would have come alive at the touch of him. Now, his touch repulsed her. "I can make you feel so fucking good. Is that the kind of convincing you need?"

He used his strong torso to hold her in place as he trailed one hand down her back and cupped her ass as he filled his other hand with one of her breasts, giving the soft tissue a gentle squeeze, massaging it through the fabric of her bra and dress.

"Derick, stop!" Amarah said more sternly as her eyes shot open at his revolting touch.

"Let me worship you. Let me prove to you that my touch is better than his could ever be. Then you'll see just how wrong you chose," Derick said, lust heavy in his voice.

He didn't have to say Liam's name for her to understand that's who he was referring to. Amarah needed to stop him before it was too late. She grasped his biceps for support and with every ounce of strength she had, she threw up her knee right into his groin. He groaned loudly at the impact, causing him to stagger back and double over in pain.

She quickly balled up her right fist and threw all her weight into a punch like her brother showed her. The impact sent Derick falling backward into her desk. She threw open her office door and ran out.

"Security!" Amarah shouted. Her loud voice carried through the entire building.

Two security officers came running toward the commotion. One of them, Charlie, was a gentleman just entering his forties. He was a few inches taller than her, but he was in surprisingly good shape for his age since running was his passion. The second guard was a few years older than Charlie, a man by the name of Tucker. He had grey peppering his hair and always kept his face clean-shaven. He too kept himself fit for his age. The dynamic duo had been guards there for over a decade.

"Amarah, what's wrong?" Charlie asked as he and Tucker came to a stop in front of the frightened woman.

"Derick attacked me." She pointed a shaky finger in the direction of her office, her voice uneven. "I never want to see that man in this building again."

Both security guards followed her finger as they saw a tall blond man lying on the floor of her office, holding his groin with pain contorting his face.

"Are you hurt?" Tucker asked as Charlie entered the office and started hauling Derick to his feet.

"No, I'm ok." Amarah spoke in a weak voice. Tucker pulled his brows together, as if not believing her. She cleared her throat and tried again. "Really, I'm ok," she said, her words stronger this time.

Both men had known her for the last four years since she started working there. She was confident they'd trust her word and knew she wouldn't lie about something like this. Each man had a hold of Derick's arm as they started to escort him outside.

As they passed by, Derick gave her a quick wink and said, "I'll see you soon, love," and blew her a kiss.

That was it for her. Amarah knew it was time to get the cops involved. She went into her office, collected her things, and walked straight to her boss's office.

Mr. Conner's office was just down the hall from hers. She knocked on the door as a courtesy before entering, even though it was always open.

"Ah, Amarah, come in. Are you ok? I just heard what happened." He motioned for her to sit on one of the chairs by his desk.

Mr. Conner was an older gentleman, in his late fifties. His father founded the company and passed the torch over to him when he was in his late twenties. He was a short, round man whose hair started thinning at a young age, so he always rocked the bald look. He always kept himself clean-shaven, too. She had never seen as much as a stubble on the man. He was a gentle soul, treated his employees with respect, and always made it a point to remember your name.

"No sir, honestly, I'm not. But it'll be ok soon. I have no idea how he found out where I worked. But I need to take some time off. I need to sort this out with the authorities. I hope you understand." She told him the truth, not all of it of course, only what he needed to know.

Amarah was quitting, she had to. Derick knew where to find her now. She knew the guards would never in a million years let him into the building again, but she couldn't risk him waiting outside for her or potentially following her home one day.

"Of course, please, take all the time you need. And if you decide you want to come back after all this is dealt with, you'll always have a job here," Mr. Conner sounded reluctant but sincere.

"Thank you, Mr. Conner," she said with a soft smile and walked out of his office.

"Would you like an escort to your vehicle?" Charlie asked as Amarah made her way to the lobby.

"Yes, thank you," she agreed with a soft smile. Once she got in her Tahoe and started it up, she booked it straight to the local police station.

CHAPTER 13

Amarah constantly checked her rearview mirror for any signs that Derick might be following her. She took a few extra turns and circled back but never saw his red truck. She finally pulled into the police station parking lot, parking in a space up front.

The building was nice and updated. The outside was a light tan brick, and there were bright, colorful flowers in full bloom and neatly trimmed bushes that ran all along the length of the building.

She climbed out of her SUV and walked through the bulletproof glass front doors of the station. The inside was updated and clean with white ceramic tile covering the floor, and a nice soft grey colored the walls. There was a large oak counter with two uniformed police officers standing behind it.

One of the officers looked up at her and smiled. "What can I do for you today, ma'am?"

"I was attacked at work today and would like to file a report." Amarah built up the courage to say.

She forced herself to stop checking behind her, repeating in her mind that she was in one of the safest places around. Derick trying anything in here would be a death sentence.

"No problem. If you follow me, I'll escort you to someone who will help." He motioned for her to pass through a metal detector and buzzed open a thick metal door that led to the rest of the station.

Once she was through, the officer walked her down a long hallway tiled in the same white as the lobby. A variety of posters and display cases lined the walls. A large room opened before them that was filled with rows of desks and more uniformed officers and detectives at work.

"Trenton!" the uniformed officer called to a detective who was writing away at his desk.

An older gentleman who looked about mid-thirties with tanned skin, neatly kept brown hair, and large brown eyes glanced up and smiled welcomingly at her. He was dressed in civilian clothes, wearing a plain black T-shirt that was tucked into a pair of blue jeans with a gun holster clipped to his belt that had his service pistol secured within.

"Yes?" Detective Trenton answered.

"This woman was attacked at work today and would like to file a report." He motioned for her to sit in the chair that was right next to Detective Trenton's desk.

Amarah sat down and thanked the officer as he made his way back up to the front counter.

"What's your name, ma'am?" the detective asked as he pulled out a paper from a filing cabinet by his desk.

"Amarah Patterson," she answered nervously, subconsciously smoothing out invisible wrinkles in her dress.

"Alright Amarah, I'll need a little more information before we get down to the details." He spoke kindly.

She gave him all the personal information he requested. Her birthday, race, social security number, home address, phone number, employer, and employer's address.

"Does the person you're reporting know of your home address?"

"No. Not that I know of," Amarah answered truthfully.

Lord, please never let him find where I live. Her house was her sanctuary, and she'd be damned if someone ever made her feel unsafe in her own home.

"Ok, I'll need some of their information. As much as you can provide."

Amarah gave Detective Trenton what she could. She didn't know where Derick lived but knew where he worked and gave the detective

Derick's phone number.

"Here comes the hard part," he said with a gentle smile. "I need you to tell me what happened. Why do you want this man kept away from you? Don't spare any details. Even the smallest things could be of importance."

She closed her eyes, took a slow, deep breath, then proceeded to tell him everything. She started with how they met and how Derick was when they first got together. Then about the subtle changes and how he hurt her, all the texts and voicemails, and lastly, the incident today.

"Are you wanting to move further and press assault charges on this man for the attack that happened today?" Detective Trenton asked, never once letting the gentleness leave his voice.

Amarah was still for a minute before answering. "Yes."

Detective Trenton was quiet as he finished writing all the information down. He gave her his business card that contained his email so she could send him the texts, voicemails, and video she recorded to put on file.

Upon examining his card, she cocked her head to the side slightly and pulled her brows together. "You're a detective? I thought y'all only worked murder cases?"

He laughed lightly. "That would be a homicide detective. I'm a police detective. There are quite a few different types of detectives that specialize in different fields like homicide, forensics, narcotics, cold cases, undercover, missing persons, etc. And now that you're pressing assault charges, I'm glad they brought your case to me."

Amarah nodded in understanding as she emailed him everything, including a photo of Derick.

"Ok, I think I got all I need. I'll get all this into the computer, attach all the evidence with it, review it, and start an investigation. This could take some time. However, I'll do everything in my power to speed things along. I'll keep you updated, but call me if you ever need anything, feel in danger, or have any questions about the progress of the case."

"Thank you, detective. I can't begin to tell you how much this makes me feel more at ease."

The fact that an investigation could take time had her nervous. She wanted Derick locked away as soon as possible but there were steps that had to be followed. She chose to remain hopeful that Detective Trenton would do everything in his power to quicken things.

"My pleasure, ma'am." He smiled. "Would you like an escort to your house?"

"No, I should be ok. I made sure I wasn't followed here. Thank you again, detective."

Amarah gathered up her stuff and made her way back out to the parking lot, feeling a little less paranoid after leaving the police station. She sent up a quick prayer that this would be over soon, and Derick would be caught.

Amarah did the same thing on her way home as she did on her way to the police station, making a few extra turns and circling back all while checking her mirrors to make sure Derick wasn't following. When she pulled into her driveway, she quickly shut off her engine and got inside fast, locking the door behind her. She triple-checked it, making sure it was locked, and did the same with her back door. Only then did she release a heavy sigh and draw herself a much-needed hot bath.

When her bathtub was full, she shut the water off, took off her makeup, put her clothes into the hamper, and climbed into the welcoming heat. She turned on the jets as she slowly sank into the water until her head was the only thing not submerged. Only then did she let herself break down. She cried. Hard.

She'd let all the fear, anger, worry, and hurt that she was feeling this last week build up till she couldn't take it anymore. She let it all out. She screamed, cursed, swore, and cried until her head ached, allowing all those emotions to wash out of her.

She was in there for almost an hour purging herself of all those feelings. Once she was done, Amarah cleaned herself up and got out of the bath. She brushed her teeth, braided back her hair, crawled into bed, and fell into a deep sleep, completely exhausted from expelling all those emotions.

CHAPTER 14

Amarah woke to the smell of coffee wafting through her room. She was so glad she remembered to set the alarm last night so it would start when she got up. She rolled over, stretched, and reached up to check her phone. Her hand hesitated when she saw her white charger not plugged into her phone.

Her brows furrowed in confusion. She always made sure to charge it every night before she fell asleep. Maybe she was too tired after her bath to remember to plug it in. She pushed the worry aside and brought her phone to her face, her eyes squinting from the brightness of the screen. It was almost 10 a.m.

She threw off her covers and slowly made her way to her bathroom. It was Saturday, which meant Travis and Sandra were having their biweekly cookout over at their house at noon, so she had to start getting ready.

She pulled her long blonde hair up into a high ponytail, not wanting to mess with it today. Her makeup was light, like usual. Just some eye shadow, eyeliner, and mascara. She entered her walk-in closet and grabbed her favorite pair of blue jeans that hugged her ass and hips perfectly and a cute, low-cut black Metallica tank top.

Amarah checked her phone and couldn't stop her brows from furrowing when she saw no messages and no voicemails from Detective Trenton. She reminded herself that it had only been twelve hours or so. It would take a bit longer than that for an investigation.

She forced herself to smile. Today would be a good day filled with family and fun. Plus, Liam and Travis would be there. There was no safer place than with those two.

After checking herself in the mirror by her front door, she put her favorite pair of black and white Converse on, grabbed her purse and keys, and made her way to her vehicle. She connected her phone to Bluetooth and pulled up her Spotify app, selecting her 1990's/early 2000's playlist.

It was a beautiful sunny day, with not a cloud in the sky, so she turned off the AC and rolled her windows down. She cranked up her radio and put on her very own, one-woman concert, dancing and singing at the top of her lungs.

Amarah was about five minutes from Travis and Sandra's house, dead in the middle of belting out the second verse of "Sk8er Boi" by Avril Lavigne, when she felt her tires go flat. She quickly turned down her music as she pulled over to the side of the road.

"No, no, no! This can't be happening. Not now of all times."

She got out and checked her driver's side tires. They looked normal. She then walked around to the passenger's side to see both the front and back tires were flat. *What the hell did I hit? I didn't see anything.* She glanced back down the road to see if maybe she just wasn't paying attention, but there was no debris. This stretch of road was bordered by wheat fields on both sides and woods as far as the eye could see.

"You picked a hell of a place to break down," she muttered sarcastically.

If it were just one of them, she'd change it and put the spare on. But she only had one, so she wouldn't be able to change both flat tires. She sighed inwardly as she grabbed her phone and called her brother. The road she was on didn't get much traffic, and she wasn't about to hitchhike either.

"Hey, sis! You on your way out?" Travis asked by way of greeting.

She could hear her nieces and nephew laughing and playing in the background and the sound warmed her heart, a smile sliding across her face, which was a rarity these days.

"Yeah, I'm about five minutes out but I blew both my passenger tires. I don't know what I hit. I didn't see any debris or anything. Ugh, who knows." She groaned.

"Jeez, Amarah, you're supposed to swerve around stuff in the road, not run over it." He laughed. "I'll leave right now and come pick you up."

She froze when she saw a truck approaching in the distance. Her heart dropped into her stomach thinking it could be Derick. Relief washed over her when she saw it was a black truck and not a red one like his.

"Hold on Travis, I think I see Liam's truck." Amarah squinted her blue eyes as she tried to get a better look at the driver. The black Chevy slowed and pulled over behind her SUV. "Yeah, it's Liam. Don't worry about it, I'll get a ride from him. We'll be there in a few," she told her brother.

"Talk about perfect timing. Alright sis, be safe. See you soon."

She hung up the phone and tucked it in the back pocket of her jeans as she started walking toward the back of her Tahoe. Liam got out of his truck and met her there.

She had to school her face as she took him in. No matter how many times she saw him, the man took her breath away. His plain dark green T-shirt played well with his bright green eyes and fit so snugly across his torso. It accentuated every muscle in his chest, arms, and shoulders, leaving little to the imagination. The artwork that covered both of his arms was on full display. The simple pair of Levi jeans he wore showed off his muscular legs and fit perfectly over his square-toed boots.

"Please tell me you didn't murder a poor helpless animal," Liam teased.

"Ha. Not funny. Both of my passenger tires just went flat, but I didn't hit anything. Did you see any debris back there?" Amarah asked as she walked with him so he could survey the damage.

"No, that's weird though. Stranger things have happened. I'm just glad you're ok." He looked at her, doing a once over as if to make sure she was unharmed. "Grab anything you need or don't want potentially stolen from your vehicle. I have a buddy who owns a tow truck and I'll have him bring it back to my place."

"Alright, thanks," she said as she grabbed a few things and rolled up her windows.

She made sure to lock her Tahoe a few times for good measure. Halfway to Liam's truck, she got a weird feeling that had the hairs on the back of her neck standing up. She could only describe it as a feeling of being watched. She paused and took in her surroundings. They were the only two out there. Not even a passing car was in sight.

"Cupcake?"

Amarah whipped her head toward Liam. "Huh?"

"Everything ok?" Liam asked, pausing with a hand on the driver's side door handle, a single black brow perched high on his head in question.

"Oh, yeah, sorry. I was, uh… I was making sure I didn't forget anything." She mentally shook herself. There was no way Derick could be out here. She would be able to see his truck if he was. "And stop calling me that!"

Amarah and Liam rode the remainder of the drive in silence. The only sound came from the radio that was playing through his speakers. She kept her gaze out the window, not really looking at anything, too lost in her own mind. Too lost in all the ways her quiet life had turned into such a messy nightmare. Before she knew it, they were pulling into her brother's driveway. She forced herself to snap out of it. She would put all her troubles with Derick on hold, even if it were for only a few hours.

"Knock, knock! Your favorite aunt has arrived!" she shouted through the home, calling to her nieces and nephew.

"Aunt Amarah! Aunt Amarah!" A stampede of kids came

rushing around the corner, jumping into her arms with enough force that it nearly knocked her backwards.

She hugged them all tightly, smothering them with kisses and then tickling them till they almost peed themselves. Liam stood there and watched, laughing and shaking his head. They reached their little arms out for him.

"Uncle Liam, help us! Save us!" they all pleaded.

"Sorry kiddos, you're on your own. I wouldn't want to go up against your aunt. She's feisty." Liam laughed.

She eventually let them go and they took off toward the backyard. Amarah and Liam walked out back onto the covered patio and greeted the rest of the family. Liam approached Travis, accepting a beer from him.

"How did you manage to get two flats, dear? Are you alright?" Charlette asked as she embraced her daughter in a hug and pulled back to look her over.

"I'm fine, Momma, I promise," Amarah reassured her.

"Good thing your knight in shining armor came to your rescue." Her mother whispered in a tone so low that only Amarah would be able to hear as she wiggled her eyebrows suggestively.

"That means the knight has never had his armor tested. Screw that. I prefer the scarred-up warrior who bathes in the blood of his enemies." Amarah smiled as she whispered back to her mother.

"Oh, my." Charlette blushed as she brought her hand to her heart in shock. "I knew I raised you well." She smiled and winked at her daughter.

"She got two flats because women are terrible drivers. She most likely plowed over some wood lying in the road," Amarah heard Travis call out from beside the grill. Steaks were on the menu this time.

"Screw you!" Amarah threw back at her brother and raised her middle finger at him.

"What does that mean, Aunt Amarah?" Carly, the middle child

who just turned five asked as she held up her hand with her middle finger up in the air, copying her aunt.

"Carly!" Sandra shouted in a shocked tone. "You know better than to repeat the actions of an adult."

"Sorry, Momma."

"It's a way to say a curse word without actually saying it," Amarah told Carly. "When you go back to school, you can show your teacher that you learned something new over summer break."

"Ok!" Carly's toothless smile beamed brighter than the sun before she ran off to join her siblings.

"Don't you dare try to get my baby in trouble. If I get a call from the school, I'm coming for you," Sandra said as she pointed a well-manicured finger at her sister-in-law. She tried to act stern, but she couldn't hide the smile and laughter that slipped out.

"Oh, trust me. I'm going to teach them all the bad stuff I know," Amarah joked.

She spared a glance over at Liam, who had remained quiet as he watched the interaction from the sidelines next to Oscar. He had a mischievous look on his handsome face as he smiled at Amarah before turning and starting a conversation with Travis.

Amarah took a minute to soak in the scene around her. Kids' laughter filled the air, Sandra gossiped to her mother-in-law about what she saw her neighbor doing the other day, and Liam, Travis, and her father caught up about whatever guys talked about. Laughter and family. That was what she needed after all the crap she'd gone through this last week.

She shoved those creeping thoughts to the back of her mind as she grabbed a beer from the cooler and engaged in conversation with Sandra and Charlette, letting all her worries go, even for just a few hours.

When Travis finished grilling up the last of the steaks, they brought all the food into the kitchen as everyone made their plates and took their seats around the family table. Amarah was listening intently to a story her brother was telling when her phone went off, scaring the daylights out of her, causing the silverware she held to fall and clink against the hardwood floors. All the color instantly drained from her face.

CHAPTER 15

Everyone at the table paused and peered at Amarah. She slowly pulled out her phone and checked the caller ID. It was Detective Trenton.

"I'm so sorry guys, I have to take this." She picked her silverware back up and placed it back on the table before exiting through the back door for some privacy.

"Hello?" she answered while pacing around the back porch, nervously chewing on a fingernail.

"Amarah Patterson, this is Detective Trenton. How are you?"

"I'm ok. Any news?" she asked, wanting to get right to the point.

"Yes, we went by Derick's place of employment. Apparently, he quit yesterday. They were able to give us his home address they had on file. We went by and searched the place, but it was cleaned out. That signals he may be on the run."

"So, he could be anywhere right now?"

Panic started to set in. Amarah tried to calm herself and not expect the worst. He could be in another state by now for all she knew.

"Yes, unfortunately. But we do have a track on his credit cards and bank accounts. So, if he makes a purchase or a withdrawal, we'll be able to track him. Also, I wanted to warn you that he could still be in town, lying low. So please be careful. And if you feel like your life is threatened in any way, don't hesitate to give me a call or come straight here to the station."

"Thank you, Detective. I'll watch my back. Just please find him soon," she pleaded with him.

"Yes, ma'am. I plan on it," Detective Trenton said, ending the phone call.

Amarah needed a moment to fully collect herself before she went back inside. She closed her eyes and took slow, deep breaths, trying to squash the anxiety that was attempting to overtake her. This couldn't be happening. She didn't understand why. Of the millions of people who use dating sites, she didn't know how she managed to attract the attention of a psycho stalker.

She prayed he left town, but that didn't sound like something he would do. Her last memory of him flashed through her mind while his threat echoed through her head on repeat like a broken record. *I'll see you soon, love.* No, she knew deep down that he was still around. Derick wasn't the kind to give up easily. He'd proven that already when he showed up at her work.

She managed to compose herself enough as she entered the home and sat back at her spot at the table next to Liam.

"Is everything alright, hun?" Charlette asked, concern filling her voice. "You looked like you saw a ghost when your phone went off."

"Oh yeah, sorry. It was my boss. Work stuff. Everything's ok though." Amarah tried to play it off, pushing her food around her plate, but after that phone call, she'd completely lost her appetite.

"Well, next time, tell him no business calls during non-business hours," Sandra said with an innocent laugh.

Liam, however, wasn't convinced. Amarah could feel his weighted gaze on her, but she refused to look at him. The last thing she needed was for him to use his training to analyze her and figure everything out. He would insist on handling Derick himself and she couldn't let that happen. *Well...* No, she couldn't have Liam kill Derick. As enticing as it sounded, this was her mess to fix on her own.

Hours passed by all too quickly, and things were starting to wrap up. "Are you ready?" A deep voice washed over Amarah, causing her body to instantly wake up.

She whipped her head around. "For what?"

"For me to take you home?" Liam asked with a half-laugh.

She groaned inwardly at the reminder of her poor SUV's fate. It had completely slipped her mind as she lost herself in family time.

"Oh, right. Yeah, ready when you are." She gave him a weak smile.

After saying their goodbyes, Amarah and Liam made their way out to his truck. Once on the road for a few minutes, Liam finally broke the silence. "Alright, spill it."

"I don't know what you're talking about," Amarah answered, sounding as if she were a thousand miles away. She forced herself to keep her eyes out the window.

"Cupcake, look at me," he said, his tone all demanding and serious. Reluctantly, she turned. Those green eyes of his bore a hole through her as if he were trying to read her mind. Thank goodness he couldn't because then he'd know of all the inappropriate things she wished he'd do to her. "The phone call. What's wrong?"

"It was nothing, really. I told you it was my boss. I, um... I quit yesterday," she managed to say.

Amarah had never been a good liar, but she didn't want to worry Liam or her brother over Derick. Travis had a wife and kids to look out for, and Liam had an entire business and his personal life to manage. The cops were handling it now. And besides, half of what she said was true, so she went with it.

Concern weighed heavily in his voice. "Why did you quit?"

"I just needed a change. Been there for a while and wasn't moving up as fast as I wanted to. Didn't foresee it happening for a while anyway. I felt my time would be best served elsewhere." She shrugged.

"Have you found another job yet?" Liam questioned further as he kept one hand on the wheel and rested his other atop the middle console.

"Not yet, but I have some listings saved. Just need to apply to them."

"Well, if you're interested, I happen to have an opening at my company. My assistant just had a baby, and she informed me she didn't plan on coming back after her maternity leave was over. Which I don't blame her for. I know you'd be perfect for the job. It's yours if you want it." He shifted his gaze between the road and Amarah.

"I don't need handouts, Liam. I can get a job on my own," she stated, meeting his gaze.

"Oh, trust me, I know you can. This isn't a handout. I know you. You have great work ethics, are trustworthy, and reliable. Plus, we get along so I know we'd work well together."

"Alright, I'm listening," she said, raising an eyebrow at him and crossing her arms under her breasts.

She didn't miss the way his vision dipped to her chest. Before she could think anything of it, he shifted his gaze back to the road.

"Monday through Friday from 7 a.m. to 3:30 p.m., most weekends and holidays off, paid annual and sick leave. Full benefits package. $1,200 a week." Amarah's jaw dropped at that number, causing Liam to do a double take. "What? Is that not enough?"

"No! No, that's plenty. Trust me."

Being single, she lived a comfortable lifestyle with minimal bills and expenses. Her previous job provided her with more than enough money, but this, what Liam was willing to pay, would give her more than she knew what to do with. Which was always a good problem to have. It just meant more damage she could do at her local bookstores.

"Well, the job is rather demanding. But I know you can handle it. You're a great multitasker, and you work well under pressure."

"Wow, Liam, was that a compliment? Can you say it again so I can record it? Who knows when that'll happen again?" She laughed.

"Nope, that was a one-time thing. Sorry," he said as he threw her a wink.

"Alright, but I only have one condition. I'm not sleeping with you to get a raise," she joked.

He teased her and gave her a wicked smile. "I don't know, I can be pretty persuasive. Plus, I have a couch in my office that's just begging to be broken in."

Amarah stared at Liam, mouth agape, speechless as her body came alive from his sinful words. A dirty picture started to form in her mind, causing her to groan and shift in her seat, forcing her to cross her legs to alleviate the building need that ached between them. He simply chuckled and went back to driving.

CHAPTER 16

After Liam parked in the driveway of Amarah's cute little duplex, he escorted her to her door as she dug for the keys buried deep in her purse.

"Your Tahoe has been towed to my house. Tomorrow morning, I'll get you new tires and put them on for you. I'll drop it off when I'm done." She froze as she stared at him in disbelief.

Although, she didn't know why she was shocked. She half-expected him to try and pull something like this.

"I can't let you do that, Liam. The Tahoe is my responsibility. I do have a savings account built up for instances like these. You can put them on for me, that would be greatly appreciated, but I'll pay. I'll also reimburse you for the tow truck."

Amarah stood her ground. It was beyond generous of him to offer. After Liam separated from the military, he took over his father's real estate and architectural firm. Lord knows he had plenty of money. So much so that new tires would be pennies to him.

"Why do you have to be so damn stubborn?" Liam sighed as he brought an arm up and ran a large hand over his black scruff. "Accepting help isn't a sign of weakness. It's acceptable now and again. I know you have the means to take care of this yourself, but you have people who care about you and want to help in any way they can. You don't always have to do everything yourself." He finished with a half-laugh.

She knew her mom was to blame for certain traits of hers. Charlette was just as strong-willed and hardheaded, always wanting to do things herself, with no help from others. Her father had dealt with it for decades and loved her all the more for it.

"That's just the way I am, I guess. Love it or leave it." Amarah shrugged unapologetically.

"Good night, Ms. Independent," Liam said with a big smile that made his green eyes sparkle playfully.

She melted internally. How could something so innocent make millions of butterflies come alive in her stomach?

"You should smile more, Liam. It looks good on you." She giggled nervously.

"Well, if anyone can make me truly smile, it's you, Cupcake."

Those butterflies had now exploded, making her feel as if she could fly. She had the sudden urge to rock up onto her toes and kiss the hell out of him like she's been dreaming about for years. The only thing that kept her rooted in place was fear. Fear that if she voiced her truths, he would finally confirm what she knew to be true as much as she knew two plus two equaled four. That he didn't feel the same way. That he had no romantic feelings toward her.

Liam's rejection would be kind and gentle. She knew he'd do everything in his power not to make her feel embarrassed, but it wouldn't soften the blow to her heart. And embarrassed she certainly would be. So much so that she'd barricade herself in her house and never leave. Or be forced to relocate to the North Pole because Amarah knew she'd never be able to face him again. Her dignity wouldn't allow it, and that would be the end of their friendship. If she had to choose between having him in her life as only a friend or not having him in her life at all, she'd choose the former.

Swallowing her feelings and clearing her mind, she lifted her chin, plastered her best 'everything's fine' smile, and said, "Good night, Mr. Pain In My Ass."

The next morning, Amarah woke up early enough so she could be at Liam's house first thing to go with him to the store. She knew he was

stubborn enough to still go against her wishes and purchase the tires himself.

There was still no word when she checked her phone. A part of her was relieved that Derick hadn't reached out in some way, but the other part of her was worried that Detective Trenton hadn't contacted her with an update either. She figured Derick must still be in the wind. Maybe by now, he had relocated to another state entirely, and she could wipe her hands clean of the creep.

She got up, padded her way to the bathroom, and got ready for the day. She braided her hair into a beautiful French braid that hung down the middle of her back and did her makeup with her favorite eyeshadow palette, which accentuated her deep blue eyes more than usual, then added some eyeliner and mascara.

As Amarah dug through her drawer, searching for a bra, she noticed two were missing from her ever-growing supply. A woman can never have too many.

"Jesus, please don't let me be going insane," she said aloud as if she wasn't alone in her room.

She pushed the growing worry away and chose a simple pair of cut off jean shorts that stopped just above mid-thigh and a low-cut, loose pastel pink tank top. It was supposed to be pretty hot, another brutal Oklahoma summer day.

She skipped her coffee this morning, knowing that she'd pass by her favorite coffee shop on the walk over to Liam's house. She was not going to miss the opportunity to stop in there. She put on her shoes, grabbed her purse, and locked the door behind her as she left. It was almost 8:30 in the morning and already quite warm outside.

Amarah strode down the sidewalk, enjoying the view and quietness of her neighborhood. It would only take her about ten to fifteen minutes to get to Liam's house. She was thankful he lived so close. Besides the occasional car here and there, the streets were quiet for a Saturday morning.

The smell of freshly brewed coffee drifted through the air, causing a beaming smile to shape her lips. Inhaling deeply, she rounded the corner and there it was. The Coffee Kingdom, her favorite little slice of heaven. It was a quaint mom-and-pop coffee shop that was tucked away on the corner of a shopping plaza. She quickened her pace a little, not wanting to wait a second longer than she had to for her coffee.

"Good morning, dear!" Mrs. Johnson said to her as she entered through the front door.

She was a short, chubby woman in her middle years, with her black hair peppered with the occasional grays pulled up into a bun on the top of her head. She and Mr. Johnson had owned and ran the shop, just the two of them, for more than twenty years. Mr. Johnson was always in the back making fresh pastries each morning. Cooking was his passion.

He never went to school for it but after tasting his treats, you would have thought he graduated top of his class from the most prestigious culinary school in the country. Mrs. Johnson said that's why she kept him around all these years. "Why would I let life-changing food like that out of my life?" she would always say, snickering.

That wasn't the true reason, though. Anytime Mr. Johnson emerged from the back with a fresh tray of pastries for the counter, he'd greet his wife with a kiss and sneak a grab of her round bottom, or even give it a little smack, wink at her and disappear into the back of the shop again.

Amarah wanted that kind of love. Passion like that, well after two decades and they still couldn't keep their hands off each other, didn't come around that often. It was rare and absolutely beautiful.

"Good morning, Mrs. Johnson. How are you?" Amarah asked as she approached the counter.

The shop was small but clean and decorated beautifully, having been fully remodeled about five years ago. The floors were extra large beautiful mocha-colored ceramic tile. Soft cream colored the walls, making the space feel brighter and more open. Large windows filled the place to let in all the natural light. Small, round dark wooden tables with metal legs, with matching chairs—two or three to a table—were placed sporadically around the lobby.

Canvases of various artwork hung on the walls, from close-ups of coffee beans to mosaic paintings filled with various shades of browns, creams, and tans. There was a long dark wooden counter along the back wall, topped with a grey and white marble countertop that had dark wooden display cases on each end filled with mouthwatering pastries.

"Well, Mr. Johnson and I both woke up this morning in good health, so pretty good. How are you dear?" Mrs. Johnson asked in a loving, motherly way.

"I've been better, but I'm doing good. I quit my job and am starting a new one come Monday. I'm a little nervous."

She came here often enough and had a wonderful relationship with the owners. They'd become like a second family to her since she found this little gem almost five years ago.

"Oh, that's exciting. Why are you so nervous, sweetheart?" Mrs. Johnson asked as she started to work on her usual—a mocha Frappuccino with extra mocha, a shot of espresso, and topped with drizzled caramel.

Maybe she did come in here a little too often. When she had the world's best coffee a short walk from her house, how could she not stop by frequently?

"It's at Godrik Enterprises. I'll be Liam's assistant. I don't know, I just feel like if I don't meet a certain expectation, he'll be disappointed. Plus, I'll have to see his grumpy ass every day. Who knows how much I can take before I murder him?" Amarah said, half-laughing.

Mrs. Johnson froze in place and looked up at her with a raised eyebrow and a smirk on her lips.

"Oh, no. Get that look off your face. Nothing is going to happen between us." Amarah knew exactly what Mrs. Johnson was thinking.

"All I'm saying is, I have read numerous books about this storyline— the boss and the assistant. Plus, you've had a crush on this man since y'all were kids. Honey, this is inevitable. Just prepare yourself and be smart. I don't want to see you get hurt. I can't leave Mr. Johnson to run this shop by himself because I went to jail for murder. He'd never survive without me."

Amarah knew she wasn't bluffing. Mrs. Johnson may look like a harmless, gentle older woman, but if you crossed someone she loved, she would make your life a living hell.

"Oh, that reminds me, can you make one for him too? Normal coffee, hazelnut creamer, no sugar. I suppose I can be nice since he is taking me to get new tires for my car this morning," Amarah told the woman, who looked at her with a questionable expression.

"Did something happen?"

"Both of my passenger tires went flat yesterday. I know, don't ask me how I managed that one." Amarah shrugged. "And throw in a delicious blueberry muffin please."

Mrs. Johnson finished making the coffees and handed them to her along with her muffin. Amarah paid in cash, giving the woman a little extra for the tip jar like always.

"Thank you! Tell Mr. Johnson I said hello and the muffin is exceptionally good this morning," she called over her shoulder as she pushed open the front door and walked out.

Once outside, that prickling, uneasy feeling washed over her again, as if she was being watched. She stopped and scanned her surroundings intently but there was not a soul in sight. *Stop it, you're just being paranoid.* She closed her eyes and shook the feeling off as she continued her walk.

CHAPTER 17

Amarah casually sipped from her coffee and munched on the mouthwatering blueberry muffin as she finished the remainder of her walk to Liam's house. She turned a corner that led into a gorgeous high-class neighborhood. Expensive mansions lined the streets, all secured by tall wrought iron fences and gates.

She ogled each house as she passed, wondering what some of these people did for work to be able to afford homes like those. Liam, of course, could buy the whole neighborhood if he wanted to. His father's company, which he took over two years ago when he got out of the Navy, had tripled in size and equity, making it a national multi-billion dollar corporation.

She finally stopped at his driveway and punched in the six-digit code for his gate: 032507. Amarah always wondered what the significance of the code Liam chose was and when she asked him about it, he simply shrugged his shoulders and said, "No significance, just a bunch of random numbers. That's the perfect kind of code." It made sense to her, but she always got the feeling there was more to it.

Though Liam had lived in this mansion of a house for two years now, and Amarah had been over more times than she could count, its beauty never ceased to amaze her. The driveway had been laid with beautiful grey cobblestones that continued up the walkway to the massive, dark double wood front doors that were accented with black fixtures.

The outside of the home was built of a light cream-colored rock and every window was framed with wooden shutters that were the same dark wood as the front doors. A black metal roof topped the mansion. Beautiful, well-manicured flower beds lined the front side of the home, and the perimeter of the land was lined with tall evergreen trees that created complete privacy from any nosy neighbors. The only way to see the home from the street was if you were standing at the gate in the driveway.

Amarah moved through the opening of the gate, making her way to the front door. She had a key, but always felt weird just walking in randomly, so she rang the doorbell.

"Good morning, Cupcake. Come on in. I'm in my office," Liam said through the doorbell camera, unlocking the front door from his security app on his phone. She pushed it open and made her way inside.

The inside was just as breathtaking. Extra large dark brown ceramic tiles covered the foyer, a light grey covered the walls and a wrought iron chandelier hung from the fifteen foot ceiling. A large square opening led into the open concept living room and large updated kitchen. A grand fireplace was centered on one wall and had floor-to-ceiling windows on each side that overlooked the large private backyard. It was furnished with modern furniture that was surprisingly still comfy and canvas art and family photos were hung sporadically on all the walls.

On the left side of the living room was a hallway that led to Liam's home office and another room that contained a personal library. That was Amarah's favorite room. The hallway branched off in two different directions. Down to the right held three large spare bedrooms, each with its own en suite bathroom and walk-in closet, and down to the left held white double doors that led to the primary suite.

Amarah walked past the living room and down the hallway. She slowed her pace as she observed the photos that hung on the walls. There were photos of Liam and his parents on vacation at different stages of his life, as well as his senior class photo. A collage frame that held photos of his time in the military always had her drooling whenever she saw it.

It displayed Liam, Travis, and their buddies on ships or in different countries they deployed to, his official Navy photo, a picture of him in his dress uniform accepting an award, and a group photo of them all in dress uniforms posing in a goofy fashion that was taken at a Navy ball he and Travis attended one year. She sighed inwardly as her body ached with need from the photos. That man had no right looking that sexy in a uniform. She caught herself biting her lip and forced herself to take a few calming breaths to settle her raging hormones.

Thankfully, she'd composed herself as she came to a stop at the open door of Liam's office, giving a courtesy knock before she entered. The space was very sophisticated, organized, and clean. Large custom bookshelves lined the left wall, every shelf filled with different kinds of books and souvenirs from all his travels.

A large window was centered on the back wall that had royal blue curtains hanging from one side, pulled back to let in the natural light. A large L-shaped oak desk was placed in the back right corner of the room with a navy blue cushy armchair positioned in front of it.

His desk housed three large monitors, a black case that held various pens, a stack of sticky notes, and a few more personal photos. One of which Amarah knew was of Liam, Travis, Sandra, and herself on a hiking trip they took two years ago. One was Liam and Travis fishing. And the last one was of Amarah and Liam on the day she graduated college.

She strolled into his office and placed his coffee down on a coaster in front of him before she took a seat in the armchair and waited patiently for him to get off the phone. From the sounds of it, it was a business call.

"Do you ever stop working? It's the weekend," Amarah questioned as he hung up.

"I've been known to take a day or two off now and then," Liam joked while taking a sip of his coffee.

Lord, even the way the man drank coffee was beautiful. *Get a grip,*

Amarah. Never going to happen, remember?

"Don't you have people who can do that stuff for you?" she asked as she finished off her drink. It was always gone too soon.

"I do, but it's Sunday, and I'm sure they have families they would like to spend time with. I don't mind the work, honestly. It keeps me busy." He shrugged as he leaned back in his computer chair.

He may have this intimidating ex-military, "don't cross me or I'll kill you and everyone you love" energy about him, but deep down, he had a caring and compassionate side. She smiled to herself, knowing she was one of the lucky few to see the true him.

"You're such a big softie," she teased.

Liam simply winked at her and took another drink.

"What brings you here this morning?" His deep voice washed through her, waking her up more than her coffee ever could.

"I'm going with you to get the tires. I can't let you pay for them," Amarah said as she forced her body and emotions back in check.

Liam shook his head silently. "Well then, ready to go?"

"Ready as I'll ever be," she responded as she stood and walked out of his office.

Amarah tossed her empty cup into the trash as she passed through the kitchen, followed Liam through the mudroom, and out into the five-car garage that was almost as big as the house. She saw her Tahoe parked and missed it already. It wasn't anything too fancy, but it was the first vehicle she ever purchased brand new and was proud to have had it paid off in only two years.

It was just her, and she didn't need quite that much room, but she loved the space. Liam, Travis, Sandra, and she generally used her Tahoe when they went camping or hiking. It fit them and all their stuff comfortably. Plus, it had four-wheel drive, which was a must in Oklahoma's unpredictable winters. But she knew new tires for her baby were going to cost a pretty penny. Fortunately, her parents always taught her to have a nice savings account for instances like these.

They loaded up in his truck and made their way into town to the Discount Tire a few miles away. Liam held the door open for Amarah as they entered the lobby.

CHAPTER 18

"Welcome to Discount Tire, how may I help you?" a heavy-set, older gentleman in his middle years called out to them with a warm smile. Chandler, his name tag read.

She opened her mouth to tell the man what she needed, but Liam beat her to it. "Picking up an order for Liam Godrik."

An order for him? He must be getting something for one of his vehicles. Amarah didn't know which one it would be for. The man owned at least seven that she knew of. Most of them were classic muscle cars that he had a passion for restoring.

"Ok, give me just a second to look it up," the man said, typing away at his computer on the front counter. "I have an order for four eighteen-inch Goodrich All-Terrain tires for a 2015 Chevrolet Tahoe. Is that correct?" Chandler asked

"Yes, sir," was all Liam said, not once looking away from Chandler.

The audacity of that man. She'd told him that she would pay for her own damn tires. Amarah even made it a point to get up early this morning so she could go with him and pay herself. What does the man do? Order them over the phone and pay before she can. Leave it to him to find a way to go against her wishes. She swore, he did it simply just to get under her skin and aggravate her. Well, guess what? It worked.

Not wanting to make a scene, all she could do was glare up at him. The corner of his mouth twitched, causing rage to boil inside of her. The jerk was trying not to smile. He knew what he had done, knew how it was affecting her, and the man thought it was comical? Oh, she was going to have a few choice words for him on their way back to his house.

"All right, since you already paid for them, we'll have a guy bring them out to your vehicle. Is there anything else I can do for you today?" Chandler asked with a soft smile.

"No, that's it. Thank you," Liam answered.

Chandler wished them a good rest of their day as Liam and Amarah turned to walk back out the front door. She was mentally preparing her speech by the time they made it back to his truck. What she wanted to say, names she wanted to call him, to tell him just how much of a stubborn ass he was being but for some reason all that came out of her mouth was, "Why, Liam?" She sighed, looking right at him as he opened his passenger side door for her.

She knew that Liam, as well as her brother, had been trained for years on how to control their emotions. Shock, anger, happiness, grief. Liam had one hell of a poker face, but she'd known him for so long, she trained herself to pick up on the slightest twitch of his muscles one would normally overlook. That's why she knew her question had surprised Liam, because of the slightest twitch of his brows.

He'd casually shrugged a shoulder and said, "Eh, call it an early birthday present."

"My birthday is months away," Amarah said flatly.

"So then it's an *extra* early birthday present." He gave her one of his devilishly handsome smiles as he ran his hand over the black scruff on his face.

Oh no, stupid hormones, we're not letting that smile get him off the hook. Not this time. Get a hold of yourself, woman. She closed her eyes, pinched the bridge of her nose, and let out a long breath.

"Why did my brother have to choose you of all people to become friends with? You irritate me to no end, you know that? I'll pay you back." She climbed into his truck.

"If you do that, Cupcake, I'll have to spank you," Liam said in a dangerously low and husky voice with the wickedest smile spread across that perfect face of his.

Amarah was speechless, frozen in place on the seat, halfway through buckling her seatbelt, with her mouth half open in shock. There was no mistaking it though, not with that look on his face and the evidence of his words pooling between her legs. Before she could say anything—if she was able to form words coherently, that is—he shut the door and walked to the back of the truck.

A younger gentleman, around her age, tall but skinny, pulled a cart behind him stacked with her tires. Liam dropped the tailgate down and loaded them in the bed of his truck. Amarah couldn't help but admire the movements of his body through the rearview mirror.

She was not about to get caught gawking at him, especially not after he just said that to her. But Lord have mercy, it was like the man was modeled after Hades himself. The way his muscles moved and flexed with the loading of each tire, his dark nature, and the threat of the delicious sins his body promised had her wanting to watch him work all day. Once Liam was finished, he climbed into the driver's seat.

Amarah made it a point not to look at the man. She, however, wasn't trained in the art of masking her emotions like Liam and her older brother. She knew her face would give her away in a hot second.

"Did you enjoy the show?" Liam asked as he put the truck in gear, enjoyment in his deep tone.

There was no way he could have known. She was so careful to be sneaky with it, but of course, he noticed. It used to be his job to notice every detail of his surroundings. Skills like that don't simply disappear overnight. She didn't say anything, just shook her head and kept her eyes looking out her window. He just laughed as he pulled out of the parking lot.

The ride back to Liam's place was quiet. Not an uncomfortable silence, never with Amarah, but a nice, calm silence with nothing but classic rock music playing lightly as background noise. He noted an unusual amount of quiet from her as he occasionally glanced over, checking for—hell, he didn't even know.

Something just seemed… off. She wasn't a Chatty Kathy by any means, but she did like small talk sprinkled here and there. He secretly loved it too and realized how much he missed it when she didn't do it. He wondered what was going through that beautiful mind of hers that had her so deep in thought.

When Liam's family relocated and he met Travis in high school, the two juniors instantly became friends and he spent a lot of time at Travis's house.

Amarah was eleven at the time. Liam cared for her in an innocent, best friend's little sister type of way, looking out for her just like her older brother did.

By the time Liam and Travis joined the Navy, Amarah was just getting into junior high school. Because of the length of SEAL school, training, and eventually all the missions they went on, they didn't get to come home often. Amarah and Liam still kept in touch, talking almost every day while he was away through emails, letters, and text messages. Both men tried to make it home on the major holidays if they were able to.

When Liam and Travis attended Amarah's high school graduation, something changed in him the day he saw her in her cap and gown. It was like he was seeing her in a whole new light. She'd blossomed into a beautiful, intelligent, strong-willed woman, with a body that could stop a truck. A body that filled out in all the right places. He knew he was done for the moment he saw her.

By the time Liam got out of the military to take over his father's company, he was twenty-six and Amarah was in college. He hoped that after being away for the last two years, his infatuation with her would go away. He thought it finally had, but the moment he saw her again, all those feelings came rushing back in full force, driving him crazy.

Being home permanently had been the hardest struggle of his life.

Every other weekend at the cookouts, he was forced to watch Amarah from afar, never allowing himself to get too close.

Every time he saw her, he wanted nothing more than to corner her in a secluded room and discover every inch of her beautiful body, but he fought against it because she was still Travis's little sister—a no-fly zone—even if they were all adults now.

When Amarah had introduced him to Derick, he felt something he'd never felt before. Jealousy. He knew she had more than likely dated before but seeing it with his own eyes was hard. After seeing that little shit kiss her and grab her ass right in front of him, something inside of himself had snapped, causing him to see red.

Liam forced himself to walk away, to calm down before he did something he couldn't take back. Like murder him right there on the spot with his bare hands. He kept reminding himself that this was her life, and she was a smart woman with a good head on her shoulders. Amarah was free to live it how she saw fit, no matter how many times his heart screamed "mine" to his brain, hoping one day it would listen.

He relived the moment he'd pinned her against the bar in his dreams each night. The way she looked and felt beneath him, the intoxicating smell of her perfume as he drug his nose across her chest and up her neck, the filthy words he whispered in her ear. Words he wished he could take back because he'd crossed a line. A dangerous line that needed to stay in place because he couldn't go there with Amarah. No matter how much he wished he could.

He had been harder than he'd ever been in his life, and the little gasp Amarah made when she felt his erection pressing into her, the evidence of what she did to him, he'd nearly claimed her mouth right then and there. But he had to dig at every ounce of will power he had to resist. He couldn't do that to his brother. He couldn't mess around with Travis's little sister, even if she was a grown woman with a mind and needs of her own.

Liam found his eyes exploring the sun-haired beauty in the

passenger seat, etching everything he saw into his memory as if he hadn't been doing that for years now. His gaze started with her slim neck and collarbone.

He'd lost count of how many times he'd pictured kissing a trail from that collarbone up to whisper the dirtiest of thoughts into her ear. He noted her makeup, light like always. Liam always thought natural beauty was the best, and the way Amarah did hers made those eyes of hers stop any man in their tracks. So deep and blue, like the most beautiful gems you'd ever seen.

He tried to force himself to stop those thoughts, to pay attention to the road but his eyes would drift right back to her soon enough. This time, it landed on the cleavage that presented itself at the top of her tank top. Amarah never showed much, but just enough to draw you in and make any man want a full look at the mystery hiding underneath her shirt.

Focus on the road, Liam scolded himself, rubbing a hand over the dark scruff of his neatly trimmed beard. *Exactly how would you explain that you wrecked because you were having the most inappropriate thoughts about your best friend's little sister?*

All too soon, he found his eyes back on her. Lower this time at her long, tanned legs that were exposed beneath her jean shorts. He'd never admit just how many times he'd imagined those legs wrapped around his neck as he buried his face in what he knew could be nothing less than heaven. It took everything in Liam to not reach over and rest his hand on Amarah's bare thigh as he drove. He gripped the steering wheel harder, fighting the urge.

Before Amarah realized it, they were pulling back through Liam's gate. He left his truck parked in the driveway so he'd have more room in the garage to put the new tires on her Tahoe.

"Tell me a little about my job duties that I'll be required to complete," Amarah said as she leaned back in a folding lawn chair and watched as Liam jacked up one side of her Tahoe.

"Well, with your degree in finance, I'll have you managing budgeted funds. I go out of town frequently to meet with potential and existing clients, so you'll also arrange my travel details. When I get paperwork from new clients, you'll create a folder for them and file all the paperwork," Liam said as he loosened the lug nuts on one of the ruined tires and removed it from the Tahoe.

"Ok, all seems manageable. What else?" she asked as she caught herself biting her bottom lip.

She cursed inwardly but was thankful he had his back toward her. She couldn't stop gawking at the way his muscles moved and flexed with each movement.

"You'll be in charge of reaching out to clients and arranging meetings so they can pitch new projects to me or discuss ongoing projects." He tightened the lug nuts on the new tire, lowered the Tahoe off the jack, moved to the back, and jacked it up again.

"Will I be answering a lot of phone calls daily?" Amarah inquired further.

"No, I have a receptionist who'll manage the bulk of incoming calls. She'll patch the important ones through to you," Liam said as he removed the second ruined tire and grabbed the new one.

"Ok. Will I be required to bring you coffee in the mornings?" she joked.

"No," he laughed. "I'm capable of getting my own."

"Mm, maybe I should have you bring me coffee each morning instead."

He finished tightening the second tire and lowered the SUV off the jack again.

"Only if you've been a good girl." Liam gave her a wicked grin before he moved to the other side and repeated the process.

"You better behave! I would hate to go to HR and have to file a harassment complaint against my boss."

"I always behave," he called from the other side of the vehicle, amusement evident in his tone.

"Somehow, I doubt that." She laughed.

Liam wrapped things up as he tightened down the last tire, lowered it off the jack, and took her Tahoe for a test drive around the neighborhood to make sure everything was good with her vehicle before parking it in the driveway.

"Thank you, Liam. I appreciate you doing this for me," Amarah said as she climbed into her SUV.

"Anytime, Cupcake, you know that." Liam winked at her, closed her door, and made his way back into his garage. She just smiled, shook her head, and made her way back home.

Amarah spent the rest of the afternoon relaxing on her couch with a good book. Before she knew it, it was 9 p.m. She showered, brushed her teeth, and climbed into bed. After setting her alarms for the next morning, she checked her messages.

No texts, no missed calls, no voicemails from either Detective Trenton or even worse, Derick. No news was better than bad news, she reminded herself as she snuggled into her body pillow and drifted off to sleep.

CHAPTER 19

The sound of Amarah's alarm buzzing at 5:45 a.m. woke her from a restless sleep. She tossed and turned all night, trying to stop her brain from worrying about the what-ifs with Derick.

Reluctantly, she got out of bed, washed her face, brushed her teeth, and braided her hair. After applying her makeup, she headed to her closet to pick an outfit for the day. She grabbed a pair of black high heels that strapped around the ankle to finish off the outfit.

She grabbed her keys, phone, and her purse, checking herself in the mirror by her front door and smiling at her reflection. Today was going to be a good day. Amarah had a new job that Derick knew nothing about, she looked fantastic, and she got to work with Liam. As long as Liam behaved, everything would be fine.

She did feel safe knowing that she'd be working with him. She always felt safe whenever she was with him. If, by some miracle, Derick did find and approach her at her new job, she knew he'd have Liam to answer to. She'd pay good money to see Liam do some damage to the man and knock him down a few pegs.

Godrik Enterprises was located downtown in the heart of the city. Thankfully it was located within a few miles of her old job, so her commute wasn't much different. Godrik Enterprises was its own standalone ten-story office building that was modernly designed with glass windows completely covering the building. There was a large four-story concrete parking garage around the back for employees.

It was one of the top-ranking real estate and architecture firms in the world. They owned hundreds of properties around the world that ranged in variety from hotels, homes, office buildings, skyscrapers, restaurants, resorts, and many more.

Because Liam had some of the most prestigious architects working for him, people from all over the world would reach out to him about something they wanted designed and built.

Amarah rounded the corner and turned into the parking garage. She found a good space not too far from the elevator, gathered her things, and began walking. About halfway to the elevator, she felt the hair on her neck stand up and goosebumps prickled on her arms. She froze in place as fear and panic swept through her.

She pivoted and looked around hastily, but like always, no one was there. *Stop it, Amarah. You are freaking yourself out for no reason. Derick's not out there.* She calmed herself down and turned back, quickening her pace, and pressing the button frantically to call the elevator.

Once inside the main building, she took in the space. The lobby was open and the wraparound windows allowed the morning sun to flood the room. It was decorated in cream, navy blue, and dark oak furniture. The floors were laid with white and grey marble ceramic tiles. Cream-colored armchairs with navy blue pillows in each one were stationed around the lobby.

Amarah approached the help desk up front, letting them know it was her first day. A kind older lady in her mid-thirties gave her a badge to be able to scan through security. All employees had one, each with a unique code that showed a picture of the person it belonged to anytime it was scanned. If security found someone using one that wasn't theirs, well… Let's just say it wasn't pretty.

She directed Amarah to the elevators that would take her to the top floor where she'd be working. Once in the elevator, Amarah reached out with a shaky hand and pressed the button for the tenth floor. *Stupid new job jitters,* she cursed at herself. She hated being the new person, not knowing how things were done, who was who, and what not to do. However, give her about a week, and it'd seem like she'd worked there for years. She'd always been a fast learner.

The steel elevator doors opened on the tenth floor, and she stepped out. It was decorated the same as the lobby downstairs. There was a large desk to the left that was manned by a woman who looked around the same age as her. She was a petite little thing with brown hair tied up into a tight bun, large, round glasses resting on a button nose, and the occasional freckles dotting under her light green eyes. The silver name plate on her desk read "Allison."

Allison smiled at Amarah as she exited the elevator. "Good morning! You must be Amarah. Am I right?"

Oh boy, she's a bubbly one. The girl was all giddiness and smiles. It wasn't even 7:30 a.m. yet. Allison practically bounced over to her with excitement.

"Yes, how did you know?" Amarah couldn't help but chuckle amusingly.

"Mr. Godrik told me he was expecting you. He gave me a description, and I knew it was you right away. Alright, let me show you around," Allison practically sang as she walked past her desk and looped her arm through Amarah's. Her head barely reached Amarah's shoulder. "This is my desk, which of course, you already knew. My job is to answer phones and direct people to where they need to go when they come up. Those doors to your right will take you into our conference room." She pointed to two thick wooden doors to the right of the elevator.

"We only have a few offices up here and they belong to the higher-ups. The head of HR, the CFO, one for each of our world-renowned architects, a filing room, and then yours and of course, Mr. Godrik's." She pointed around the open space to the offices that bordered the walls, each of their doors leading to a large middle section that held a rather large dark wooden conference table that seated twelve comfortably.

"Further on, straight back," Allison pointed with a tiny, well-manicured hand, "is your office and Mr. Godrik's."

She walked Amarah past the other offices and around the conference table to where there was another set of large double doors. Just before the doors, tucked away to the left, was a nook that housed a large dark wood desk complete with a computer, two monitors, and basic office supplies.

A solid black computer chair that looked very expensive and comfortable sat behind the desk. There were floor-to-ceiling bookshelves that lined the wall behind it. Ideas flooded Amarah's mind with what she could put on them to personalize her space. This space was significantly smaller than her old office, but she didn't care one bit. She found the area cozy and quiet. The perfect combination.

"Mr. Godrik is waiting for you in his office. If you've got any questions about anything at all, you know where I'll be. Good luck, you'll do great!" Allison gave her a little squeeze of the arm she still held on to, smiled big at her, and practically skipped back to her desk. Amarah shook her head slightly while giggling to herself as she opened one of the double doors to Liam's office.

CHAPTER 20

Amarah gasped as her vision drifted around Liam's office, taking in the space that was flooded with the morning sun lighting the sky. She was expecting the same color design scheme as the rest of the building, but this space was something completely different.

Dark hardwood floors were spread horizontally, making the room appear bigger, and covered with an oversized blood red area rug centered in the middle. The walls were painted flat black and a large, framed world map hung centered on the right wall, with photos of some of the most beautifully architecturally designed buildings from all over the world placed around it.

The entire back wall was buried behind white built-in bookcases littered with books and knickknacks, much like his home office. A large white desk sat in the middle of the space facing the door containing only the bare minimum of equipment on it. Two monitors were angled off to one side, a black mouse and keyboard, and a large silver nameplate sat in the middle.

Amarah's eyes couldn't help but drift to the left wall that was nothing but windows. *Oh, the view,* she thought. She wondered how he ever got any work done when he had that to look at. The city spread out before them—buildings of different colors, styles, and heights that had no right to go together, blended perfectly with each other. Each had its own special characteristics that made it beautiful.

Her vision drifted to the last place she had yet to discover and instantly her eyes grew twice as round. A large white microfiber sofa with black and red throw pillows was sitting between two white wood end tables, each topped with a small wrought iron framed lamp with red shades.

Her mind recalled what Liam said about that couch, how he had one in his office that needed to be broken in. Heat instantly rose within her and color flooded her cheeks as she pictured him bending her over it, with her skirt hiked up to her waist and her hair balled up in one of his large hands.

She clenched her thighs together with need and turned away from the couch, shaking those thoughts off, only to find a pair of piercing green eyes centered on a god-like face with the most devilish grin spread across those full, kissable lips. Instantly, her thong dampened with want.

The moment Amarah entered his office, Liam knew he messed up... Big time! As she took in the room, he took her in, raking his eyes all over her body. He made a mental note to inform her that her new dress code would be sweats and a hoodie, because with her dressed like that, he wouldn't be able to focus and get any work done. Him or any other guy in the building.

It should be illegal for clothes to form perfectly around a woman's body, and that's exactly what she had. Gone were the days of a skinny, preteen, stick figure. Her body had blossomed into that of a mature, sexy, curvy woman who knew the exact effect on men she had.

Her dark purple blouse was pulled tight to accentuate her beautifully perky tits and shrank around her stomach to show just how small her waist truly was. That black pencil skirt showed off the full curves of her hips, and damn, when she turned around to look at the couch, her ass could be what wars were fought over. The slit in the back was nothing but a tease that made Liam groan inwardly.

He started to feel blood rushing to a certain extension of his body. The effect she had on him was clearly evident by the bulge now straining against the zipper of his suit pants, begging to be set free to play. He leaned back in his chair, stretched his legs out, crossed them at the ankles, and interlocked his fingers behind his head.

As her gaze swept over the couch, he saw her body tense, knowing all too well she remembered what he said to her. He wanted nothing more in that moment than to rip that skirt from her body, bend her over the arm of the couch, grab her hips tightly, and pound deep into her warm center.

Liam could tell by the slight clench of her thighs, the flush of her cheeks, and the now unevenness of her breath, that she wanted it too. Unfortunately, that territory was prohibited, but he could still have some fun and torment her. He wasted no time putting his best devilish grin on full display.

"Good morning, Cupcake," Liam said in a low and humorous tone. "That outfit complements you well."

"Really? You don't think it's... inappropriate?" Amarah asked hesitantly.

She knew all her clothes were perfectly acceptable, but Derick's negative words repeated in the back of her mind, making her self-conscious.

"Not at all." Liam sounded almost shocked that she even asked. "I'll have to inform the men that you're off-limits though, but that won't stop them from looking. Why do you ask?" He raised an eyebrow in question.

"No reason. I just wanted to make sure I looked the part," Amarah lied.

"You definitely do. But you look a little flustered. Is everything ok?" A sly grin pulled at one side of his full lips.

"What? Oh... A... Yeah, I'm good," she said, miserably failing to get herself under control. She knew the burning in her cheeks was a dead giveaway.

Amarah watched as Liam stood from his chair and slowly stalked toward her, like a lion approaching its prey, and she quickly realized that *she* was the prey. It was as if her feet grew roots, anchoring her to the floor. She couldn't make herself move. All she could do was watch this sexy man, dressed to kill in an all-black suit that molded around every muscle in his large arms and chest and spread tight across his broad shoulders. His black hair looked as if it'd been freshly cut while the strands up top were brushed back as if he'd just run his fingers through it.

Her body betrayed her with each step he took, her core growing tighter and her underwear growing wetter. Her body was reacting on its own, like it always did, getting ready for what it truly wanted, whether her mind wanted it or not. Even though it always did and always would. She clenched her thighs tighter, wishing the throbbing ache would go away.

He stepped close to her, so close she could feel the heat from his body and smell the woodsy scent of his body wash. "Are you sure? Maybe you should sit down. I have a couch right over there that's pretty comfortable."

Oh, this asshole. Amarah knew exactly what he was doing. Knew he was reading her body language, a skill he'd mastered, and knew he was toying with her. Instead of being the lamb, she would be the lioness. He wanted to play? Alright, two can play that game. She had no idea where she got the courage from, but she was going to run with it while she had it.

She laid her hand ever so gently against his strong chest as she tilted her head up, looking at him with those big blue eyes of hers. "Maybe I should. Would you like to join me? It's big enough for the both of us."

CHAPTER 21

Liam's expression changed. A flicker of surprise flashed through his eyes for a split second before they darkened. If Amarah hadn't been looking right into them, she would've missed it. With a blink of his green eyes, his face went hard, showing no emotion.

She knew it was a shielding tactic that meant he wanted no one to know or see what was going through his mind. But being physically close to Liam, she didn't need to see his face to know what he was feeling. With her hand on his chest, she could feel his heart beating a little quicker.

A small growl emitted deep within his chest, and Amarah found herself wishing she had an extra pair of underwear with her. The ones she was wearing were completely drenched now.

She leaned into him ever so slightly and started walking two fingers up his broad chest until she was rubbing the palm of her hand through the dark scruff on his cheek. She'd fully expected him to pull away but instead, he surprised her by turning his head into her touch as if he loved the feeling of her soft delicate hands on his rough features.

"You better be careful, Cupcake. If you play with fire, you might get burned," he warned in a husky voice.

"Maybe I want to be burned," she returned in a sensual voice of her own—one she'd never heard before.

No sooner did the last syllable leave Amarah's lips, she found herself being uprooted off the floor. In one fluid motion, Liam scrunched up her skirt around her thighs, hoisted her up by her plump ass, and placed her right on top of his desk, standing dangerously close between her legs. He held her face between his large calloused hands, forcing her to meet his penetrating gaze, those green eyes of his searching her soul for who knows what.

"Be careful what you ask for. You might just get it," he growled into her ear, sending a wave of pleasure coursing through her body at the thought of being taken by him.

Amarah sent up a silent prayer that there wouldn't be a puddle on his desk when she got up. Who knew simple words—when structured together just right—could have such a huge effect on someone? It made her body come alive in ways she didn't think possible.

Liam leaned into her, causing her to lay back flat atop his desk. He placed his elbows down on each side of her head and laid his chest on top of hers, not putting his full weight on her, but wanting her to feel his hard frame against her soft curves.

Amarah's eyes grew wide as she felt his rod pressing into her lower stomach. She couldn't judge how long it was, but that didn't matter because she felt just how thick it was, rock hard and ready for her. Her imagination ran wild, trying to picture exactly what it looked like, what it might taste like even.

"I always get what I want," she whispered, not sure how she was still able to speak coherently. She was a puddle of emotions lying atop his desk.

She wanted this, wanted him, in every way possible. She'd loved this man since they were kids, and though she never wanted to admit it to herself, the reason she never had sex with anyone was because she wanted to give that one special piece of herself to him. Liam already held her heart, whether he knew it or not.

You're going way too far with this, Liam thought to himself. Playing a game and teasing was one thing, but he was dangerously approaching a line that there would be no coming back from once crossed. However, when Amarah flipped the script on him, playing into it instead of shying away like usual, he got a taste of *what if.*

Questions he never should be thinking of danced through his mind. What does she taste like? What would she look like underneath him? How tight would that sweet pussy of hers grip his cock?

He found himself wondering where she got her confidence from. He loved it and cursed it at the same time. He was forced to become a master of his emotions—he had to, or it would've meant an early grave for him on operations—but he never understood how this woman, this tiny five-foot-seven goddess could make him lose all control. The amount of pull she had over him was dangerous if she ever learned that.

Liam knew Amarah could feel his member pressing into her stomach and saw the shocked expression in her eyes. *Yes, Cupcake, this is what you do to me. The power you have no idea you have over me. Fuck it,* he thought. They were all adults. If Travis had a problem with it, he could get over it.

He wanted her so badly in that moment, had wanted her for a very long time now, and knew for certain that she wanted him too. The evidence of exactly how badly she craved him would be present between her legs. Liam couldn't wait to explore that uncharted territory.

"Are you sure this is what you want?" Liam removed one arm from his desk and brought it to her left leg as he slowly and gently trailed a path with the tips of his fingers up the inside of her thigh.

He watched as her eyes drifted closed. "Yes," she pleaded in a breathless moan.

It's actually going to happen, she thought, *right here in his office.* This wasn't exactly how she pictured her first time, but she wasn't about to refuse. No way in hell.

A soft moan escaped her lips as he grazed the sensitive flesh of her inner thigh, approaching her core with agonizing slowness. She knew he was teasing her. This was torture, but she loved every second of it.

"Will I find the evidence of just how badly you want this between those sexy legs of yours?" Liam asked in a lust-filled voice as he buried his face in the crook of her neck and inhaled her sweet scent.

"Yes," Amarah whimpered.

"Dirty girl." He chuckled wickedly. A tortured groan escaped his throat as his fingers rubbed the outside of her soaked thong. "Fuck, Cupcake."

"Liam," Amarah pleaded no louder than a whisper. She hoped his name on her lips told him exactly how badly she wanted him, how badly she craved more of his touch.

Just as he was about to pull her thong to the side and explore her heated sex, a knock sounded at the door, snapping them both out of bliss and back to reality.

"Motherfucker," Liam growled in a low and dangerous voice.

He straightened up, fixed his clothes, and composed himself again as if nothing ever happened. As if he wasn't just about to fuck his best friend's little sister on his desk.

A small whimper escaped Amarah's lips at being interrupted, but she quickly composed herself too. He held out a hand, helping her off his desk. She fixed her clothing before she walked over to the door, waiting until Liam was sitting behind his desk before she opened it.

Allison was standing there with a tall gentleman dressed in a blue suit, with peppered hair and a matching beard.

"I'm sorry to interrupt, Mr. Godrik, but Mr. Lemming—your 8 a.m. appointment—is here to see you," Allison said with a big smile.

Amarah wondered if the girl had been born smiling.

"Good morning, Mr. Lemming. I'm Amarah, Mr. Godrik's personal assistant. It's a pleasure to meet you. Please come in and make yourself comfortable." She was completely in business mode now, giving him a nod of her head and a genuine smile.

She didn't miss the way his eyes went from her face, down her body, and back up again a little slower than usual. Mr. Lemming gave her a big smile in return.

"Thank you, ma'am. It's a pleasure to meet you as well," he said, stepping into Liam's office.

Amarah stepped out and closed the door behind her, but not before meeting Liam's gaze one last time. A hint of lust still lingered as well as something else she thought she detected. Sadness, perhaps? She quickly dropped her gaze, closed the door, and went back to her desk to get to work.

She needed the distraction, big time. She couldn't believe what had just happened. That went further than she'd planned. She didn't feel guilty though. She only wished that it *had* gone further. Much further.

CHAPTER 22

It'd been two days since Amarah started working for Liam, and nothing remotely sexual had happened between them again. They both had a silent agreement to pretend that it never even happened. Simply chalking it up to getting caught up in the moment. Amarah had started to relax more. She hadn't heard a peep from Derick at all.

Detective Trenton did call her on Wednesday morning to update that they did have Derick on camera at an ATM withdrawing a large sum of money from his account. By the time they got a squad car there, he was gone. They tried tracking him with cameras through the city, but after he'd disappeared into an alley, the trail went cold.

Derick now had cash, which meant he wouldn't be using a card anytime soon. Unless someone reported a possible sighting, the police had nothing more to go on and were at a standstill. Again. That could also mean he was planning to leave town. She remained hopeful, something that she found almost futile nowadays.

Amarah had just parked her SUV after returning from lunch and was making her way to the elevator in the parking garage when she got that feeling again. The feeling that made her stomach churn and the hairs on her body stand up. Instantly, a deep chill ran down her spine. She steeled herself as she turned around to check her surroundings.

Getting that feeling once could be written off as paranoia but getting it twice, in the same parking garage, couldn't be a coincidence. She didn't find anyone though. She never did when she got that feeling.

Maybe they were just delusions, something her mind had created from the strain of so much stress and fear. She hoped the authorities found Derick quickly. She was tired of looking over her shoulder everywhere she went.

She sighed loudly, turned around, and took a step only to walk into what felt like a brick wall. "Oh, shit!" Amarah screamed as she stumbled backward, tripping over her heels, and braced for impact on the hard concrete floor.

Only it never came. One large hand reached around and supported her back while another gripped her bicep. Not aggressively, just enough to keep her upright. She frantically looked up and met the piercing gaze of beautiful green eyes.

"Someone's jumpy," Liam joked as he peered down at Amarah.

He'd come down to the parking garage and saw her standing there looking around. Her back was to him, and she didn't answer when he called out to her. As he reached her, she turned around and bumped right into him.

Thanking his fast reflexes for being able to catch her, Liam held her there for a moment longer, liking the look of her in his arms. Those deep blue eyes stared up at him, registering who caught her. Amarah sighed a breath of relief as he stood her upright, making sure she was steady before letting go.

"You scared the crap out of me," she said to him while slapping his chest.

"What were you looking at?" he asked, pinching his brows together and searching past her, trying to see anything out of place.

"What? Oh, nothing. Parking garages just give me the heebie-jeebies is all," she said. "You heading out to catch your flight?"

Liam wasn't convinced. He knew Amarah was hiding something, he just hadn't figured out what yet. Most people wouldn't see anything different, but his eyes were far from untrained, picking up on her changes in behavior.

He'd noticed that whenever they were together, she'd been checking her phone more often as if she was expecting horrible news about a sick family member. She had become jumpy, as if seeing her shadow would send her into hiding. She'd lost a bit of her light, like some monster in the shadows was trying to swallow her up and she was clinging on to the remaining rays of light for dear life. That bright smile she always wore had dimmed, and the way she acted after her phone call last Saturday was weird.

Amarah claimed it was just her boss, but he didn't buy it. And now this? Something was definitely going on with her and he couldn't put his finger on it. He wished, more than anything, that she'd just talk to him about it.

"Nice subject change," Liam said flatly. "Yes, I'll be back Friday morning. I have a work function to attend that night. A charity ball. Would you like to be my plus one?"

Amarah looked at him for a second, stunned. Was he asking her out? No, he said it was a work function. He must need his assistant with him for whatever reason.

"I don't own anything fancy enough to attend a black-tie event."

"No worries. Take the company credit card and get a dress, and shoes to match if you need them. It *is* technically a work-related expense." He chuckled.

"Oh no, I couldn't—"

"Are you arguing with me?" he asked, arching a brow and lowering his tone.

"No, sir," Amarah said, knowing it would get under his skin just as it gets under her skin anytime he teases her with innocent flirtation.

"That's what I thought." He gave her his famous wicked smile and started off towards his truck.

She turned and watched him walk away, glaring at the back of his head. That man was going to be the death of her. She made her way back up to her office, only having a few more hours left in her workday before it was quitting time.

Amarah hadn't heard much from Liam while he was out of town. He texted her to let her know he had landed and had gotten settled into his hotel. The next day he texted with some details from his meeting with a potential client for her to get some paperwork started, and then texted again on Friday morning.

> **Liam:** Good morning, Cupcake. These last few days have been dull without you here to annoy. I'll pick you up tonight at 7 p.m.
>
> **Amarah:** I don't know if I'll be able to make it. My boss is kind of a dick and the last thing I want to do is spend my Friday night with the man.
>
> **Liam:** Either you're ready by 7 p.m. or I'll call you into my office Monday morning, bend you over my desk, and spank you as punishment.
>
> **Amarah:** See, he's a dick! UGH FINE!

Without Liam there to distract her, she had a productive day: worked through a bunch of emails, got invoices organized, and updated some budget spreadsheets. Each day she felt less and less like the new girl. Everyone was very friendly and helpful in answering any questions she had.

No word from Detective Trenton and still nothing from Derick. It'd been a week, so maybe he truly was gone. Amarah stopped by the dry cleaners, picked up her dress, and booked it to her hair appointment at a beauty salon to get it styled for the night. She described her dress to the short, plump hairdresser.

The lady advised that her hair in an updo would be best with that style of dress. Amarah didn't argue. The hairdresser was the professional after all. The lady went to work and put her hair up into a bun that had a thick braid wrapped around it. She had left a few strands on each side of Amarah's head down and curled them to frame her angular features.

Amarah had to do a double take. Her hair looked fantastic. She paid the woman and drove home to get started on her makeup. On special occasions like this, she paid a little more attention than usual. She put on some foundation and powder, did a smokey eye, and topped it off with bright red lipstick and shimmery gloss over top to make it sparkle.

Amarah pulled her beautiful dress out of the garment bag and stepped into it. The dress was solid black and strapless, which pulled her boobs up tight, front and center. It was form-fitting and hugged her waist and hips, showing off her curves. The back did a crisscross pattern to expose a good amount of skin and tied off right above her ass. There was a long slit up the left side that stopped at the top of her thigh. She knew it was pretty risqué, but the moment she saw it, she knew it was the one. She smiled at her reflection, satisfied with her appearance.

She looked at the clock and noted that she had five minutes before Liam would be there. He was *always* punctual. Another habit he gained from the military, but she always knew exactly when to expect him. She cleaned up her mess, put everything back in its place, and sprayed the Obsession perfume she loved so much on her wrists and a little on each side of her neck.

To pull her outfit together, she grabbed a pair of diamond earrings out of her jewelry box. Her hand paused halfway to her ear. Some of her other jewelry had been moved as if someone picked up each piece and didn't set them back down in their correct location.

A sickening feeling churned her stomach as a horrific thought entered her mind. A few articles of clothing had mysteriously gone missing, some of her books had been rearranged, and now her jewelry had been touched. Had someone broken into her home and messed with her belongings? Did Derick know where she lived?

No, he would've made his presence known to her. He didn't seem like the kind to lurk in the shadows. He seemed more of the in-your-face type. She closed her eyes, tried to roll the tension off her shoulders and took a few slow breaths as she made her way to the front door.

Amarah grabbed a black clutch she found in her closet, making sure she had her ID, some cash, and her phone. Lastly, she slipped on a pair of black open-toed high heels that strapped around the ankle—completing her ensemble—and showed off her freshly painted red toenails to match her lips.

Right on time, Liam rang her doorbell at 7 p.m. sharp. Amarah took one last look at herself in the mirror by her door, smiled, and opened it.

"You know, sometimes your punctuality is scary," she said as she shut and locked the door behind her.

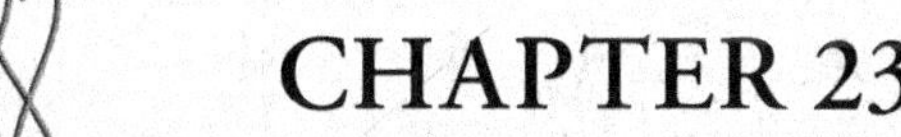

CHAPTER 23

If this were nineteenth-century England, the moment Amarah had opened her door, she would've swooned. Her heart rate spiked, and her lungs momentarily forgot how to function. Liam stood there in a black-as-night suit with a dark purple dress shirt underneath and a black tie. Her core tightened instantly as she looked upon her god of death.

His suit was pulled tightly over his broad shoulders and large arms. Even his pants were expertly tailored to form around his ass and tall, muscular legs perfectly. His black hair was freshly cut with a medium fade and styled with a little bit of gel up top, and his dark beard was trimmed close to his tanned skin, leaving a good amount of stubble to ogle over.

Time had ceased to exist. It could've been seconds or minutes she was gawking at Liam. When she finally brought her eyes up, she only prayed that her face wouldn't betray her thoughts. But she had nothing to worry about because his eyes weren't on her face, they were raking down her body. Before she could accurately gauge if that was lust in his gaze, he'd blinked, cleared his throat, and schooled his features behind his usual calm mask.

"Ready?" he asked, extending his elbow to her.

Amarah nodded, knowing her lack of voice would give away the effect he was having on her right now. He escorted her to his truck, opened the door, and held her hand as she climbed in. She closed her eyes and took a deep breath to steady herself before he opened his door and climbed in too.

They rode in silence, and before she knew it, they were pulling under the covered entrance of a high-end hotel, parking at the valet stand. A kid who looked straight out of high school, dressed in black slacks and a red polo shirt with a golden name tag labeled "Jack," walked around to meet Liam by the front of his truck. They exchanged the keys for the valet ticket.

Liam walked around, opened the door for Amarah, and held out a hand to help her down. He extended his left elbow, and she looped her arm through his, loving the feeling of her hand resting on his muscular bicep, fighting hard not to give it a firm squeeze.

She was thankful that he was escorting her because she was too busy ogling over the high-end décor placed throughout the lobby to pay attention to where she was going. Her eyes drifted up to watch the light bounce off the crystals of multiple chandeliers that were suspended from the ceiling. She stopped dead in her tracks as her mouth gaped open in shock. She thought the lobby was beautiful but the ballroom… The ballroom was magical, making her feel as if she stepped right into a fairytale.

Men and women all dressed in their finest gowns and suits stood around in small groups, chatting or dancing. Rows and rows of tables were draped with a light ice blue fabric with dark wooden chairs circling them. Each table was topped with the most beautiful bouquet of a variety of red and white flowers placed in crystal vases.

Each vase had a white and ice blue ribbon wrapped around it. There was a stage up front where a string quartet played one of the most beautiful melodies her ears had ever heard. A wooden dance floor littered with twirling couples lay at the foot of the stage.

Amarah couldn't stop her eyes from darting up to see if the same crystal chandeliers hung in here as in the lobby. They did, but something even better caught her eye. Thousands of white twinkling lights were strung across the ceiling, creating a beautiful and elegant glow that played well with the crystals of the chandeliers.

Servers dressed in white, long-sleeve button-up shirts tucked into black slacks walked around carrying silver trays lined with long-stemmed glasses containing sweet red wine. Liam grabbed two glasses from a server passing by and extended one toward Amarah. Her gaze dropped from the ceiling to his beautiful green eyes. The way he was looking at her as if she were the only person in the room made her heart skip a beat.

"Stay close, ok? There can be a lot of grabby old pervs at these types of events," he said, leaning in close to whisper in her ear.

She just giggled and sipped from her glass. But Amarah did just that as different men introduced themselves and their spouses, if they had one. That's how it always was, others approaching Liam. He never had to seek anyone out to talk to. People just tended to gravitate toward him, and he always greeted them with a smile and introduced her to everyone they met, never once making her feel invisible or forgotten.

"Let's take our seats. The auction is about to begin," he said as he placed one of his large hands on the small of her back to lead them to their table.

The moment his hand made contact with her exposed skin, butterflies took flight in her stomach. Liam led her to a table up front where they found name cards written in elegant calligraphy. They took their seats as Amarah snagged another glass of wine from a server passing by, placing her empty glass on their tray. It was so good, she couldn't stop drinking it. This was her third.

"Feeling adventurous, are we?" Liam raised a teasing black brow at her.

"I'm spending my Friday night with my boss. I'll need at least two more just to get through the night. What's being auctioned off anyway? Handsome eligible bachelors for a night of fine dining?"

"No." He chuckled softly. "Why? Would that be something you would be interested in?"

"Who wouldn't like being romanced by a rich man for a night? If that's the case, I'm using the company credit card for my bids. This is technically a work function," Amarah teased.

"You think I'd let you go on a date with a random stranger?" Liam asked as two deep creases formed between his brows.

"Isn't every first date technically with a stranger?" She laughed and then hiccupped quietly. "And sorry to burst your bubble, but you have no control over my life."

"It's not control, Cupcake. I just want to protect you. My body count is high enough. I'd hate to have to add another number to the total because someone hurt or disrespected you in any way."

"Your body count? Like sex partners?" Amarah asked, confused, as she cocked her head to the side.

Though she knew he was most likely well experienced in the art of sex, the last thing she wanted was to think about him engaging in the act with other women. Women who weren't her. It made an ugly green monster try to roar to life deep within. And she had no right. Liam wasn't hers. He'd never be, no matter how badly she wished he would.

"No." He laughed as a wicked grin pulled at his lips. "Death count."

"Oh..." She wasn't sure what else to say.

What Liam said should have sent her running for a cab. He just confessed that he's killed men, as in multiple, but all it did was cause her to clench her thighs together with want. The fact that he'd kill just to protect her, to keep her safe? What woman wouldn't want the man they loved to be willing to go to such extremes? Curiosity had her wanting to ask just how high a number his death count was, but she knew better. That wasn't something anyone should dare ask a service member. Ever.

"Every year, I purchase artwork from local artists and then auction it off here to the highest bidders. All the proceeds are then donated to charity."

"Wait, this is your event?" Amarah asked in total surprise.

Liam winked at her, took a swig from his glass, and walked on stage. She followed him with her eyes, waiting for some kind of explanation.

"Good evening, ladies and gentlemen." Liam spoke into a black microphone as everyone quickly found their seats. "Thank you for getting all dressed up and spending your Friday night here with us. I hope you all brought your checkbooks because the auction will be starting soon."

"About five years back, I attended a function just like this and was amazed at the turnout they received, and it inspired me to do the same with my own company. Every piece you see tonight has come from local artists. Every dollar raised will be donated to a charity I hold close to my heart—the Vet's First Foundation. It's an organization created with a single goal in mind: to place veteran men and women as the priority, helping them with anything they may need—housing, job placement, counseling, medical treatments, and more. So please, enjoy your night, buy some art, drink some wine, and dance the night away. Thank you." The crowd clapped and cheered as he exited the stage and took his seat next to a very shocked Amarah.

"If I wasn't on my third glass, I would be totally upset that you've never mentioned this before. You really are a big softie, aren't you?"

"Alright, I'm cutting you off. Water from here on out."

"Ha! You're not the boss of me. Oh, wait..." Amarah paused in realization. "You actually *are* my boss now. Why do you have to ruin everything?" She pouted.

CHAPTER 24

The auction was a huge hit. Every piece sold for thousands above the starting price, making the total donation amount well over $150,000. After the last piece had been sold, the quartet started up again, allowing people to mingle and dance some more. Amarah was still sitting at their table when a man approached her.

"May I have this dance?" A smile spread across his slim face.

She peered up at the man who held his hand out waiting for an answer, his chocolate eyes studying her. He wore a tuxedo that formed around his slim frame snugly. His brown hair was cut short, and he was clean-shaven. He was cute. She observed no ring or tan line in sight, and she wanted to dance.

As she took his hand, she looked over at Liam to let him know where she would be, but he had his back to her, talking to someone about who knows what.

The stranger didn't give her time to get a word out before he was pulling her toward the dance floor. "What's your name?" he asked as he took one of her hands in his and placed the other on her lower back.

"Amarah," she answered as he began swaying them around the dance floor.

She was thankful that he knew what he was doing. Not the greatest, but at least she wouldn't get a broken toe from the man stepping on her foot.

"A beautiful name for a beautiful woman. Mine's Brandon," he said in a sensual tone, slowly creeping his hand lower to rest just above her ass.

That got her attention quickly, finding his touch revolting. She reached around and moved Brandon's hand up her back to a more appropriate spot.

"Apologies. Sometimes they have a mind of their own," Brandon said lightheartedly and shrugged as if it were no big deal.

But roaming hands, especially uninvited ones, are a huge deal. Not even ten seconds later, a deep voice spoke from behind her. She didn't have to turn around to know who that beautiful voice belonged to. Her body recognized it anywhere, coming alive as it always did.

"I believe it's my turn." Liam's presence consumed her, wrapping around her like a warm blanket.

Brandon halted their dance, glaring at Liam. Most likely for having the audacity to interrupt, however, Amarah couldn't find it in her to be upset. She was glad their dance was now over.

"Sorry man, she's dancing with me right now." Brandon picked his foot up to take a step, wanting to continue, only to be halted in his tracks when Liam placed a hand on his shoulder. Not in a mean or aggressive way, just casually, which is what made it all the more threatening.

"I think you misunderstood me. I wasn't asking," Liam said flatly, rocking his world-famous expressionless face.

Brandon let go of Amarah and leaned in to say something quietly to Liam, who still had a hand on the man's shoulder. She tried to hear what Brandon was saying, but his voice was too low to hear over the music.

He'd turned his head from her so she couldn't read his lips either. She tried reading his body movements but that didn't work. She turned, thinking she could study Liam's face instead. Maybe his reaction would help her understand what was being said. That was futile, though, because the man never showed what he was thinking. She gave up in the end and waited patiently to see how this was going to play out.

Once Brandon finished, it was Liam's turn to respond. Amarah noticed Liam's grip on Brandon's shoulder tighten, turning his knuckles white. Brandon tried to act tough and hold in the pain he was clearly feeling. Whatever Liam said to him had Brandon pulling back, his face contorted with fear.

"I'm sorry." Brandon held up his hands defensively as he looked back at Amarah. Then without another word, he turned on his heels and practically bolted off the dance floor.

She was more confused than ever as her gaze followed Brandon's retreating body until he faded into the crowd. She turned back, only to be met with Liam peering down at her.

"May I?" Liam offered his hand.

"I thought you weren't asking." He grinned and his eyes sparkled with amusement. "You know how to dance?" She raised both brows at him in equal amounts of suspicion and surprise.

"I know a few steps," he said with a casual shrug.

She took his hand hesitantly and without missing a beat, he stepped into place and started leading her around the dance floor. All she could do was gawk. A few steps? The man was so swift on his feet, hitting every step with accuracy, not faulting once.

"I'm pretty sure the military doesn't teach you how to ballroom dance. Where'd you learn how to move like this?"

"My mom taught me. She said one of the ways to a woman's heart is to dance with her. So she made sure I knew how."

His mother wasn't wrong. There was something so personal and intimate about dancing and when you had the right partner, it could be downright magical. Amarah never let her smile waver as Liam led her around the floor, occasionally spinning or dipping her. She trusted him completely and let go, just following wherever he led her.

Before she knew it, the song was over, and disappointment washed through her. Amarah didn't want that moment to end. Ever. The band followed up with a slower song and without speaking, Liam pulled her in close and began to sway. There was nothing fancy about this dance. It was more about feeling the closeness of your partner.

Amarah didn't protest and slid her arms up, resting them around his neck as Liam placed both of his strong hands on her back. In a more appropriate position than Brandon had.

Always the gentleman. She didn't want that though. Why was it that the men you want to cop a feel on you, don't, and the ones you don't want to, do? It was always backward.

Because of that delicious wine, Amarah had some liquid courage working in her favor or she would have never done anything so bold. She left one hand up around Liam's neck as she brought the other to rest gently on his chest. She moved in closer, pressing her soft front into his hard frame. She was the perfect height, her head even with his chest.

She closed her eyes, rested her head against his strong pec, and listened to the rhythm of his heart beating in her ear. She felt Liam's body tense for only a moment before he relaxed into her and wrapped his arms around her snugly, resting his chin on the top of her head.

Damnit, Liam cursed inwardly. He never understood how this woman could make him lose all control. Only Amarah could make his heart and body react this way—wanting to throw caution to the wind, wanting to say fuck it and jump headfirst into uncharted waters.

He hadn't taken his eyes off her all night, for more reasons than one. Most of those reasons were very selfish and dirty. How could he not when she was dressed the way she was? He'd nearly gone into cardiac arrest when he picked Amarah up at her house. The moment she opened her front door and stepped out, every intelligent brain cell fled his mind. He couldn't breathe, couldn't speak.

All he could do was move his eyes over every inch of her perfect body. The dress made her voluptuous cleavage stand front and center, making them look truly inviting. And when she'd turned to lock her door, he got a good look at the back and how it showed off a large amount of her gorgeous, smooth skin.

He'd thought he had finally composed himself enough by the time he got into his truck, but his eyes happened to wander across to the goddess in the seat next to him. The slit of her dress was presenting itself by exposing so much of her tanned and toned leg, all the way to the top of her thigh.

A thigh he found himself between just a few days ago. A thigh he wished to be buried between until she screamed his name so much that her voice went hoarse. The exposed skin was enough to tease any man, married or not, and leave them wanting to know what the pot of gold at the end of the rainbow looked like—tasted like, even. That dress on anyone else would look plain, but on her... There were no words. He knew all eyes were going to be on her tonight. And who could blame them? His would be too.

It may have seemed like he wasn't watching, but he was always paying attention, especially if she was around. Liam saw that sleazeball ask Amarah to dance. He wasn't a jealous man by nature, but when it came to that woman, he wanted to strangle Brandon for even thinking about touching her.

Liam refrained though, because she willingly agreed, but the moment he saw Amarah remove Brandon's hand from her ass, Liam saw red. Brandon fucked up and crossed the line by touching her like that without her permission.

Something about dancing with her just felt right and when she pulled in close and rested her head against his chest, he couldn't fight it anymore. He let himself go, consequences be damned, and wrapped her up snugly against himself. All the voices in his head quieted, and the dark acts he'd done in the military faded away. For the first time in years, he was truly at peace. That was where she belonged. Right there in his arms, forever.

Amarah's favorite place to be was in Liam's arms. It was hard to explain, but when he held her, she felt like nothing in the world could ever hurt her. She took a deep breath, loving the woodsy scent of his body wash, and felt all her worries and fears leave.

Gone were her troubles with Derick. Gone were her worries with the case and Detective Trenton. Gone was the paranoia of looking over her shoulder, wondering if she was being watched. Her mind was quiet for once, something it hadn't done since that night at the bar, solely focusing on the rhythm of Liam's heart playing sweet music in her ear. She wished she could stay in this moment forever. But all too soon, the song was over.

Reluctantly, she pulled away. She allowed herself to let go completely, just for one song, to experience what it would be like if they were a real couple. Amarah knew it would never happen, knew Liam didn't think about her like that. She hated doing this to herself, letting her heart have hope, no matter how many times her brain scolded her for it.

All it did was hurt her. Yes, he'd teased her, and they had a few intimate encounters, but all that was just from getting caught up in the moment. Nothing more, unfortunately.

"Thank you for the dance. Remind me to thank your mom the next time I see her." Amarah said as she turned, not wanting to give away anything she was feeling toward Liam.

She thought she heard him groan in frustration, but it was too quiet for her to hear over the music. She turned to glance at him, but he was composed and back to his normal guarded expression.

"It's getting late. Are you ready to leave?" he asked.

"Ready whenever you are," was her only response.

CHAPTER 25

Liam pulled into Amarah's driveway and shut off the engine. He walked around, opened her door, and held out his hand to help her down. They walked to her front door in comfortable silence, only the sounds of her heels clicking against the sidewalk filling the air around them.

"Thank you, Liam. I surprisingly had fun tonight," she said as she reached for the keys in her clutch.

"Me too. Your company isn't as bad as I thought," he joked, earning an eye roll as she playfully slapped his chest. He chuckled. "Good night, Cupcake."

"Good night, Liam." She closed the door behind her, locking it.

Once Liam heard both locks click into place, he made his way back to his truck. He didn't leave though. Not yet. He found himself on autopilot, moving without really thinking as he started up his truck, pulled out of the driveway, and parked along the side of the road two houses down. He became lost in his own thoughts, his mind playing through how Amarah had been acting differently as of late.

Still, within clear view of her house, he sat there and watched. Not sure what he was looking for though. A boogeyman to lurk around the corner. For her to leave her house after knowing he was gone so she could sneak off to some undisclosed location. A man to stop by that she was carrying on a secret relationship with.

Amarah had always been a private person, so her having a boyfriend that no one knew about was a possibility. That thought had him gripping his steering wheel unusually tight. When he realized what he was doing, he let go and released a long breath.

His mind flashed back to that night at the bar two weeks ago. To the guy who had kissed her so possessively and grabbed her ass right in front of him, clearly trying to mark his territory. The poor, insecure excuse of a man tried way too hard to get a reaction from Liam.

Maybe Amarah was still seeing him. But she did end up drinking by herself at the bar, clearly upset about something. If she were still with him, she wouldn't have let herself get caught up in the moment with Liam the other day in his office. One thing he knew for certain about Amarah? She was faithful to her core.

Had their breakup been what was affecting her? Her actions weren't signaling a broken heart. She seemed... scared. Something had to be going on to explain the change in her. Liam had known Amarah since she was a kid.

She was always peppy and cheerful, always optimistic, and hopeful. Growing up, she always wore a big smile on her face. Amarah was the kind of person who would go out of her way to help a stranger. Even if it meant she would go without.

Whatever it was had affected her hard. She wasn't the same, and Liam would give anything to get that sweet, innocent, bright-eyed girl back. Sure, she still smiled a lot, but a smile can hide a broken soul if practiced enough. Her actions had become different as well.

He could see the trouble that haunted her, swirling around in those beautiful blue eyes. Like her soul was trying to scream for help from deep within, no matter how brave a face she put on. Liam had a gut feeling that something more was going on. Those gut feelings had saved his skin more than once while out on operations with the SEALs. He'd learned to listen to them, and listening he was as he watched from his truck.

Amarah hung her keys on the rack by the door as she placed one hand against the solid wood, bracing herself so she could slip her heels off.

They dropped to the ground with a loud thud as she unfastened each strap, letting out a sigh of relief at the sudden pleasure she felt once they were off. Once the second heel hit the floor, she found herself abruptly being shoved against her front door.

"He's just a friend, huh? Nothing romantic has ever happened between y'all? Well, that's not what it looks like," a deep menacing voice mocked as an unwelcome guest held her down against the door.

That voice, she knew it all too well.

Oh no… No… How is this possible?

How was he in her home? How did he find her? Panic rushed in as she tried and failed to fight against Derick.

"Hello, love. I told you I'd see you soon," he said as he spun her around and pressed her back flush against the thick wood, putting his weight on her to hold her in place as he brought one of his large hands up to grip around her throat.

"How…" Amarah choked out, gasping for air.

It felt as if all her breath had been stolen from her, and her voice along with it. She hadn't been losing her mind. Someone had been coming into her house and messing with her things.

"I told you. I have my ways." Derick smiled.

A smile she used to love, that used to send butterflies to her stomach, but now only sent chills down her spine and her stomach churning.

"Now, be a good girl and answer me," he warned her in a threatening tone. "Why the fuck did you lie to me about… What was his name again? Liam?"

"I… never… lied to… you… Derick."

"Did you let him touch you? Did you let him touch what's mine?" he seethed.

She tried to get free, to push him off her, but he was stronger. Anytime she tried to fight against him, he would continue to tighten his hold around her neck. She tried clawing at his hand, anything to release his grasp on her throat. She was running out of time as black spots started to cluster on the edge of her vision.

Calm down, Amarah. Think. If you can't overpower him, outsmart him. You can talk your way out of this. She could, at least until he let go, and then she could make a break for her room to get the gun still lying underneath her pillow. Images of what happened between her and Liam in his office earlier that week flashed through her mind.

"No," she choked out, trying desperately to gasp for air.

He released her and took a step back. Sweet air flooded her lungs as she clutched at her neck with both hands. She couldn't take deep breaths fast enough. Being too preoccupied with catching her breath, she didn't see the hand heading toward her face until it was too late. A slap landed on her cheek that sent pain radiating through her face. She held her stinging cheek and looked at him with a shocked expression as tears threatened to fill her eyes.

"What the fuck, Derick!" Amarah yelled.

"I don't like being lied to. Do you take me for a fool?" Derick seethed through gritted teeth as he clenched and unclenched his fists at his sides.

"I promise you, nothing's going on. We had a work function tonight. Liam is my boss!" Amarah tried to plead with Derick.

How could she get him to see that? Before she could finish that thought, another slap landed across her cheek just as fast as the first one. This time, the pain was so bad that a tear unfortunately escaped. She quickly wiped it away, not wanting to give him any satisfaction.

"Your *boss* calls you Cupcake?" His words were like venom as he tried hard to contain his rage.

Still cupping her stinging cheek, Amarah opened her mouth to argue but closed it when she realized she didn't know what to say to that.

"This is why I told you that you weren't allowed to hang out with other men. All they want is to get between your legs, and yet you still disobey me. On top of that, I've told you time and time again that you weren't allowed to wear clothing like this in public. It gives men dirty thoughts about you," Derick chastised as he motioned down her front with his hand.

"And I remember telling you that you have no control over my life. Jesus, you act as if I fuck every man I talk to!" Amarah shouted in frustration.

"You told me you weren't ready for anything physical, and I respected that. That you were a virgin. Yet you dress like a whore. As if you crave male attention. Is that what you want, love? Some male attention?" He asked with a devilish grin pulling at one side of his lips.

Derick took a step toward Amarah and she recoiled, her back hitting the door. With him so close, there was nowhere for her to go except through him.

"Stay away from me!" she spat, but he ignored her.

"Let me show you what you've been missing out on. Then we can go away for a while. Just you and me so we can rebuild the relationship you so easily tossed aside for another man when I asked you to choose. I'll show you just how wrong you were to choose him over me."

Total fear set in as he finished that last sentence. Derick was going to force himself on her. She tried to calm herself so she could think, but the thought of him putting any part of his body on hers made her want to scald her skin off in the hottest of showers.

"I would rather die than allow you to stick your pathetic, shriveled-up, disease-infested dick inside of me," Amarah seethed.

Derick's smile turned downright sinister. "I never said you had to allow it. But I promise you," he said slowly, continuing to move closer toward his prey, "once you get the taste of me inside you, you'll find yourself unable to get enough."

CHAPTER 26

Before Amarah knew it, Derick was on her. His hands ravaged her body while he peppered her neck with kisses. He inhaled deeply before he spoke, his tone heavy with lust. "God, you smell fantastic!"

Amarah struggled to get out of his grasp, wiggling around so much that her left leg ended up between both of his, and she didn't waste a second in thrusting all her weight up into his balls. He brought his legs together, catching her knee before it made contact.

"You thought you could get me with that again? You're going to have to try harder than that." He laughed, mocking her.

He was playing with her now, toying with his prey. Without thinking, she dug both of her thumbs into pressure points below his ears, a trick Travis and Liam had taught her in some self-defense lessons. He grunted loudly, letting go of her knee, and grabbed both of her hands, using his muscles to easily pry them away from the sensitive pressure points.

Amarah smiled internally, knowing he would fall for the distraction. She thrust her knee up again, this time, hitting its target. Derick let out another grunt and stumbled backward, dropping to a knee. She didn't waste a beat and pushed herself off the door toward her bedroom, but Derick caught her by the leg, causing her to trip and fall.

He had a hold of her ankle and started to drag her back to him, but she kicked with her free foot, hearing a loud crack as her foot hurtled into his nose. He let go for a second and stood, allowing just enough time for her to reach for the decorative glass plate she had displayed on her coffee table. Using all her strength, she threw it toward Derick, but he dodged it, causing it to shatter against her window.

Amarah turned and made a break for her bedroom, but only made it a few steps before Derick threw his arms around her, his weight sending them falling to the floor. He flipped her over on her back, handling her as if she were a rag doll as he positioned himself between her legs and landed a right fist on the left side of her jaw.

She cried out as he hit her a second and a third time. The force of those punches stunned her, causing her body to go limp. Not wasting a single second, she heard the sound of fabric tearing as he ripped the slit of her dress up further to give him better access.

Amarah tried kicking, swinging her fists, or clawing at him, anything to get him off her, but he swatted her actions aside, as if she were a child trying to fight their parent. Derick gripped both of her small wrists and held them down in one hand above her head. He smiled down at her, as if satisfied to have her right where he wanted. Blood trickled down his face from his broken nose.

This was all a sick game to him. The more she fought, the more pleasure he got out of it. How many times had he done this? How many innocent women had fallen victim to this lunatic?

"This doesn't have to be unpleasant, you know. I could make this rather enjoyable for you if you'd let me," Derick said as he slid his tongue from the base of her neck, up the side, and sucked on the bottom lobe of her ear, all while his free hand slid down between her parted legs.

"Fuck you, you piece of shit!" Amarah screamed and spat in his face.

He wiped his face across his shoulder as he gave her another sinister smile. Lord, how she wanted to punch that smile right off his stupid face.

Derick made circles, rubbing his free hand on the outside of her panties. "Mmm, you are starting to get wet for me. Your brain may not want this, yet, but your body certainly does." He chuckled into her ear.

Amarah tried to wiggle her hips out of his grasp, but it was no use, his weight held her in place. He pulled her thong to the side as he ran his fingers up and down her center, teasing her.

"I hope you rot in Hell, and I'll be the one to put you there!" she snarled.

"I may spend eternity in Hell, but this right here," he said, slipping a finger deep into her, "is Heaven."

Amarah gasped at the sudden intrusion.

Derick moaned into her ear. "Love, you're so fucking tight!" He didn't waste any time as he slid another finger inside, spreading her out more. "It makes my dick throb knowing my fingers are the only ones who've been inside this virgin pussy of yours. God, if it feels this good now, I can only imagine how tight your walls are going to grip around my cock."

He pumped his fingers in and out of her. She refused to give him any satisfaction. She didn't scream. She didn't cry. She merely looked at him with all the hatred in the world.

Liam was brought out of his thoughts by the sound of glass breaking. He glanced around the perimeter of Amarah's house and saw that the blinds on her front window were now askew. He jumped out of his truck and sprinted to her front door.

Liam put his ear against the wood as he listened for anything inside that would indicate a problem. He could hear muffled voices and knew that she wasn't alone. Whoever it was, they weren't welcome, seeing as how they didn't use the front door.

"Amarah!" he called for her.

"Liam!" Amarah screamed back.

When he heard the degree of panic in her voice, it sent his blood boiling. He was already in fight mode, reverting to his Navy days as if no time had passed. He stepped back and sent his left foot hurtling into the wood, as close to the doorknob as possible, causing it to splinter and burst open on the first try. A figure moved in his peripherals, drawing his eyes up to her back door in time to see a man rushing out of it.

Liam took off after him, but by the time he reached the back door, the stranger was already disappearing into the woods behind her house. It would be child's play for Liam to track down and catch the stranger, but that would mean leaving her there all alone. And after the quick once-over he did on her as he ran through the room, he knew she couldn't be alone right now.

Reluctantly, he let the intruder go, returning to Amarah. He sat down on the floor, scooped her into his lap, and wrapped his strong arms around her protectively. Now that he had more time, he took in her disheveled state a little more thoroughly, checking for any serious injuries.

He noted the tear in her dress, her busted lip, some bruising starting to show slightly on her cheek, and the loose strands of golden hair that escaped her bun. *I will make that fucker wish he was never born for hurting you, Cupcake. I promise.*

He held and rocked her slowly in his arms as he tried to calm her down, trying to keep her from going into shock.

"I want a name," was all Liam said in a tone he'd never used in front of Amarah before. He could tell it affected her because he felt the way her body shivered against him.

"Derick…" was all she was able to get out in a weak, shaky voice.

So, it had been about that sleazeball she introduced him to at the bar. What the fuck happened between those two that would lead to this? He wanted answers, and he wanted them now.

"How… Why…?" Amarah tried and failed to get the simple question out.

"I know you better than you know yourself, Cupcake. I could tell that something has been off with you since that night at the bar. After dropping you off tonight, I had a gut feeling that something wasn't right. So, I waited outside."

"Thank God for those gut feelings," she said through hushed, shaky words as she fisted his shirt and leaned into his chest.

At least she was able to form proper sentences now. She let the rhythm of his heart play her a calming melody as she willed her adrenaline to settle. She always found comfort in his arms and knew that if Derick was stupid enough to come back tonight, he wouldn't be able to touch her again. Not with Liam around. She knew Liam would kill Derick before he ever came within arm's reach of her.

"Can I borrow your phone?" she asked hesitantly. She knew he would want answers now, but she needed to report what had just happened to Detective Trenton. "I need to make a call. Then I'll tell you whatever you want to know."

Liam released one arm from around her to reach into a pocket of his suit pants and pulled out his phone. She felt cold and empty where his arm had been, immediately missing contact between them. He handed it to her and returned his arm around her, pulling her a little closer against his chest.

"2872253," he spoke softly, telling her the passcode to his phone.

"Just a bunch of random numbers. That's the perfect kind of code." Amarah impersonated him jokingly as she wiped away a lonely tear that fell down her cheek and swiped open his phone.

She quickly opened the dial pad and punched in Detective Trenton's number, praising herself for memorizing it in case she ever needed to get a hold of him but didn't have her phone. She pressed the call button and put the phone up to her ear as she rested her head back against Liam's strong chest.

"Hello, Detective Trenton, it's Amarah Patterson. I'm sorry to call so late, but Derick attacked me in my home."

She knew Liam would demand answers, but she had to report this as soon as possible. With how quiet it was in her house, she knew that

Liam would be able to hear the entirety of her conversation. She was going to have to finally tell him the truth. She might as well go ahead and let him in on this conversation.

"What?! Are you ok? Do you need an ambulance? I'm on my way!"

"No, I'm ok. A few minor bruises are all." Amarah focused what strength she had left into her voice. It was hard though. She just wanted to break down and lose herself after what she had just survived. "No need to come here. Derick ran out my back door and disappeared into the woods behind my house."

"I'll get some officers to case the surrounding area. Hopefully they catch the bastard. Are you able to come down to the station and give a statement, or do you need a ride?" Detective Trenton asked.

"I can get myself there. I'm leaving now," she informed him.

"Ok, I'll be waiting. I'm glad you're ok, Amarah." Detective Trenton ended the call.

Amarah braced herself for the storm she could feel brewing inside the man who held her. She could feel how tense every muscle that touched her body had become over the course of that phone call. She knew she was in for it now.

CHAPTER 27

With her eyes closed, Amarah nestled her head a little further into Liam's chest, letting his woodsy scent fill her nose and the rhythm of his accelerated heartbeat play a soothing song in her ear.

"Something you care to share with me, Cupcake?" Liam said in a deep, calm, no-nonsense tone.

A tone that had her wincing a little because she knew of his dislike for secrets. Secrets get people killed, he'd always say. This secret could've gotten her killed tonight. That thought alone had bile rising in her throat and her stomach churning with unease. She allowed herself one more deep inhale of his scent to calm her further.

"Derick's been stalking me," she admitted out loud for the first time.

A long sigh escaped from her, knowing there was no sugarcoating this. Liam went completely still. If her head hadn't been on his chest, listening to his heartbeat, she would've feared he died.

"Tell me everything, no matter how minor you might think it is." His voice was clipped, the strain evident in his fight to contain his anger.

So, she did. She told him about how they met. About how everything was great at first, aside from the occasional comment from him about who she could hang out with and her clothing choices, until that night at the bar. She felt Liam's muscles tense when she told him how Derick grabbed her and hurt her, but he stayed quiet, letting her get everything out.

She went on to tell him about how some of her clothes had gone missing, and how a few objects had been moved or rearranged. Then about the text messages and voicemails she got from Derick that she never responded to. And lastly, about how he found her at her old job and attacked her.

Amarah kept her head on Liam's chest, unable to bear looking at the man right then. It was easier for her to talk about all that happened as if she were merely talking to the floor and not another person. She continued the story about going to the cops and the assault charges she filed against Derick. About how she felt like she was being watched that day in the parking garage, and then about the silence she had this week, thinking it was all over... Until tonight.

"Jesus, Amarah! And while all this was going on, you never once thought to ask me or Travis for help?"

Oh, Liam was pissed. She'd seen him mad before, but never at her. She didn't like being on the receiving end of his anger. Amarah could see the internal battle he fought so he didn't scream at her.

"Travis has a wife and kids to think about. I was not going to involve him and risk exposing them in any way to that psycho. And you have your own stuff going on."

"You're my family," he stated firmly. "If you're in trouble in any way, I want to know about it. Period."

"I know, but I figured I could handle it on my own. With the cops on board, I thought it would be over quickly."

"And how's that working for you?"

"What did you expect me to do, Liam? Come to you and say, 'hey, turns out my new boyfriend is a creepy stalker with control issues. Can you clean up my mess for me?' No. It's not your responsibility, it's mine."

"Yes, that's exactly what you should've done. Had I known about it from the beginning, that night at the bar would've been the last time you saw or heard from him, ever."

Liam didn't voice it, but it was implied. He would've ended Derick for laying a hand on her. A strained silence fell between them.

"You aren't safe here anymore. Clearly, he has resources if he found where you worked. What made you think he wouldn't find where you lived next?"

Amarah didn't speak. What could she say? He was right. She thought about that too but had said to herself over and over that there was no way that was possible. She'd convinced herself it was true. Denial was a powerful thing. She always kept a loaded gun nearby, but look how much that helped her tonight.

"Pack a bag. Two weeks' worth of whatever you need. You're staying with me until Derick is caught or dead. I pray for the latter, but I'll take what I can get."

"Liam, I…" Amarah started to protest, but he shot her a look that froze her and cut off any further words from spilling out of her mouth.

"I said pack. A. Bag," Liam clipped out through gritted teeth. "I'm not going to let you stay anywhere alone after what happened tonight. I have plenty of space, so you'll have your own bedroom and bathroom. Also, my security system is top-of-the-line. I'd love to see him try to get around it without triggering it. If by some miracle he does, I have multiple weapons in every room of my house."

She knew there was no point in arguing. Once Liam put his foot down on something, it would be easier to move a mountain than convince him otherwise. Instead, she did as she was told.

The instant Amarah stood, she mourned the blanket of warmth his body radiated. She numbly walked into her room, grabbed her largest suitcase, plopped it down on her bed, and began filling it with clothes and items from her bathroom.

As she passed through her bathroom, she caught her reflection in the mirror and grimaced. She took in the light bruising on her cheek and the split lip she had with dried blood around it. She wanted nothing more than to jump in a hot shower and vigorously scrub every inch of skin Derick touched, but she knew that had to wait. Detective Trenton would want to see and record the damage done to her for the police report.

Liam had not let her out of his sight since she got up and started packing, but she didn't mind. In fact, she loved how protective he was being. It helped her feel safe in her own home again, after Derick so rudely shattered the security of her sanctuary. He pushed off the doorframe he was leaning against as she took in her appearance, gently grabbed her shoulders, and turned her towards him.

"Stop it. Whatever is going through that head of yours, stop. You went through something that not all women survive. Those are your battle wounds. You fought like hell and should wear them with pride. Don't let him make you feel any less about yourself."

"Easier said than done," Amarah mumbled as her gaze sank to the floor.

Liam gently grabbed her chin and tilted her head so her sapphire eyes peered into his. "I wish you could see yourself the way I see you."

"How do you see me?" she asked breathlessly.

"I see a strong, brave, intelligent, beautiful woman with the biggest heart I know."

A lonely tear cascaded down Amarah's cheek, and Liam swiped it away gently with his thumb. His words constricted around her heart almost to the point of pain.

"If I were half of those things, I would've never found myself in this situation," she whispered.

"Everyone makes mistakes now and again. There are no perfect people in this world," Liam spoke softly. Not a hint of judgment could be found in his tone. "Come on, we shouldn't keep Detective Trenton waiting. Do you have everything you need?"

Amarah did not trust herself to form coherent words at the present moment. All she did was nod. He grabbed her suitcase in one hand as if it weighed nothing and wrapped his free arm around her tightly, leading her out of her house.

CHAPTER 28

It was almost midnight by the time Amarah and Liam finished talking with Detective Trenton and pulled into Liam's driveway. She let out a sigh of relief as they walked through the door of a familiar, relaxing place. It was as if there was a barrier at the threshold, and as she passed through, all the weight of worry lifted from her shoulders.

Peace of mind settled over her knowing she would be safe here. That Derick wouldn't be able to catch her by surprise again. She almost wished he would try to break in, just so she or Liam could kill him, and she could be done with that creep indefinitely.

After locking the front door and arming his security system, Liam picked up her suitcase and led her down the hall to one of his spacious spare bedrooms.

"You can use this room. Mine is right down the hall through that door if you ever need anything," he said, opening the door for her and pointing down the hall towards the double doors that led to his bedroom.

Amarah slowly walked inside, taking in the space. It was decorated differently from the rest of his home. Purple, black, and grey colored the space. Three of the four walls were painted a concrete grey, the last a black accent wall.

The back wall housed a large four-poster king-sized bed made of wrought iron that was twisted into a spiral design, covered in a dark purple bedspread, and two black nightstands resided on each side. Drapes shaded in the same dark purple covered the windows.

A large black six-drawer wooden dresser with a mirror on top was placed along the right wall and two white doors to what she assumed was a closet and the bathroom hung on the left wall.

Amarah was taken aback by the bold design choice. She turned to look at him with both eyebrows raised.

"What? A man can't like the color purple?" Liam said casually, as if there was nothing wrong with his style in a bachelor's pad. He placed her suitcase on the bed and asked, "Are you hungry or anything?"

"No." She shook her head as she wrapped her arms around her middle and bore a hole into the carpet.

After being forced to relive the horrific incident when she told Detective Trenton every excruciating detail of what happened, with each passing minute, she found herself slipping closer to the edge of a cliff that would lead her straight into a nasty breakdown. Derick's parting words played like a broken record in her head.

"You may think you can get away from me, but you're wrong. You belong to me and me alone," Derick said, looking her dead in the eyes as he spoke in a low, threatening tone. He sucked on the two fingers he had inside of her, licking them clean, and finished with a wink. "We'll pick up where we left off next time, love." He slammed his lips down on Amarah's, stealing one last kiss, before he took off out her back door right as Liam kicked in the front door.

She didn't want there to be a next time. She never wanted to see that man, hear his words, feel his eyes on her, or feel the way his presence turned the air heavy ever again. Not after what she just survived, the violations he did to her. If he got to her again, she knew it would be a thousand times worse, and the thought made her want to vomit.

"Do you want me to help you unpack?" Liam offered, concern filling his voice. Most likely noticing the shift in her body language and mood.

"No," Amarah's voice cracked as she reached the edge of that cliff, one step away from losing it. Her eyes filled with unshed tears.

"Fuck, Cupcake. Tell me what I can do to help." He dropped his shield, his face showing every emotion he was feeling. He appeared as if someone had ripped his beating heart right out of his chest.

"I just need to be alone. Please," she pleaded with him as her body began to tremble.

"I can't," he whispered. "If you need to scream, then scream at me. If you need to hit something, hit me. If you need to cry, let me hold you while you let go. But I will not leave you alone to drown."

Amarah couldn't hold it in anymore. She closed her eyes and let out an ear-piercing scream that shook her body, forcing her to curl in on herself. Strong arms caught her as she began to drop to the ground. Liam went down with her and pulled her into his lap as she began to cry.

A cry that wrecked her entire body. She threw her arms around his neck as she clung to him as if he were the rope that would pull her back up the cliff. With each tear that fell, she felt all the stress, worry, fear, sadness, pain, and violations done to her that night slowly begin to lift off her shoulders.

With one arm wrapped around Amarah, holding her head against his chest, Liam rubbed gentle and soothing circles across her back. He didn't tell her everything was going to be ok, and he didn't try to give her advice that might help her heal. He simply held her, allowing her to purge her body of all the things she had let build up for too long.

After a while, Amarah's cries began to soften and eventually stopped altogether. He released his hold on her only when he felt her start to pull away. Liam easily shifted her weight around, as if she were a mere child, so he could carry her bridal style as he walked her into the attached bathroom, setting her down atop the counter. She didn't fight or protest. She was too exhausted.

He opened the glass door to the shower and turned on the water before returning to her. "Get cleaned up, ok? I'll unpack your stuff."

"Ok," she said in a weak voice as he left, mostly closing the door to the bathroom, leaving only a thin crack.

She didn't pay any mind as she numbly climbed off the counter and undid her hair, letting the sunny strands drop freely down her back. She stripped out of her dress, the ruined material pooled on the tile floor before she opened the glass door to the shower and stepped in. The water was a welcome relief to her aching muscles.

A light knock against the door drew her attention away from the water. "I have all your bathroom things and some pajamas. May I come in?"

"Yes," she called out in a weak voice.

She watched as Liam pushed open the door and forced his eyes to the floor. He kept his back to her as he handed each item over the top of the glass. Amarah placed each one on the tiled shelf in the shower, and a weak smile pulled at a corner of her lips when she noticed he made it a point not to look at her. *Always the gentleman,* she thought.

He then placed her pajamas on the counter before he walked out and closed the door, again leaving only a small crack. It was as if her body was on autopilot, mindlessly going through the motions of shaving, soaping up, and washing her hair. After she had scrubbed every inch of skin that Derick touched, she started to feel like herself again. She got out of the shower and dried off before she wrapped the towel around her wet hair and got dressed.

Amarah brushed out her hair and braided it back. Then, took in her reflection and sighed. Her makeup was washed off, the dried blood from her split lip was gone, and her eyes were puffy from crying. She averted her gaze, turned off the light, and froze in the doorway.

She expected Liam to have left but he was sitting on the edge of her bed, his forearms resting on his knees and his hands clasped together as he focused on an invisible spot on the carpet. His head snapped toward her, and he gave her a kind smile.

"You're still here?" Amarah asked from her spot in the doorway.

"Always," Liam said as he stood up and pulled back the covers.

His suit jacket was draped over the edge of the bed, he had ditched his tie, his sleeves were rolled up just past his elbows, and a few buttons on his dress shirt were undone, causing the shirt to gape open and expose his tanned and strong tattooed chest.

"Get in bed."

Amarah didn't protest. Her body was running on empty as she padded across the carpet and slid under the covers. He brought the covers back up, tucking her in before he rounded the bed and propped himself up against the headboard, tucking a pillow behind his back as he stretched out his legs and crossed them at the ankle.

"What are you doing?" Amarah asked as she rolled over and peered up at him.

"Don't worry," Liam said with a small chuckle. "I'm only staying until you fall asleep."

"Oh, ok." She snuggled into her pillow and brought the covers up around her shoulders. "Thank you," she said, peering up at him through her thick lashes.

"For what?" he asked with a raised eyebrow.

Amarah half-laughed. "Where do I start? Thank you for saving me tonight, for letting me stay with you, for not letting me break down alone. Sorry that you had to see that. I'm not a pretty crier."

"You're beautiful no matter what you do." Liam's bright green eyes bore into hers, where she saw the honesty of his words.

"Thank you for unpacking my things."

Her deep blue eyes widened around the edges, and her cheeks started to color. A wicked grin that pulled at one side of his face said he knew what she had just realized.

"You unpacked my things… All my things." It didn't hit her when she was getting dressed that he had brought her underwear with the pajamas he set in the bathroom.

"All of it, and might I just say, you have great taste in undergarments. Laced thongs and bras, who knew?" Liam teased her.

"Shoot me now!" She groaned as she buried her face in her pillow, trying desperately to hide the massive blush that was stinging her cheeks.

Liam laughed fully, most likely at her embarrassment, and the sound healed her heart a little.

"Get some sleep. Goodnight, Cupcake," he said as he crossed his arms over his chest and tilted his head back, resting it against the headboard.

"Goodnight, Liam," she said as she turned over, putting her back to him.

CHAPTER 29

Nightmares plagued Amarah's dreams. She found herself back in her living room, fighting for her life as Derick violated her body. The sickening words he said to her ran like a broken record. All she could do was scream for help, but no one answered. So, the torment continued, repeating in an endless loop until she was shaken awake. Strong hands held her by her shoulders as a deep voice called her name.

She jolted awake, sitting upright, and sucked in deep gasps of air as if she couldn't fill her lungs fully. Liam was perched on the side of her bed in nothing but a pair of grey sweatpants with a look of worry in his eyes. Even still, he was the most beautiful man she had ever laid eyes on.

His muscles were on full display along with the artwork that covered both arms and spread across his broad chest and back. And those sweatpants didn't leave much to the imagination either.

"Hey, it's ok. You're ok. Deep breaths, Cupcake. You're safe now," Liam spoke, coaxing her out of her frantic state.

"Please tell me this is real. That this isn't some sort of dream when, in reality, I'm still back in my house with Derick," Amarah choked out, a single tear cascaded down as she looked into his big green eyes.

"Do you feel that?" he asked as he took her hand and placed it against his bare chest. She could feel the warmth radiating from him, the rhythm of his heart beating, the smoothness of his skin against her palm. "I'm real. This room, this bed, it's all real. You got out. It was just a bad dream." He tucked a few golden strands back behind her ear.

All Amarah could do was nod, not trusting that her voice wouldn't crack if she tried to speak.

"Try to get some more sleep. Your body needs the rest," Liam told her as he went to stand.

"Wait…" Her voice cracked with emotion. She cleared her throat and took a deep breath before she tried again. "Can you… stay with me? Just until I fall back asleep. I don't want to be alone right now." She felt embarrassed that she had to ask.

"Of course."

Liam climbed on the bed, making sure to stay on top of the covers. He propped himself up on the headboard next to her, stretching his long legs out and placing one of his arms back behind his head. Amarah eased herself down and snuggled back into her covers.

"I'm sorry if I woke you up."

"Don't be. We all get nightmares now and again."

A comfortable silence fell between them as Amarah slowly drifted back to sleep. Liam watched her, hating the fact that she was in pain, hating how she kept this from him. He didn't agree with it, but he understood where she was coming from. He sent up a silent *thank you* for his gut feelings. It made him think of what would have happened to her had he ignored them and gone home.

Though he knew exactly what would've happened. The thought of it made him see red and want blood. Liam hadn't left Amarah's side since the incident, so he heard every word that happened as she filled the detective in at the station. The fact that Derick had violated her body in the way he did was bad enough.

No woman should ever have to fear being attacked by a man who couldn't control himself. He wouldn't let that happen again. He admired her courage, only allowing herself to break down in private, keeping a brave face for everyone around.

Amarah never believed she was strong, but he wished she saw

herself the way he saw her. She had put up with a stalker and survived not one but two attacks from him. She survived, and given time, she'd be ok.

He wanted nothing more than to crawl into bed with her, pull her onto his chest, and hold her tight. But he knew she needed space. Comfort, but space. Instead, he lay there, watching her chest rise and fall with each breath as she drifted back to sleep, his own eyelids growing heavy as well.

Amarah stirred as the sounds of birds chirping outside her windows filled her silent bedroom. When she noticed that she didn't have any more nightmares after falling back asleep, she found herself in a better mood upon waking. She kept her eyes closed as she snuggled into her pillow. A pillow that was surprisingly warm, and firm but soft as well, and… Wait… was it moving?

She slowly opened her eyes and observed that it wasn't a pillow she was lying on, but Liam. He had sunk down to lay flat on the bed atop a pillow and somehow, sometime during the night, she must have rolled over and snuggled into him. Her head was now resting on his chest, and he had a strong painted arm draped around her shoulder.

As she slowly looked up, she was met with a pair of piercing green eyes staring back down at her. His other arm was bent and resting behind his head, and he wore a humorous expression that suggested he was getting enjoyment out of this.

"Good morning, Cupcake," he drawled.

Amarah sat up abruptly and scooted away from Liam. Her awkwardness pulled a genuine laugh from him.

"Don't act like you didn't enjoy it."

"Don't flatter yourself. I won't be held accountable for what my body does on its own while sleeping." She rolled her eyes, keeping her face turned so he wouldn't see the coloring that started to paint her cheeks.

"Maybe your body just knows what it wants, even when your mind is asleep." His words sent a shiver down her spine at how unbelievably correct he was.

Amarah's body had always reacted on its own whenever Liam was around, and she cursed herself for it.

"You have absolutely no effect on my body," she lied.

"I don't? That's weird, because I distinctly remember a moan escaping from that little mouth of yours when I had you pinned to my desk earlier this week."

Her cheeks were on fire now, but that didn't stop heat from flooding her core at the memory his words brought up. She quickly grabbed her pillow and swung it at him, but he blocked it, swiping it away like it was nothing. Then he grabbed her wrists, pushed her onto her back, and hovered over her, pinning her wrists on each side of her head.

"Did I strike a nerve?" Liam said with a wicked grin on his face.

Amarah was frozen with shock. He had her on her back in two seconds flat, before she could even process what was happening. This man she'd loved since they were kids now had her pinned to a bed, hovering over her half-naked.

"No, you just aggravate the hell out of me."

She couldn't stop herself from taking him in. The way his muscles popped in his arms and shoulders as he held her, the elegant inked artwork he wore down each arm and across his chest, the contours of his prominent abs, and oh Lord, her eyes went wide as she took in the erection clearly visible in his sweatpants.

Look away, Amarah. Look at something else, anything else. But she couldn't. Her imagination was running wild with wonder.

"See something you like?" Liam teased.

Amarah's eyes snapped to his instantly, but she was speechless, her mouth agape. She should be panicking right now. After what happened to her last night, being pinned down with a man on top of her should be terrifying, but she found herself not scared at all.

This wasn't just some man. It was Liam. A man whom she had known for so long. A man she knew would never push her or do something that would hurt her. A man she loved with every fiber of her being. Things were different when it came to him.

"I don't see anything, actually," she said breathlessly.

His wicked grin widened at her lie as he slowly lowered himself down between her legs and rolled his hips so she could feel the full length of his erection that pressed into her pelvis and lower stomach.

"Do I still have no effect on your body?" Liam asked with what she swore was pure hunger in his voice. Something she'd only heard once before, when he had her pinned to his office desk.

Amarah sucked her bottom lip between her teeth to fight off the moan that wanted so desperately to escape. She watched as his eyes darkened and drifted down to her mouth. She couldn't lie again. Her voice would easily betray her, so she just shook her head no.

"You're a terrible liar." He chuckled.

"Liam, I..." she started to ask but clamped her mouth shut, unsure of how to go about voicing what she needed. Unsure *if* she should even voice it.

"You what?" Liam challenged her as his gaze shifted between her eyes and her lips.

"I need you to do something for me," Amarah whispered, her chest rising and falling in a faster motion as her heart rate began to spike with nerves.

"Anything."

She closed her eyes and took a slow breath. "I need you to take the memories of Derick away."

Liam was quiet, as if he was battling against whether he should do this or not. "And how exactly would you like me to do that?"

"Replace them with memories of you." Amarah met his gaze, pleading with him not to pull away.

She was confident that he'd know what she was asking. This was different from what happened in his office. That was them getting caught up in the moment, teasing each other until it went too far, but there would be no one to interrupt them and pull them back to reality this time.

Wanting something so badly to happen and actually being presented with that possibility were two totally different things, and still, with every fiber of her being, she prayed he'd give her the answer she so desperately needed.

"Are you sure? With everything that happened last night, I—"

"Please." Her voice cracked again. "I know you won't hurt me. I trust you. I need this and I think you do too."

He paused and Amarah waited with bated breath. "With pleasure." He grinned wickedly.

CHAPTER 30

Amarah didn't think Liam would agree, but then she saw the unmistakable lust that darkened his eyes, shaped that grin of his into something wicked, and tightened every muscle in his naked torso with anticipation.

"If it gets too much for you or you want it to stop for any reason—no explanation needed—just say so, ok?"

"I trust you," she said with a small smile.

Her nerves were all over the place. A part of her was scared but her excitement and anticipation quickly overpowered it.

Liam brought his lips down as he began to place soft kisses on the column of her neck. She let out a small moan and arched her back, causing her perky, full breasts to press into his chest, gaining a groan from him.

He let go of one wrist, only to snake his hand beneath her tank top and grab a handful of one of her breasts, kneading her already hard nipple between his finger and thumb. She pushed herself further into him, wanting him to keep working her tit as she moved her hips up and began to slowly grind against his erection, needing more to relieve the aching need between her legs.

"Someone's greedy," Liam said in a husky voice.

He pulled up to smile down at her. Her pulse quickened and all she could do was watch as he pulled her shirt up over the planes of her stomach and chest to finally free her breasts.

He grabbed a handful of soft tissue and sucked her hard nipple into his mouth, swirling his tongue around it, licking and biting playfully.

His other hand began massaging her other mound, making sure it wasn't left out. Amarah gripped a handful of his raven locks with one hand and his shoulder with the other, digging her nails into his flesh. He swapped his mouth for her other breast and repeated what he did with his tongue, turning her into a moaning mess.

Liam moved further south, placing gentle kisses along her flat stomach. He hooked his fingers into her shorts and underwear and tugged them down. She arched her hips off the bed so he could get them off quicker, but not quick enough. The anticipation was killing her. She was now bare from her breasts down as he discarded her clothing to the side. Liam raised up on his knees, still between her legs to admire her.

"You're so fucking beautiful. I know this pretty cunt of yours is going to be my salvation," he confessed as he lowered his head towards her middle.

Holy shit, how can words be so hot? she thought. However, her body got wetter by the second just from his words alone. His fingers grazed her entrance, and she jerked at the sensitive sensation.

"Fuck! You're dripping wet for me." He growled as his tongue started to slowly lick up and down her center.

Amarah's hands instantly held on to his head as she peered down at the man who had his face buried between her legs. The scruff from his black beard brushed against the sensitive skin of her inner thighs as his tongue tasted and explored. He pulled back and stuck his middle finger into his mouth, wetting it before he slid it inside her.

She gasped, nearly coming off the bed. "Oh God, Liam!" she moaned.

Panic tried to take over, but she forced it back. This wasn't Derick doing this to her. It was Liam. He wasn't doing this to her against her will. She wanted this, very much. She repeated that to herself a few times and made it a point to keep looking at Liam's face, so her brain would finally understand that this was ok, to just relax and enjoy it.

"I love the sound of you moaning my name." He impaled her with his finger, easily slipping in and out from how wet she was. He licked and sucked on her clit before he inserted another finger. "You taste fucking amazing! Do you like that?"

"Yes! This feels so good," Amarah moaned, grinding her hips against his fingers. She could feel her orgasm start to build at the base of her spine.

He hooked his fingers, hitting that sensitive spot that had her eyes rolling in the back of her head. He continued his assault on her clit with his tongue as he reached his free hand up to play with one of her mounds, massaging it and rolling her hard nipple through his finger and thumb. That trifecta would be her undoing.

"Right there! Don't stop!" Amarah pleaded with him, getting closer to the edge.

"I won't stop until I feel your tight pussy squeezing around my fingers. Now come for me. I want to drink you in and lick you clean."

His demand had her coming undone five seconds later. A powerful orgasm hit her like a freight train, rocking through her entire body.

Amarah moaned his name over and over as she ground her hips against his face, pushing his head down as if to smother him between her legs. Judging from his enthusiasm, he was loving every minute of it. His tongue continued its exploration, licking up every last drop of her finish.

When Amarah finally came down from the high of her orgasm, he finished cleaning her up with a few more licks, groaning as if sad it was over already. He came back to lay between her legs, gazing into her eyes. She could only imagine what she looked like right now, but a part of her didn't care. This was Liam. She could be sweaty, covered in dirt from working in her garden all day, and she was sure he'd still find a way to compliment her. It was one of the qualities she loved so much about him.

She peered up at him and smiled. "That felt amazing. If I knew it would be this good, I would've done that a long time ago."

"What do you mean?" Liam cocked his head.

"I'd rather not say. It's kind of embarrassing."

"I was just buried between those sexy legs of yours with my fingers and tongue inside you as you came all over my face. I think we're beyond that point with each other."

That statement alone sent her blushing. So matter-of-fact with him but damn did it sound good leaving his mouth, the same mouth that had just brought her the best orgasm of her life. Her small, handheld vibrator never made her feel anywhere near that satisfied. And that was just from him going down on her. She could only imagine what an orgasm brought on by sex with him would be like. Fresh heat started to pool in her core, and she could feel herself already getting wet again, ready for more.

"I'm a virgin," Amarah admitted nervously.

"What? Surely, you've done other things though, right? Like messed around or oral sex before?" Liam questioned in disbelief.

"No, nothing further than makeout sessions with roaming hands and the occasional grinding, but always fully clothed."

She didn't understand how she was speaking so freely about it to Liam, but she didn't argue.

"Derick wanted to take me away for the weekend. Well, before he went all crazy on me." Oh great, now she was babbling nervously. *Shut up Amarah, shut up!* But unfortunately, she couldn't stop once she started. "You remember last year when we went hiking in Arkansas at Lake Ouachita? Do you remember seeing that beautiful log cabin across the lake? Well, apparently his family owns that. I was thinking about agreeing and thought it would be romantic and the perfect place to take our relationship to the next level. Thank goodness he decided to let his true colors show before I made that mistake."

"How come?" was all he could manage to ask, studying her face intently, like she was someone he needed to interrogate to get sensitive information out of.

"I… I was saving myself," Amarah said sheepishly as she tried to control her breathing.

"For marriage?" Liam prodded further, furrowing his brows.

She shook her head and let out a long sigh. "For you," she finally admitted, looking deep into those green eyes of his.

CHAPTER 31

Well, there it was, out in the open now. The ugly truth of a young girl naïve enough to fall for her older brother's best friend. A statement that would either show just how much Amarah loved Liam or how foolish she was to think he would want her in that way. She prayed he saw it was the former.

Liam's body tensed on top of hers, his face unreadable. Her heart sank into the pit of her stomach. It felt as if time had stopped moving from the anticipation of his reaction to her very personal confession. What was only a matter of seconds felt like minutes.

Had she ruined things? Messed up by speaking her most coveted secret? Did she just lose not only a best friend, but the only man she'd ever loved? Before her mind could run wild with fear, the unexpected happened.

His mouth was on hers in an emotional, hungry way, as if he needed to feel the contact with her, feel the connection between them. She could taste herself on him, and it turned her on even more. She'd been kissed before, quite a few times, but never like this. He ran his tongue along her lips, seeking entrance. She granted it and their tongues danced in a rhythm together, fighting for dominance.

She lost all sense of time as she closed her eyes and enjoyed the taste of him, loving the exploration her tongue went on of his mouth. Amarah reached her hand between them as she gripped the throbbing erection in his sweatpants. Liam moaned at the feeling, but he gently grabbed her hand and pulled it away.

Finally breaking the kiss, she said, "You made me feel good. Now let me return the favor."

"This wasn't about giving something to get something. This was about you and helping you heal."

Amarah pouted, pushing her bottom lip out. He just chuckled and bent down, resting his forehead against hers.

"All in good time, Cupcake. I promise."

Detective Trenton had called later that morning, informing Liam and Amarah that they were unable to locate Derick. They'd brought in a police bloodhound to track his scent from her house.

The K-9 led them through the woods, but it lost the scent when they came out on the other side, to a large parking lot next to a public park. Derick must've gotten in a vehicle and driven off.

She could hear the frustration in Detective Trenton's voice. He wanted that bastard behind bars as much as she did. She let out a frustrated sigh. She wasn't upset with the police; she knew they were doing everything they could to try and find him. There was even an APB out for his arrest. No matter what city he was in, if an officer found him and ran his name, it would pop up that he was a wanted man.

Liam forced her to relax the whole day. He kept telling her she needed rest—body, mind, and soul. She grabbed one of her current reads, a spicy romance, and curled up on the couch under a cozy blanket. He spent most of the day in his office, attending to work calls or emails. She didn't mind. A part of her welcomed the solitude a little. After what he did to her that morning, her cheeks heated and her core clenched with desire every time she saw the man.

Liam ordered them some Chinese takeout for dinner. After handing food containers to a very flustered Amarah, he flashed one of his knowing smiles at her and retreated to his office again. She let out a breath she didn't realize she was holding. She ate while she read some more, then cleaned up her mess and put the leftover containers away in the fridge. After reading all day, her eyes burned and were so dried out that it hurt to close them.

Not realizing how late it was until she glanced at the clock, she placed the bookmark in her book and made her way to Liam's office. The door was wide open as he typed away at his computer. Amarah stopped at the doorframe, leaning against it with her arms crossed over her chest.

"You didn't have to stay in here all day. This is your house, you know."

"It's ok, I had a lot of work to get done anyway."

"Mmhm," she said, not believing him one bit.

Amarah knew he was just trying to be helpful by giving her space. She found herself thinking that maybe she could've read in her room, so he didn't have to hang out in his office all day.

"Well, it's getting late. I'm going to bed. Good night."

"Good night, Cupcake. Sleep tight, don't let the bed bugs bite," Liam called back, his tone light with amusement.

"I'm going to a very expensive, five-star hotel that you'll pay for if I find you have bed bugs," she joked as she turned and made her way to her room, the sound of his laughter trailing behind her.

After a very relaxing, scalding shower, she got dressed and crawled into her fluffy bed. She plugged her phone in and checked for any notifications one last time before rolling over. Nothing. Maybe Liam had scared Derick off for good. But again, she wasn't that lucky.

Amarah figured Derick was probably lying low for a while until he was ready to try again, once all this had blown over and everyone grew complacent, thinking it wouldn't happen again. The thought made her stomach churn. She rolled over and snuggled into her pillows, where sleep had found her easily that night.

Amarah woke suddenly, clutching at her chest and gasping for air. She didn't remember her dream, but if her current state said anything about it, it wasn't a happy one. She looked at the alarm clock on top of her dresser. The glowing red numbers illuminated 12:20 a.m., and she groaned. The sound boomed in the deafening silence of the night.

She rolled back over, trying and failing to go back to sleep. She glanced back at the clock again. 12:50 a.m. She gave up at that point, feeling frustrated, and made her way to the kitchen. The house was dark, and Liam was nowhere to be found. *He's probably asleep,* she thought as she passed by his empty office veiled in shadows.

She padded her way to the pantry and snorted when she saw his cereal options. Fruity Pebbles, Coco Puffs, and Cinnamon Toast Crunch. You'd think young children lived in the house, not a man on thirty's doorstep. She grabbed the box of Coco Puffs, a bowl from the cabinet, and milk from the fridge.

As Amarah was pouring her food, a deep voice sounded from behind her. "Midnight munchies?"

The hairs on her neck stood up, a shiver flooded down her spine, and her heart dropped to her stomach. She was frozen, her mind screaming at her to turn around, to yell, to grab a weapon, something, but she couldn't move a muscle. Her body was locked up in fear. She felt his presence creep up behind her as he trailed the tips of his fingers up both of her arms, stopping at her shoulders.

"Mmm, I've missed you," Derick spoke as he slowly turned her to face him.

A combination of shock and horror covered her face, her mouth slightly parted, her body still unresponsive.

"How?" she choked out, glad that at least her voice was willing to work right then.

"You might need to be a little more specific." He chuckled lightly.

"How do you keep finding me?" she asked, her voice quiet.

"I've told you before, I have my ways," Derick said with a shrug of his shoulders. He gently ran the backside of his hand down her cheek as he continued, "I'm starting to get rather frustrated that I keep finding you with… him. You belong to me and me alone, remember? Now, where did we leave off? Oh yeah, that's right. I had my fingers buried deep inside that tight pussy of yours." His voice dripped with lust.

As if Amarah was jolted back to reality, she regained control of her body as she pushed him away with all her might, causing him to stumble backward into the cabinets. She spun around and reached for a knife from the set that rested on the counter, unsheathed a large carving blade, and spun back around to point it at Derick.

He had recovered and was now stalking toward her, chuckling softly while a wicked grin slid across a face that she once found so handsome.

"Come now, love, be a good girl. Put the knife down. I don't like hurting you," he said, holding both hands up as if to show he wasn't going to hurt her yet, but give her one more chance.

"Stay the fuck away from me!" Amarah spat at him, gripping the knife so tight her knuckles turned white. "Liam!" she shouted.

Derick's smile only widened, and his chuckle turned into a full menacing laugh, a sound that sent goosebumps up her arms.

"You think your white knight will come to your rescue again? I learned from the first time." Derick pulled out a knife of his own from behind his back.

Her eyes widened in horror as she took in a blade that was covered in bright red. *No! No! It can't be true,* she screamed inside her mind.

"I took care of him first. Slit his throat while he was asleep. Some bodyguard you got there. You should've seen his eyes—the shocked expression as I watched his life fade from them. Now there will be nothing in the way of *us*."

"No!" Amarah screamed as tears welled in her eyes. She dropped to her knees as her knife slipped from her hand and clanged against the kitchen floor. "No! Liam!" She tried screaming again at the top of her lungs through the rivers falling freely down her cheeks. "This can't be real! He can't be dead! You're lying, Liam has to be ok!" But this time, she didn't hear Liam's beautiful voice shouting her name in response. All that answered her was agonizing silence. "You sick fuck! How could you?"

Derick spoke to her in a calm, unnerving tone. "I gave you a choice. You chose him over me. I told you that you picked incorrectly. His death is on you."

"No matter what you do, Derick, I'll never choose you!" Amarah screamed through her tears.

"Shhh," he cooed, setting his knife down on the counter as he crouched down to cup her face with his hands. "It'll be ok, I promise. I'll give you a good life and as I watch your belly swell with each new life you bring into this world, our family will become more complete. You'll see," he reassured her, brushing his thumbs over her cheeks to wipe away the tears before he stood up and began to unzip his pants.

More tears flowed freely down her cheeks as she just knelt there, numbly, utterly empty inside, as if she lost the will to fight, to live. She watched him unsheathe himself from his pants and didn't protest as he pushed her back with his hand until her back was lying flat on the kitchen floor.

CHAPTER 32

Amarah was shaken awake and pulled into a pair of strong arms. "Hey, shh, wake up. It's just a dream. It's not real. Look at me." Liam spoke in a soothing and gentle tone.

She pulled back, peering at him through watery eyes. She frantically grabbed his face in her hands as she looked him over, checking for any wounds. Her eyes went right to his throat, not a scratch in sight.

Liam was here, really here, sitting on the side of her bed in his grey sweatpants looking as breathtaking as ever. A nightmare, that's all it was. It wasn't real. Derick had not found her again, had not broken in, had not slit Liam's throat. She breathed heavily as she threw her arms around his neck and crushed him against her. Tears spilled down her face with horror from the nightmare but also relief that it was over.

"You're alive," she cried.

"Of course, I am. I'm not going anywhere," he said as he climbed under the covers and pulled her down to lie on top of him, her head now resting on his chest.

Liam wrapped both of his arms around Amarah protectively and traced delicate swirls down her back with the tips of his fingers over the thin fabric of her tank top.

"Do you want to tell me about it? I've found that talking about your dreams helps you not relive them as often." He placed a soft kiss on the top of her sunny hair.

She knew he was speaking from personal experience. She could only imagine the nightmares that plagued his mind from everything he'd seen and done for our country, for the sake of freedom. After taking a deep breath, she told him what happened in her nightmare.

"The feelings were so real. As if I truly lost you. I never want to feel that again, Liam. I couldn't handle it if I did." She snuggled closer to him.

"Fuck, Cupcake, you aren't going to lose me. I'll be here to annoy you for at least another fifty years. If by some freak accident that did happen, I never want you to lose the will to live. You keep fighting until your last breath, do you hear me? Don't ever let that fucker win."

Amarah knew he was right. She craned her neck to look up. His eyes were already on her, worry swirling through them.

"Thank you, Liam. Honestly, it means the world to me."

"You're my family," Liam answered, as if that simple sentence explained everything.

Well, almost everything. She didn't know where she pulled the courage to make the first move, but she needed to know. For Amarah, this was their make or break moment. All the flirting, touching—she needed to know if anything more was to ever happen between them. If not, she would force herself to grow up and move on from her first love, finally accepting that it would never happen.

Amarah slowly slid her hand down his torso, loving the feel as her fingers slid over his muscles. She felt him tense beneath her, as if unsure where this was going. She didn't stop until her hand rested on his cock. She was surprised to find it was fully hard and ready to go. Her core heated, her thighs clenched, and her mouth watered with anticipation.

"Careful," Liam warned in a low and husky voice. "If you don't remove your hand, I won't be able to stop myself from flipping you over and finally claiming you."

"Bullshit." She didn't sound as confident as she planned. "If you wanted to fuck me, you would've done it by now."

"What would you say if I told you I've fucked my hand countless times to the thought of your tight, pretty cunt?"

Stand strong, Amarah. He's testing you back. "I would say prove it."

She steeled her spine.

"You want to watch me play with myself? Do I get to come all over those pretty tits when I'm done?"

You can come on me, in me, down my throat, she thought. That single question from him had her dripping wet now.

"If you've done that to the thought of me, why not have the real thing? I think you're scared."

Amarah was surprised she was able to speak coherently, even if it still came out breathlessly.

"And what would I be scared of exactly?" Liam's emerald gaze pierced into the sapphires of her eyes.

"That if we do sleep together, things will change between us. Either it'll be the wrong thing to do, causing a rift between us and you'll lose me as a friend. Or it'll be so good that you keep coming back for more and this—us…" She motioned between them. "We become more than friends."

Without warning, he pushed her onto her back and nestled himself between her legs, propping himself up on his elbows. She gasped at the sudden change but didn't protest. If anything, she spread her legs wider to give him more room to lie between them.

"So, which is it, Liam? What are you afraid of?"

"Neither," he finally admitted.

"Then why do you hold back?" Amarah asked, raking her gaze over his handsome face, trying to find any sign that would give away what he was thinking. She knew there had to be more to this.

"When I saw you in your cap and gown, something shifted inside me. I became infatuated with you. The next two years I was away, I hoped it would leave my system but the moment I saw you again, it all came flooding back to me. I've spent the last two years in an agonizing Hell, seeing you all the time, and not being allowed to touch you. Your heart is so full of light and joy. It's innocent in the purest of ways, and I'll be damned if I let my darkness taint that or dim it even in the slightest." Liam spoke softly, tucking a few golden stray hairs back behind her ear.

"Darkness is no match for the light. There isn't a place darkness can hide where the light won't reach and snuff it out," she said as she cupped his cheek, loving the feeling of his scruff against her smooth skin.

"After everything I've done, the amount of evil I've carried out in my lifetime, only you can soften my razor-sharp edges and spark warmth into my cold heart. Let's test that theory of yours, shall we?" And without any warning, his mouth was on hers, his tongue seeking entrance right away.

Amarah obliged and Liam didn't waste any time exploring her mouth. He slowly rocked his hips back and forth as he ground his throbbing erection into her core, driving her crazy. The gentleness of his movements and the friction from the clothes were almost too much. She needed them gone.

"I'm a virgin, not a glass doll." She laughed lightly as she broke their kiss to look him in the eyes. "You don't have to take it easy on me."

"Because you're a virgin is why I need to take it slow with you. I don't want your first experience with sex to be me hurting you," he confessed.

"You won't hurt me." She cupped his cheek. "Liam, I've dreamed of this for years and now that it's finally happening, I need you. All of you."

"If it's your first time, how do you know what you need or will like? What if by fully being me I do something that you aren't into, and it scares you?" he asked, cocking his head to the side half in amusement and half in curiosity.

"I read romance books, Liam, the majority of which are dark, with very graphic and explicit sex scenes. I've pictured you doing all those things to me, and each time I do, I come harder than I ever thought possible. So, yeah, I think I know what I like."

"Just so you know, you asked for it," Liam warned her with his famous devilish grin.

He crushed his mouth back over hers in a hungry and dominating possession. One of his large hands reached for a fist full of hair as the other groped one of her voluptuous tits over the fabric of her shirt, working her already perky nipples between his fingers and thumb. He put more force behind grinding his erection against her and she moaned against his mouth.

Amarah gave it right back, matching his energy. Her hands were roaming his body, loving the feeling of his muscles beneath her touch, until they found his firm, round ass and she squeezed, trying to pull him closer to her. She arched her back to give him better access to her breasts and rocked her hips to match his. They both broke the kiss, needing air, only to have him start nipping and biting her neck and ear.

She loved every minute of it. Loved the tingling sensation she got anywhere his mouth connected to her skin. Loved the way her body reacted to his. Loved the way her soft and delicate form molded against his hard manly exterior like two pieces of a puzzle.

Liam lifted his hips slightly, causing Amarah to whimper at the loss of contact, but soon gasped as he slipped his hand under the waistband of her shorts. The tips of his fingers passed teasingly through the slickness at her center.

"I love how wet you get for me," he growled. "Do you want me to play with that virgin pussy of yours?" he asked between kisses and bites to the sensitive skin at the base of her neck.

"Yes, please!" She gasped, pushing her hips further against his hand hungrily.

"So needy." He chuckled wickedly as he slid two fingers straight into her. She moaned and instantly began grinding herself against his fingers. "Do you have any idea how many nights I've dreamed about this?"

He didn't give her time to answer, his fingers leaving her middle. Before she could protest, he had both hands on her tank top and the sound of ripping fabric filled the space around them, baring her breasts. She didn't care one bit. Clothes could easily be replaced. Within a matter of seconds, his fingers were back inside of her, gaining another gasp at the sudden shift.

Liam's mouth made quick work on one mound, licking and sucking on her hard nipple, biting down to the point of pain but expertly easing the sting with his tongue. She smiled inwardly as she quickly realized he was indeed the predatory beast she pictured as she pleasured herself to the thought of him. He was knowledgeable and confident in his skills and her body was putty beneath him.

Amarah could feel her orgasm building rapidly. "Don't stop. I'm so close," she panted.

As if reading her body like a book, Liam hooked his two fingers up into the soft spot inside her that he knew would send her over the edge, and he was right. Within a few seconds of hitting it, she was coming all over his hand.

"Oh, God!" Amarah screamed as her body convulsed.

He didn't let up on his movements. Liam kept pumping his fingers into her core as she rode the wave of her high. Once her body stilled and her breathing started to normalize again, he withdrew from her and sucked his middle finger clean, groaning with pleasure.

He brought his hand to her mouth and grinned. "Do you want to taste yourself?"

She didn't hesitate and opened her mouth as she licked and sucked his index finger clean of her finish, loving the tangy taste of herself on him. Her eagerness gained a low groan from him.

CHAPTER 33

As Liam climbed off the bed, he pulled Amarah's shorts and thong off in one smooth motion. He grabbed the torn tank top off the bed and tossed it aside with her shorts. She was now lying there bare as the day she was born. He raked his eyes all over her body as if trying to commit every curve, every freckle, every muscle to his memory.

Looking at her, he pointed to a spot on the floor in front of him. "I want to see how much of my cock that pretty mouth of yours can take."

Amarah sheepishly climbed off the bed and knelt on the floor before him. She was more than happy to comply but nervous as this was her first time doing anything like this. The last thing she wanted was to do something wrong and for him not to enjoy it. She wanted to please him as he had pleased her.

He slid his sweatpants down, just enough to free his erection. It was her turn to rake her eyes over him. Her mouth indeed started to water as she gazed upon his hard cock. Not too small, but not too long that it would hurt and rearrange her insides. He was perfect and very thick, with veins running down his length. She couldn't wait to play with it.

He stepped up to her and he grabbed a fist full of her hair so he could work her head how he wanted. "Do you want to taste my cock?" he inquired.

"God, yes," Amarah whispered as she ran her tongue across her bottom lip in anticipation.

"Tap on my leg if it gets to be too much, ok?"

Her only response was a nod. He took his throbbing cock in his hand and gave it a few tugs, causing pre-cum to bead at his swollen tip. Liam angled her head up as he rubbed the swollen head across her cheek, grazed her lips, across the other cheek, and down her jawline, smearing his pre-cum across that pretty face of hers.

"Open up," he instructed. Amarah obeyed instantly. "Take a deep breath," he continued as he pushed his cock inside.

He groaned, her tongue going to work right away along his shaft. She'd never done this before, but she'd read enough from her books to know the basics of what to do. He stilled. At first, she'd thought that she had done something wrong but quickly realized that he was allowing her time to adjust to his size. The hunger in his darkened eyes confirmed that he was indeed enjoying this as much as she was.

After a minute, he had both hands on the back of her head, gripping handfuls of hair as he thrust his hips into her, lightly at first, as if allowing her time to acclimate.

"Fuck! You suck this dick so good," he encouraged.

Pride blossomed through her at knowing she was pleasing him in a way he liked. He must've seen that she was ready and eager for more because he pushed his dick in further. Before she knew it, he was hitting the back of her throat, and a deep, satisfied groan rolled up his throat.

Amarah's eyes were watering, but she never tapped out. She ground her thighs together, needing the friction. Her arousal leaked down her legs. He was very demanding with her, but she loved it. She found herself loving the salty taste of him as she constantly ran her tongue along his length, tracing the trails of thick veins with her tongue as he fucked her mouth.

He finally pulled out and angled her toward his balls. She didn't need further instruction and went to work licking and sucking all over them, gaining another groan of pleasure from his throat.

Liam tugged on her hair slightly, signaling that he wanted her to stand. He removed his sweatpants and boxers completely and then grabbed her by the ass, hoisting her up. Amarah instinctively wrapped her legs around him as he walked to the bed and laid her down on her back. He positioned the head of his cock at her slick entrance and began rubbing teasing passes.

"Last chance to back out because once I get the full taste of you, you aren't going anywhere."

She let out a small moan at the threat. No way was she backing out. She'd wanted this for years now, and she found this better than any fantasy she could ever imagine.

"Please, Liam. I need you inside of me," Amarah begged.

He pushed inside of her heat, pausing briefly when he was met with resistance, but with a quick thrust of his hips slid fully inside of her, claiming her innocence for himself. She grunted softly from the pain, but being lost in the throes of passion helped to alleviate the majority of it.

"It'll only hurt for a moment. Then I promise I'll make it feel good." Liam settled and waited for her body to relax around him.

She took the minute he allowed her to adjust to him. He was thick and filled her almost to the point of pain. After a minute, she felt her muscles begin to relax. When she was ready, her hands found his firm ass again and she pulled him into her, signaling that she wanted more, needed more.

He didn't hesitate as he pulled out to the tip, and pushed back in again, over and over. Long, slow thrusts at first, then his pace quickened, and he roughly pounded her into the mattress.

He never once let up as if he couldn't get himself deep enough inside of her. Pain was quickly replaced by immense pleasure and she moaned his name and various curse words time and time again.

He suddenly pulled out, flipped to his back, and grinned. "Climb on, cowgirl."

Amarah scrambled to her knees as she straddled him and positioned the swollen tip of his cock back at her entrance. She slowly sank down, taking time to adjust to the new position. Once he was buried inside her again, she began riding him in a front to back motion, grinding her overly sensitive clit against his lower pelvis. He reached up and cupped both hands around her full mounds, loving how they filled up his hands.

"God, I love the way you ride my cock," he said in a deep voice that sent another flood of arousal coursing through her, loving that she was doing it right and pleasing him so much.

She switched up her movements to an up and down direction, bouncing herself on his shaft. She began to feel another orgasm start to build when he suddenly lifted her off of him.

Amarah pouted at the rudeness, but he just pointed in front of him and chuckled, "We're not through just yet. Get on all fours." Again, she obeyed with a smile on her face.

He repositioned himself behind her and thrust without warning. He grabbed a handful of her hair as he thrust roughly and smacked her ass. She yelped at the sudden sting but then moaned at the pleasure it brought her.

"Does someone like being spanked?" Liam asked with hunger thick in his deep voice.

"Yes, please," she begged.

"A glutton for punishment, are we?" He peppered her ass with more, switching off between sides. She moaned and pushed back into him after each one. "Do you want me to come all over that round ass of yours?"

"Yes! Come all over what's yours." She moaned as she buried her face in the covers.

"Shit! Then you better come for me now." He groaned, thrusting into her as he reached a hand around to stroke circles against her swollen bundle of nerves.

She bucked at the sensation, but after a few more thrusts of his hips slamming into hers, the combination had her clenching around him.

"Oh, fuck! Liam!" she screamed into the covers as she fisted the fabric tightly in both hands.

He quickened his pace and after a few more thrusts, he was pulling out, gripping his cock that was now coated with her juices, and spilling his release all over her ass and up her back.

"Amarah! Shit..." Liam groaned as he pumped himself a few more times, milking every last drop onto her.

When he had finished, he reached over and grabbed her torn tank top, wiping his come off her.

Liam collapsed on the bed, and Amarah fell right next to him, cuddling to his side as she rested her head atop his chest. That was better than she could ever have imagined. He brought the covers up and wrapped his arms around her as they both worked to get their breathing under control.

"I wasn't too rough with you, was I?" he asked as concern started to fill his voice.

"Not at all. I mean, I'll definitely be sore tomorrow, but damn, was it worth it." She snuggled into his chest.

"I'm glad you enjoyed yourself." Liam laughed lightly as he tightened his hold on her.

"What about you? Did this change things for you, for us?" Amarah held her breath, waiting for his answer. She prayed she didn't just lose the only man she'd ever loved.

"It definitely changed things between us." His tone was serious.

Her heart cracked slightly, fearing the worst. She craned her neck, forcing herself to meet his gaze. "Meaning?" Amarah asked hesitantly.

"We can never go back to being just friends. I've wanted this for so long and now that I finally got a taste of it, of you..." Liam paused as if searching for the right words. "I'm never letting you go, whether you want it or not. You're stuck with me, Cupcake."

She let out the breath she held and almost cried in joy. She feared the worst, but things couldn't have turned out better. He placed a kiss on the top of her head as exhaustion overtook them both, and they drifted off into a peaceful, dreamless sleep.

CHAPTER 34

Amarah stirred awake the next morning, finding herself in a very good mood. Had last night truly happened, or was it all just a wet dream? Did she really have sex with the man she'd known for over a decade, the once cute boy who moved into their neighborhood?

She got the pleasure of watching him grow up to be one hell of a man, her first love, and with each passing day, she grew deeper and deeper in love with him. The bit of soreness between her legs confirmed that it was, in fact, reality.

Being able to get that intimate with Liam last night was better than she ever thought possible. Now he'd have a piece of her to carry with him for the rest of his life. A part of her that she saved just for him, all this time, and it was well worth the wait.

She revisited her memories and found that addictive tingling deep within her core was starting to awaken her sleep-ridden body. She was ready for another round, soreness be damned, and knew she'd never tire of that man inside of her.

Liam's strong, painted arms were wrapped around her middle, and his front was pressed snuggly into her back. She craned her head around to find his eyes still shut. His steady and even breaths tickled the back of her neck as she began to pry herself out of his grasp, careful not to wake him, but needing a shower after last night.

The evidence of her multiple orgasms was dried up on the inside of her thighs. Her core heated further at the memories. She tried, only to be pulled tighter against him.

"Where do you think you're going?" Liam mumbled in a groggy

voice as he nestled his face in her hair and neck, breathing in the scent of her.

"To go shower." She laughed as the scruff on his face tickled her neck.

"Is that an invitation?" he purred in her ear as he pushed his erection into the crevice of her round ass.

She let out a breathy moan as she wiggled against him, wanting all of him again. Eventually, he let go as she stretched and climbed out of bed, still completely naked. Red caught her gaze as she took in the small drops of blood that stained his sheets. Her brows pulled together, knowing her cycle wasn't due for a few more weeks. Then realization hit her.

"Oh, God. I'm so sorry." Her face heated.

Liam cocked his head, then looked down, following her line of sight. "You have nothing to be sorry for, Cupcake." He chuckled. "It's just a bit of blood. You were a virgin. It's natural for that to happen. Get in the shower and I'll clean it up."

Emotions constricted around her heart at his words and how gentle and understanding he was being. She gave him a small smile before walking into the bathroom, feeling the slight soreness between her legs with each step.

Liam joined her in the shower a few minutes later. Amarah grabbed a loofah and began to wash him, taking her time and scrubbing circles over every inch of his broad, muscular body, loving the way the soap ran over and down his muscles. She squatted down to wash the lower half and she licked her lips as she came eye level with his hardened member.

"Is that what you'd like for breakfast?"

She nodded as Liam rinsed the soap from his body. He grabbed a fist full of golden hair as he glided the tip of his cock across her full lips.

"I'm happy to oblige." He grinned wickedly. "Open that pretty mouth of yours for me."

She tilted her chin and opened wide as he pushed his hard cock in, filling up her mouth until he touched the back of her throat. He slowly withdrew and eased it back in, repeating that for a few more passes as she worked her tongue up and down his shaft. Her eager moans sent vibrations down into his balls, causing him to place a hand on the tile wall for support.

"Damn, you're such a good little cock sucker."

Liam picked up the pace and began fucking her mouth. She felt spit run down her chin, and the dirtiness of it further turned her on. After a few more thrusts he withdrew, angled her head towards him, gripped his cock in one hand, and came all over her face.

Amarah closed her eyes and welcomed every drop that landed on her cheeks, nose, chin, and a little across her heavy breasts. Liam moaned her name the entire time. When she was sure he was done, she opened her eyes and ran her tongue around her mouth, licking up any nearby come.

"Fuck me!" he growled, his eyes hungry for her.

She gave him a sultry smile and stood, rinsing off her face and chest. It was his turn to wash her up now. He vetoed the loofah, and she couldn't help but wonder if it was because he wanted to run his hands all over her. She hoped so because she very much wanted that.

Liam soaped up his hands as he began to massage her skin, up her arms, down her back, paying extra attention to her perky breasts and down her flat belly. He crouched as he ran his hands up and down her legs in a slow teasing manner, grazing his fingers across her wet center with each pass.

After rinsing the soap off herself, Liam, still crouching, positioned her against the cool shower wall and tossed one of her legs over his shoulder. He began peppering the inside of her thighs with kisses as he inched his way toward her middle.

Amarah laced her fingers through Liam's wet raven hair as she watched him intently, loving the view of his face between her legs. His tongue jetted out and licked up and down her entrance, gaining soft moans from her.

"I'll never tire of your taste on my tongue," he said as he sank deeper into her.

He ate her out like a starving man. His fingers took over so he could focus on her clit, nibbling and sucking hard as he finger-fucked her tight cunt. She felt her orgasm building and began grinding her hips against his face.

He chuckled and picked up the pace with his fingers, and when he felt her core clenching around him, he hooked them into that sensitive spot, sending her over the edge as she screamed his name, gripping his hair tighter and fucking his face as his tongue licked up every bit of her finish.

As she came down from her orgasm, he stood and smashed his body into hers in a passionate kiss, making her taste herself on him. He gripped the back of her thighs and hoisted her up, pinning her against the shower wall.

Amarah gasped as Liam placed his already hard cock against her entrance. Without warning, he pushed inside her, burying himself.

He began to impale her over and over again. Mind melted from her orgasm, all she could do was wrap her arms around his neck and hold on for dear life. She peered down between their slick bodies and watched him thrust in and out, loving the view. She could feel another orgasm building as he picked up his pace, chasing his own as well. They came together in an explosion of passion.

Her cries of pleasure and his groans echoed off the tile walls as she dug her fingernails across the painted flesh of his back. He continued his thrusts, making sure he got every drop deep inside of those tight walls of hers, as if he wanted to mark it as his. Which she was perfectly ok with.

Liam rested his forehead against hers as they caught their breath. He then placed a gentle kiss on her forehead as he sat her back down, making sure her shaky legs were sturdy before letting go. She took pleasure in knowing that he made her literally weak in the knees.

"Just so you know, I'm on birth control," she said as she finished getting cleaned up.

"For now," Liam winked as he stepped out of the shower.

The sinful threat sent a delicious shiver down her back. She'd pictured Liam being the father of her children since she was a kid herself, and to hear him want it too made her over the moon happy. But there was no rush. She was still young and wanted to enjoy time with it just being the two of them before they started bringing kids into this world.

"What time are we meeting Travis and Sandra for lunch?" Amarah asked as she brushed out her wet strands, deciding to leave her long hair down today.

"Noon," Liam answered as he toweled off and ran his fingers through his wet hair, brushing it back.

"You know we have to tell them about us, right?" She tried to mask the grimace that wanted to surface.

Telling her brother that she was sleeping with his best friend was going to be a touchy subject.

"I figured as much," he said calmly.

"You aren't worried?" Amarah asked, halting her mascara application to peer at him.

"No." He laughed. "We're all adults and if Travis has a problem with it, he can put his big boy pants on and deal with it."

"Well, I know my mother and Sandra will be happy for us. Not sure about my dad though, that could go either way," she shrugged as she resumed applying her eye makeup.

"Your father gave me his blessing last year," Liam said casually before he turned and walked out of the bathroom.

"What? Wait, hold on!" Amarah followed him down the hallway to his room. "You can't just say something like that and then walk off. Elaborate, please."

"Last year at one of the cookouts, Oscar pulled me aside and said that he'd noticed the way I looked at you and asked if anything was going on between us," he said as he strode over to his closet and pulled down a pair of Wrangler blue jeans.

Amarah asked as she watched his muscles flex with each movement as he tugged the denim over his muscular legs. "What did you say?"

"I told him that nothing was going on with us. I told him that I cared for you, but he didn't buy it. He knew there was more to it, but he didn't push." He grabbed a maroon T-shirt that fit over his torso snugly. "Then he said that if anything ever did happen between us, he approved, knowing that I'd do anything to keep you happy. That's all he's ever wanted in a man for his daughter."

"Oh." Amarah was speechless.

Love and appreciation flooded her heart for her father and pride that Liam met her father's standards.

"Now go get dressed before we miss our lunch date because I tossed you on my bed and worshiped your body all day long," he threatened with a wicked grin and promise in his green eyes.

Amarah reluctantly went back to her room, finished her makeup, and threw on a pair of blue jeans and a loose baby blue tank top that played well with her eyes. When they were ready, they exited Liam's home.

CHAPTER 35

Amarah and Liam made their way to a bar and grill in town that was known to have the best farm-to-table food. They walked inside to find the place bustling with people chatting, drinks being poured, waiters delivering food, and people cheering for sports games on the numerous large flat-screen TVs mounted along the walls.

She spotted Travis and Sandra already sitting at a bar-height table with drinks in front of them. Liam must've located them, too, because he placed his hand on Amarah's lower back and began steering her through the crowd of tables and waiters.

Travis greeted his sister with a tight hug, then shook Liam's hand and pulled him in, each of them slapping each other on the back. Amarah and Sandra smiled and hugged before everyone took their seats again. A waiter came by, placing chips and dips on their table and grabbing drink orders for the two newcomers.

"How have y'all been?" Amarah said as she scooped a chip through the salsa and ate it, thankful that no one noticed her face.

It had healed a little over the last few days, but she still had to cover the small damage Derick had done to her with makeup. Apparently, she did a good job, because no one said anything.

Liam reached over and rested a hand on the top of her thigh. She inhaled sharply at the sparks that filled his touch—a touch that made her core heat—and she cut her eyes at him. How could he be doing that right then? They hadn't even told them yet. What if Travis saw?

Liam was sitting there, casually sipping his beer without a care in the world, looking calm and confident as ever, which only turned her on even more. A small twitch on the side of his mouth was his only indication that he knew what his touch was doing to her, and he was finding enjoyment in it.

"We've been good. The kids are keeping us busy. How have you been?" Sandra responded in a chipper tone, scooping her frozen margarita with a spoon and eating it.

"The last few weeks have been… interesting, but things are looking up," Amarah said with a twinkle in her eye.

Sandra cocked her head to the side, pulling her fiery brows together, but it was Travis who spoke next.

"Is everything ok?" her brother asked, concern filling his voice.

Amarah took a deep breath, mentally preparing herself for what was about to happen. This was going to go one of two ways. Either they would be happy for them, or Travis would try to kill Liam. She prayed for the former. She didn't want to see two of the most important men in her life fighting each other. Especially in a restaurant filled with people.

She dropped her hand to where Liam had his resting on her thigh, turned it over, and laced her fingers through his. When she glanced over at him, silently asking if he was ready, she was met with an encouraging wink. With a deep breath, she peered back toward her brother and sister-in-law, who shared matching expressions of concern, and gave them a large, genuine smile as she raised their interlocked hands above the table.

Well, there it was, on full display for everyone to see. Not realizing she was holding her breath, Amarah waited impatiently for any kind of response. Cheers, clapping, plates being flung, punches being thrown, curses being spewed, anything.

Travis examined their clasped hands, shifted his gaze to Liam, then back to his sister. "I'm confused… What's that supposed to mean?"

"You idiot!" Sandra shouted, smacking her husband on the shoulder. "They're trying to tell us they're together. Finally!" She squealed while clapping her hands together. She jumped off her stool, rounded the table, and threw her arms around Amarah. "Took y'all long enough, but I am so happy for you, sis."

"Thank you!" Amarah laughed, hugging her back just as tightly.

She knew Sandra would be for Team Liam. She's been wishing they'd finally get together for years now. Travis was the questionable one. Travis and Liam hadn't moved at all. Her brother's gaze slid from watching the girls over to his best friend.

"You're sleeping with my sister?" Travis schooled his face into a calm statue, only allowing one eyebrow to rise a little higher than the other.

"Jesus, honey. You could've stated that a little better. They're both grown adults, free to make their own choices." Sandra shook her head as she spoke to her husband, still at Amarah's side.

"That's a pretty great perk, but that's not the only reason I'm with her," Liam stated, meeting his best friend's gaze.

"Well, I have always wanted the best for her. Unfortunately, she chose you. Are you sure about this, Amarah? I mean, it's not too late for you to try and find someone else," Travis teased his sister, a smile finally sliding across his face.

"Nah, I think I'll stick with this one for a while." She rested a hand on Liam's shoulder.

"Congrats brother, I'm truly happy for y'all," Travis said as he raised his glass to his best friend. "I knew it was only a matter of time. You held out longer than I thought."

Sandra returned to her seat, and they all toasted to the new couple. Food was delivered, more drinks were poured, and the conversations flowed from topic to topic.

After a while, Amarah excused herself, making her way to the bathroom, feeling Liam's eyes on her the whole way. She rounded the corner and went down the hall to the ladies' room. She heard the door open as she washed her hands and glanced up in the mirror, expecting to see a woman come in. Dread filled her and she was frozen with fear as she gazed upon the evil face smiling back at her.

Derick…

Dressed in a blue T-shirt that drew out the true depths of his eyes and clung to his lean and muscular torso, a pair of light-wash blue jeans, and his black Converse shoes. His face was clean-shaven, allowing nothing to disrupt the view of his tanned skin and strong jawline. His blond hair looked freshly cut on the sides and the top was brushed back, as if he had just run his fingers through it.

She whirled around and stared at him, too shocked to speak. She could only watch as he reached for the lock on the door, securing it with a click so loud it was like a sonic boom in the deafening silence. He slowly prowled towards her as he sported a wicked grin that had her lunch wanting to reappear.

"Hello, love," he purred. "You look surprised to see me so soon."

Amarah was done letting this man have so much power over her. Sick of how he made her so scared that her body would lock up. Well, not anymore. She wasn't going to be a victim. She wasn't going to be just another statistic. She was going to fight until her last breath if that's what it took to stop him. Because even if she was lucky and managed to get away from him, the next woman he did this to might not be so lucky. And she couldn't live with that on her conscience.

"Bold of you to try something so public, Derick. All I have to do is scream and someone will be here in seconds." She steeled her spine, standing her ground.

"You won't do that. In fact, you are going to walk out the back door with me, quiet as a mouse." He never let his smile falter.

Like hell she would. Had this man lost his mind? Well… Of course he had. No sane person would stalk someone.

"What makes you think I'd ever do that?" Amarah choked out a half-laugh, raising one brow in amusement.

"Because you wouldn't want anything to happen to those precious nieces and nephew of yours, would you? Or what about the owners of the coffee shop you frequent? What were their names again? Oh yeah, that's right. Mr. and Mrs. Johnson. It'd be a shame if one of them had a tragic accident or their store suddenly caught fire. Or God forbid something happened to your parents. How are they enjoying their cruise?"

Her breath hitched and her heart dropped to her stomach. How did Derick know about them? How did he know so much about her? How did he keep finding her when the police couldn't find him?

"If you touch one hair on their heads, I'll gut you like a fucking fish," she snarled. "How the fuck do you know so much about my life, my family, where I work, where I live?" She threw her arms up in frustration, done playing his sick and twisted games.

Derick shrugged one shoulder as he answered, "I placed a tracker on your vehicle when I walked you to your car after our first date. I've been following you for a while now."

He spoke so nonchalantly about it, as if tracking and stalking people were normal human behavior. He was right in front of her now, raising a hand to grip her chin gently, forcing her eyes to meet his.

"I know you're trying to find a way out of this, but do yourself a favor and don't. It'll only make me angry, and you won't like what I'll do to the people you care about if I'm angry. You'll leave alongside me out the back. You'll not make a sound, and you'll not fight me anymore. Understood?"

Her brain was racing so fast, trying to come up with a plan, but he had her at checkmate. There was no way she would ever risk the lives of her nieces and nephew or anyone she cared deeply about. Even if he was bluffing, she couldn't take the chance. She *wouldn't* take the chance.

What if Derick wasn't acting alone? With anger welling up inside of her like a dam about to burst, Amarah did the only thing she could do. She nodded her head in acknowledgment of his terms.

"Good girl. That makes me so happy. Now, let's get out of here, shall we?" He placed a kiss on her lips in a possessive way, as if marking what he believed was his.

She felt her lunch creeping back up her throat, but she clamped her mouth shut and closed her eyes, wanting nothing more than to scrub her lips raw to erase any trace of him.

Derick broke their kiss as he unlocked the bathroom door and motioned for her to go first. She willed her feet to move and made her way to the back door at the end of the hallway that led to a staff parking lot. He placed one hand on the small of her back and the other held onto her small wrist as they walked. She found his touch acidic as he led her to a small, worn down, older model Toyota Corolla.

It made sense that he'd ditch his truck. The cops would be looking everywhere for it. He popped the trunk, and a spasm of fear shot through her. *Is he going to put me in there?*

He saw her terror and tightened his grip. "I have to punish you, love, for hurting me the way you did in your house," he said, what sounded like true remorse in his tone. Which was hard for Amarah to believe. "Please know I don't like doing this, but you force me when you don't obey. It's your fault, really. Now climb in the trunk or I'll put you in there myself."

Amarah could tell by his face that he meant what he said. She took a deep breath, beat back her panic, then reluctantly climbed in.

"That's my good girl," Derick cooed as he stroked her silky strands.

Amarah glared at him. Then, without warning, he removed a rag from his pocket and quickly covered her mouth and nose. She jerked and tried to scream, tried to call for help, but her actions were futile. He grabbed her by the back of her head with his other hand, and no matter how hard she fought, she couldn't dislodge the foul rag.

She sucked in a ragged breath and gagged at the sickly sweet taste of some chemical she didn't recognize. Her feet drummed on the trunk floor. The edge of her vision began to blur and as the darkness closed in, the last thing she heard before blackness took her was Derick's crooning voice.

"Don't worry, love. When you wake up, everything's going to be perfect. You'll see. Just perfect."

CHAPTER 36

Liam checked his watch for what felt like the tenth time. It'd been exactly twelve minutes and Amarah had not returned from the bathroom yet. Either something didn't agree with her stomach, or something was wrong.

"Dude, please don't tell me you have separation anxiety already, because that's not healthy." Travis laughed.

It wasn't a surprise that he noticed Liam checking his watch every minute. Travis received the same training Liam did, and they both managed to keep themselves and each other alive on numerous operations. They were good at their jobs.

"Screw you," Liam said over his shoulder as he glanced in the direction of the bathrooms, hoping to see Amarah round the corner any second.

A bad feeling started taking root in the pit of his stomach. Surely Derick wouldn't try anything here, but to dismiss that thought was stupid. He was desperate to get his hands on her. It wouldn't be surprising for him to try in public.

"Is Amarah in some kind of trouble?" Travis's tone took on a serious edge.

Sandra froze, her arm half-stretched to take another drink, when she shot her eyes toward her husband, as if she knew that tone all too well. Then her eyes darted toward Liam, who sighed heavily and turned back around to face them.

Liam filled them in about everything that happened between Amarah and Derick. Occasionally, Sandra would gasp in shock as a new piece of the story was revealed, but Travis kept a guarded mask. The only emotion that showed was the occasional tick of his jaw or the flare of his nostrils.

The moment Liam finished, Travis was up and moving towards the bathrooms with Liam falling into step beside him.

"Hey, wait!" Sandra called as she hopped down from the table and jogged just to keep up.

Neither man said a word the whole way. Travis rounded the corner and pushed open the women's bathroom.

"Amarah!" The only answer he received was his own echo bouncing off the tiled walls.

Liam was already moving toward the back door that led to a staff parking lot. A reflective glint caught his eye as he took in a phone on the ground. He picked it up and recognized Amarah's smashed phone. He looked up at Travis.

"Fuck," they both said in unison.

"What? What's wrong? Did he get to her?" Sandra asked, shifting frantically between both men.

"Only one way to find out," Liam said as he angled his head towards the camera mounted on the side of the building.

The three of them went back inside, making their way to the manager's office. A balding, short round man in his later years was sitting at his desk when both men came barging into his office.

The man jumped up. "Hey! Y'all can't be—"

Liam closed the space between them in two large strides. "Show me the security footage of the back parking lot," he demanded.

"I don't know who y'all are but if you don't leave, I'll call the cops."

It was hard to sound serious when your voice cracked. Liam towered over the man, forcing him to stumble backward and fall back down into his chair.

"Now," Liam clipped in a tone that he hadn't used since his time in the military.

"Ok… Ok… When?" the manager asked as his trembling hands worked his mouse and keyboard.

"The last twenty minutes," Liam answered.

The man typed away and pulled up the footage. Travis was right beside him, watching the monitors. It showed nothing at first, so the man fast-forwarded a little bit.

"Stop," Liam demanded. The poor guy jumped but did as he was told. "There," he said, pointing to the screen.

It showed Amarah and Derick walking to a car and opening the trunk. They watched as she climbed in, Derick drugged her, tied her up, smashed her phone, closed the trunk, and drove off.

"He put her in the fucking trunk!" Travis roared in anger.

"Why would she go with him? Why not shout for help? This place is packed and y'all are both here," Sandra asked, looking between them frantically.

"He must've threatened her. Used something against her that had her not willing to risk trying to call for help." Travis sighed as he ran a hand through his long blond hair.

"This man had already proven how resourceful he could be. Who knows what he used against her to get her to leave with him," Liam spoke over his shoulder to Sandra. "Rewind that one more time. Where he was driving off." The manager did as he was told. *Smart man,* Liam thought. He looked closely at the monitor. "Older model Toyota Corolla. T3X000 as the plate? Is that what you see?"

Travis leaned toward the screen and squinted, studying the image. "Yep," he agreed, and Liam already had his phone out, dialing Detective Trenton. They left the office and made their way to their vehicles.

"Detective Trenton," the man answered after the first ring.

"It's Liam Godrik. Derick has Amarah. He kidnapped her from Sports Hub Bar and Grill about fifteen minutes ago. CCTV footage shows him putting her in the trunk of an older model Toyota Corolla, license plate T3X000."

"Fucking hell… Ok, I'm putting out a BOLO for the vehicle." There was a brief pause before he continued, "How exactly did you manage to view the footage? On second thought, never mind. The less I know, the better. Did you happen to catch which direction he went?"

"No. The camera was an older model. It had shitty area coverage. I'm surprised I was able to get as much as I did."

At least they had some kind of camera. Something was better than nothing, especially in those types of situations. Any little bit helped.

"Alright. I'll call you the moment I learn anything." Detective Trenton paused. Liam could hear the hesitation in his voice. "I pulled what I could on you. I wanted to make sure Amarah would be safe with whoever she was staying with during all this. I learned that you were in the Navy SEALs, but your file is rather thin. Which means either your military life was quiet and boring, or your past is classified. I'm willing to bet you have a lot of buried secrets, Mr. Godrik."

"Your point, detective?" Liam said in a flat tone.

"Whatever you plan on doing, just be smart about it and be careful."

The detective would be foolish if he believed that Liam was the kind of man who would sit back, wait, and let the cops handle this. Liam Godrik was not that kind of man. The skills he'd acquired, resources he had access to, and questionable contacts he could call, he's the kind you wouldn't see coming until he had you at checkmate.

Liam let a smile slip across his lips—a wicked smile as he thought about what exactly he planned on doing to Derick.

"I haven't the slightest clue what you're talking about, detective."

"No, of course not. One last thing. Do you know of anywhere Derick might go? Some place he could take her that's quiet and remote. He'll want as much privacy as possible until he can get her under control and cooperative."

Liam thought about it for a moment, but he knew nothing of the guy. Only what Amarah had told him about Derick.

"No, sorry."

"Alright, I'll be in touch," Detective Trenton said, hanging up.

"What's the plan?" Travis asked before Liam could fully put his phone back into his pocket.

Liam let out a long sigh as he ran a hand over the scruff of his beard. "Let's go back to your place. I need a computer and y'all need to get back to the kids. We don't know what he used as blackmail but threatening to hurt kids is usually a common scumbag go-to."

They all loaded up and Liam followed in his truck behind a speeding Travis as they made it back to the house in record time.

CHAPTER 37

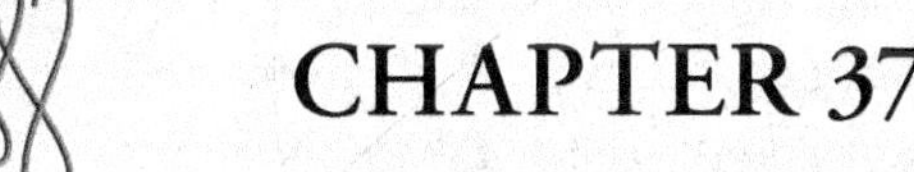

Liam, Travis, and Sandra practically ran inside to find the kids and babysitter on the couch in the middle of a movie. They sighed a breath of relief as Sandra paid the sitter and Liam made his way to Travis's office.

He pulled up the internet and searched "Derick Watland." A few social media accounts popped up. He scrolled through the list of possible Derick's until he recognized one from a photo Amarah showed him. He clicked on the link, and it took him to the man's Instagram account.

"What are you looking for?" Travis inquired as he came through the door carrying two glasses of scotch. He handed a glass to Liam while taking a heavy drink of his own.

"I'm not sure. Something… Anything that'll help me figure out where he's taken her. I know almost nothing about the man, only what Amarah told me. But he has to have somewhere he can take her. I doubt he would take her to a motel. It'd be too risky, too hard to keep her quiet. No, he must have private space somewhere. I'm hoping I can stumble upon something on one of his social media accounts. People post way too much information about their private lives on these things." Liam spoke as he scrolled through numerous posts.

Travis walked around to stand behind Liam as he scrolled through an Instagram account filled with nature photos and pictures of Derick on different adventures. Liam picked up his glass and downed it in two gulps. He paused his scrolling when he came across a photo of Derick on a boat on a lake.

What caught Liam's attention wasn't the man or the boat, but the cabin on the shore behind him. Then it hit him—he remembered the conversation they'd had the other day. Amarah told him that Derick wanted to take her away for the weekend to his family's cabin. And Liam knew exactly where it was.

"You know where he's taking her, don't you?" Travis asked.

Liam turned and stood. "It's just a hunch, but yeah, I believe so."

"Alright, let's gear up and go." Travis said, setting his now empty scotch glass next to his best friend's.

"No. Just me, brother," Liam said in all seriousness.

"Bull-fucking-shit! That's my sister he has. You really think I'm going to sit this one out?" Travis protested.

"Yes. Derick has already proven he knows a lot about Amarah and her life without her telling him. Who's to say he isn't planning on hurting Sandra or the kids to get to her? Or using them as leverage?"

"He already has her," Travis protested. "Why would he go after Sandra and the kids now?"

"You're probably right, but can you take that chance? Think like a SEAL, Travis. Think like a SEAL and not like a brother," Liam snapped and Travis stiffened. "Think like it's just another high-stakes operation. Maybe the target is where we think he is, maybe he isn't. Maybe he's one step ahead of us again like he has been this whole fucking time. Think, brother. We protect our rear while we push forward."

Liam took a deep calming breath, laid a hand on his friend's shoulder then continued more softly, "We need you to stay here and protect the rest of our family. Only then can I do what must be done. I promise you on my life, I will get her back." He gave Travis's shoulders a gentle squeeze.

Travis was quiet for a long moment. Liam knew the intense battle that must be raging inside his friend's head. Amarah was his little sister, his only sister. Travis had a responsibility to take care of and protect her. But the family he created with Sandra must be protected as well. Liam knew, deep in his bones, that he was right. Who knew what Derick had over her? It had to be important enough to get her to willingly go with him.

Travis let out a long sigh. "Don't come back without her, Liam, or I'll take pleasure in hurting you," he threatened, staring Liam dead in the eyes.

"You can have him after I'm through with him, honey. Although there won't be much left when I'm done," Sandra added after walking into the office.

Liam laughed inwardly because he knew she wasn't lying. Redheads have a stereotype for a reason, and Sandra *was* one crazy redhead.

"I'd die before I came back without her."

Travis gritted his teeth but nodded his head in silent agreement.

Liam drove like a madman back to his house, breaking traffic laws left and right, not caring about the people honking at him as he flew past. The whole way there he made a mental list of what he would need to grab and tried to remember everything he saw about that cabin, even though he only glimpsed it for a minute or two.

Barely waiting for his gate to open wide enough, he squeezed his truck through by the skin of his teeth, threw it in park in front of his garage, and practically sprinted into his kitchen. He opened his pantry and stepped in, turning towards the left. The pantry was twice as deep as his kitchen cabinets that hung along that same wall.

Looking at it, no one would think anything of it, but it hid a secret. Pushing on the shelves, a doorway appeared that led to a long dark alcove that ran down the length of the wall.

He reached for the light switch and a dim yellow glow flooded the space to reveal dark wood bottom cabinets that ran the whole length of the space and were topped with the same white and black marble countertops that decorated his kitchen. Resting atop the counter was a fully stocked ammo reloading station, a magazine rack containing a few editions of guns and ammo books, and clear plastic containers stacked on top of each other, filled with empty shell casings that hadn't been reloaded yet.

A mounted pegboard covered the wall from the top of the cabinets to the ceiling and spanned the width from one wall to the other. Over the years, he'd built up his collection of weapons, ranging from a variety of common guns to collectible swords. On metal hooks hung pistols, shotguns, and rifles, ranging in all different sizes. There was even a section that contained different swords, katanas, machetes, and knives.

Liam opened one of the cabinet doors and pulled out a black plate carrier vest. He draped it over his shoulders and secured the Velcro sides that connected the front and back pieces, making sure it was snug around his torso. Derick was most likely armed, so not wearing a bulletproof vest would be suicide. He didn't know what kind of firepower that pathetic excuse of a man had access to, so he needed to be prepared for the worst.

He grabbed his solid black pistol holster from a drawer and secured the top and bottom buckles to hug around his thick thigh. He pulled the straps tightly to make sure it was snug against his right leg.

He grabbed a Glock 9mm off the pegboard, quickly loaded the magazine with ammo, slid the magazine into the gun until it clicked into place, and racked it back. Loaded and ready to fire, he slid the weapon into the holster. He strapped a knife sheath to his left leg and grabbed a KA-BAR knife from among the collection of blades that hung before him.

He carefully thumbed the blade, testing the sharpness of its edge. A grim smile touched his lips as he thought of all the creative ways he was going to use it on Derick. He twirled it around in his hand and deftly slipped it into the sheath.

Liam grabbed a few extra magazines, loaded them each with ammo, and slid them into the pockets of his vest. Not knowing how crazy this fight might turn out, he wanted to make sure he had plenty.

A pair of black high-grade military binoculars hung on a hook by the door. He grabbed them and turned off the light to his secret room, swung the shelves back into place, and closed the door to his pantry. Liam climbed into his truck, threw it in reverse, and started his journey to Arkansas.

He did have plans to call Detective Trenton, but not until after he confirmed Amarah was in fact being held there at the cabin. The thought of her alone in a space with that nut, not knowing what he could be doing to her or if she was ok, made his foot fall heavy on the gas pedal and his knuckles turn white around the steering wheel. He had a four-hour drive before he could get to her. *Just hang in there, Cupcake. I'm on my way.*

CHAPTER 38

Amarah's eyelids felt like lead as she tried and failed to open them. Against all odds, she managed to crack them open as blinding light flooded her vision, searing into her sensitive blue irises, and forcing her to shut them again instantly. She turned her head to the side, away from the light, and tried again. Successful this time around, she found herself looking at a bedside table that contained a small lamp that had what looked like deer antlers as a base with a red shade topping it.

She pulled her brows together from unrecognition. Then her eyes widened as she observed a glass vase sitting next to the lamp, filled with vibrant flowers. Flowers that looked an awful lot like the ones from her garden.

She looked past it and intently took in the rest of the room. The walls were built out of large wooden logs, and a light logwood dresser topped with a mirror spanned across one wall with wilderness photos hanging around it. She swept her gaze across the room and found the source of the light as she took in a set of French doors that led to a large balcony and were framed by red curtains with thick rope tying them back. An open doorway snagged her vision that led to what she figured was a bathroom.

She dropped her eyes and found herself lying atop a king-sized bed that was cased in a thick bed frame made of the same light wood as the other bedroom furniture. It was draped with a red comforter the same color as the curtains. *Where the hell am I?*

Amarah started to get up, only to be halted in place. *What the...* She turned to look over her shoulder and fear began to rise within her, prickling her flesh with goosebumps as she found both of her wrists secured to the headboard in Velcro restraints.

She tugged against them, pulling with all her might, but the restraints didn't budge. Memories flooded their way back into her mind like a dam that had burst as she recalled what happened to her. Derick had found her and cornered her in the bathroom of the restaurant.

She vividly remembered the threat he used to get her to leave with him out the back door, and then she recalled climbing into his trunk as he smothered her with a rag that was most likely soaked in chloroform.

Amarah figured this must be the cabin he told her about. The décor validated her assumption. Relief washed over her as she noted the jeans and tank top she was still wearing from that morning. The thought of him touching her or God knows what else while she was unconscious made bile rise in her throat.

She clamped her mouth shut and forced it to stay down as she closed her eyes and willed herself to calm down. *Don't freak out, that's how bad things happen.* She listened intently for any kind of noise that would signal Derick was somewhere in the cabin, but it was quiet. She had to get out of there.

Trying again to pull at her restraints, she failed a second time. An idea struck her that had her slipping off her socks. If she could grip the strap with her toes, she could undo them. She brought her knees up to her chest and rolled back onto her shoulders a little as she tried to stretch a foot to her left wrist. She gripped the strap between her toes and was about to pull it up and free her wrist, but she froze in place as she heard footsteps creaking their way up a set of stairs.

Fuck! She cursed as she flattened herself out right before the door to the bedroom swung open and Derick stepped through.

"Oh, good. I was hoping you were awake." A smile crept across his face.

As he got closer, Amarah found herself sitting up and scooting herself against the headboard, bringing her knees to her chest. Derick perched himself on the side of the bed.

"Where are we?" she asked.

"My family's cabin. I told you I wanted to take you here one day. This is the perfect place for us to focus on our relationship with no distractions from the outside world," he said as he reached his hand up and tucked a few golden strands back behind her ear.

She tried to pull away but there was nowhere to go. "Why do you need these?" She tugged at her restraints. "You can't keep me locked up forever, Derick."

"No, just long enough for you to calm down and start to see reason. Once I see that you've learned the error of your ways and I know you don't plan on trying to escape, I'll take them off and you'll be free to roam about the cabin."

"Was me leaving the restaurant with you not enough? You made your threat very clear. You hold all the cards, and I would be stupid to try to run away. I'll not allow you to hurt the ones I love. If that means I must submit, then it's a price I'm willing to pay to keep them safe." Amarah watched as his shoulders dropped slightly.

Yeah, that's right, drop your guard. I'll play your little game and act like the perfect obedient girlfriend you want me to be, and when you least expect it, I'm going to murder you in your fucking sleep.

That thought made her feel a little better. Thinking of all the different ways she could end his miserable existence on this earth. That was what she would hold on to. That was what would get her through and allow her to endure what she had to. She would make sure Derick never got the chance to hurt another woman ever again. Even if it was the last thing she did. Her face remained calm, but she wore a wicked smile on the inside.

"Good girl. I knew you'd come around sooner or later," he said, leaning in to kiss her on the lips.

Amarah had to fight the urge to pull back or turn away from it. A piece of her died a little bit as she forced herself to kiss him back. She had to make it look real or he would never trust her enough to untie her. *Forgive me, Liam,* she thought. *But I have to if I'm to ever make it out of here alive and back to you.*

Derick pulled away with a large smile spread across his handsome face. "Do you like the flowers?"

She followed his gaze to the vase sitting atop the nightstand. "Are they from my garden?" Amarah asked hesitantly.

"They are." He beamed. "You have a gift with plants that I hope you'll put to good use here. This place could use some life put back into it."

Amarah took a deep breath and bit down the snarky comment she wanted to say. She had a part to play and her devotion would've won her an Oscar if this were Hollywood. "I love them. Thank you."

That pleased Derick greatly, as his smile only grew. "Dinner will be ready shortly."

With that, he rose and walked out of the room, closing the door behind him. The moment he was gone, she wiped her lips across her shoulder, trying to erase any remnants of him. She could try to undo the straps again, but that wouldn't get Derick to trust her. Instead, she sat there and lost herself in the thought of all the ways she could kill him.

CHAPTER 39

Amarah looked out the glass doors as she watched the setting sun paint the sky in shades of red and orange. She closed her eyes and whispered a prayer.

"Liam, please remember me telling you about this place. I'll do what I can here, but I don't know how long I can keep up the charade. Please, come quickly."

The door groaned on its hinges as Derick pushed it open, causing her to jump in surprise. "Dinner's ready. Are you hungry?" he asked, stepping into the room carrying a tray full of food and a bottle of red wine tucked under his muscular arm.

Food was the last thing she wanted right now. She had no appetite, but she knew she'd need her strength, every bit of it, if she was to defeat him.

Derick sat at the foot of the bed, placing the tray between them. She sat upright, crossed her legs, and looked over the spread of food he had prepared for them. On each of their plates sat a small steak, some steamed broccoli and carrots, and a slice of French bread. He pulled the cork from the bottle, causing a loud pop to echo off the log walls. He poured some into her glass before filling his own.

"This looks and smells good. Are you going to untie me, or do you plan to feed me?" she asked, keeping her voice light, which she found very hard to do.

He chuckled softly as he rose and moved towards her. Her natural reaction was to recoil away from him, but she forced herself to stay put as he approached. The sound of Velcro ripping apart filled the room as she tried hard to contain a smile at finally being free from them. He moved to the other side of the bed and undid the second strap. She couldn't help the small sigh that escaped her lips as she rubbed at the markings left behind on her sore, reddened wrists.

"Thank you," Amarah managed in a voice so quiet he almost missed it.

Derick took up his position opposite her atop the bed, picked up his utensils, and began cutting into his food. She did the same, and they sat and ate in agonizing silence.

"We need to set some ground rules," he finally said. "One, you do not ever leave this house without me. Period. Two, the phone has been disconnected, so don't try calling for help in the middle of the night. Three, you'll do as you're told, when you're told. Four, if you ever try to run away, your nieces and nephew will pay the price. Understood?"

Amarah froze with her fork halfway to her mouth. She couldn't stop herself from gaping in shock. Was he serious? She had to fight back her natural response of laughter at his audacity. But she had a role to play, and she'd play it dutifully until it was time to make her move.

Setting her fork down on her plate, she made eye contact with him as she whispered, "Yes," and then dropped her gaze to the bed, revealing a small sign of submission.

Amarah felt his fingers gently cup her chin, pulling her gaze to his. "Thank you. I promise you I'll treat you like a queen, and you'll never want for anything. Given enough time, I'll prove to you just how wrong you were to choose Liam. He'd never be able to love you as I do. You'll see."

All she could do was nod her head, signaling that she understood. How was that living? How could anyone be happy with that kind of life? He didn't want a partner; he wanted a puppet to manipulate. That wasn't a relationship, it was a prison. But it would only be for a short time. She could and would endure it because she had to stop him.

"It pleases me to see you finally coming around."

With his hand still cupping her chin, he leaned over the tray and kissed her with such possession it almost hurt. But she didn't wince. No, she endured it and kissed him right back.

"Now, let's finish our dinner. I think you've earned a hot shower."

Amarah welcomed the chance to wash him from her skin and get a little separation from his suffocating presence. They finished the rest of their meal in silence, both of them emptying their glass of wine as well. Once done, Derick piled their dirty dishes back onto the tray and placed them on top of the dresser by the door.

"Time for that shower."

"I don't have anything to change into." She didn't have anything here, actually. No clothes, no shower stuff. Hell, she didn't even have a toothbrush.

"Don't worry, I made sure to stock this house with anything you could ever need." Derick motioned towards the dresser.

That caught her attention. She scrunched her brows together and slowly rose from the bed, making her way toward it. Hesitantly, she pulled open the top drawer. She was growing rather tired of how many times this man could shock her, and not in a good way.

It was fully stocked with socks, thongs, and lace bras. A few were hers, and she was certain that when she pulled open the other drawers or looked in the closet, the rest of her missing clothes would be there.

Before she could stop herself, the words slipped out. "Why did you take my clothes?"

"I knew you'd need stuff to wear during our time here," he said with a sly smile.

Disgust and unease washed through her like a violent tsunami, sending a visible shiver over her body that she couldn't contain. Just how long had he been planning this? Not knowing what he touched or worse, she wanted nothing more than to burn every piece of clothing she owned.

Amarah closed the drawer and forced herself to pull the others open with shaky hands. One drawer was designated for sleepwear, filled with a variety of nightgowns and pajama sets. The next drawer was filled with comfy lounge clothes like leggings and workout clothes in all different styles and colors.

She then proceeded to the next row of drawers and opened the top one, curious as to what else he filled it with. But what she saw froze her to her core. The last three drawers were filled with his clothes. She took a deep breath and tried to wield steadiness in her voice.

"Are we sharing this room?"

"Of course. How are we to repair the beautiful relationship you so easily tossed aside if we don't spend as much time together as possible?" Derick asked. His tone seemed to be filled with genuine curiosity.

Amarah didn't designate that with a response. What was she supposed to say?

"I'd be lying if I said the thought of waking up with you next to me didn't excite me. I can't wait to see just how radiant you look in the mornings." He pulled open the top drawer and grabbed a black lace thong, opened her pajama drawer, picked out a maroon nightgown, and handed it to her. "Wear these tonight."

She had no words. All she could do was nod her head as she tentatively accepted the clothes from him and padded across the room to the bathroom. It too was stocked with all the items she used at home, down to the exact brands. The bathroom was decorated much like the bedroom, with the same wooden logs forming the four walls.

After the horror faded from her eyes, she turned to find Derick's watchful blue gaze on her as he casually leaned against the bathroom counter with his arms folded over his lean chest.

"I'll be out in a few minutes," Amarah dismissed, but he didn't move, not even an inch.

"And give you a chance to try and escape? Trust is earned, love, and you have a long way to go before I trust you again. Another way you betrayed and hurt me." Pain flashed through his irises, but he blinked and it was gone. A wicked smile started to slide across his face as he said, "I'm not letting you out of my sight."

Her heart dropped into her stomach and yet another shiver fell down her spine. It was alright though. She knew this wasn't going to be easy. Sacrifices would have to be made to get him to drop his guard enough for her to kill him.

Amarah took a deep breath as she set her nightgown atop the counter, opened the glass shower door, and turned the water on. While the water warmed, she began to strip out of her clothes. His eyes never once left her body, as if trying to memorize every inch of her. She could feel his gaze raking all over her figure as each piece of discarded fabric pooled on the bathroom tiles.

She stepped into the shower, never once sparing a glance toward her captor. She knew that if she did, the disgust and hatred in her eyes would give her thoughts away. The whole time she was in there, she felt his piercing and weighted gaze on her. She quickly went through her normal routine of washing up, needing to get out and clothed as fast as possible.

Once finished, Amarah turned off the water, grabbed the towel, and secured herself in it tightly. She then brushed out her golden strands and hurriedly dressed herself. Even after she was clothed, she didn't feel any better. No amount of clothing would ever be enough to hide her body from him now that he'd finally seen all of her.

"You're so beautiful, you know that?" Derick said with admiration in his voice.

"Thank you," she said timidly, keeping her eyes downcast as she picked at the hem of her nightgown.

He gently cupped her chin and forced her to look up. "I mean it. You truly are the most exquisite creature I've ever had the pleasure of knowing."

Their blue eyes clashed as her mind and heart waged war against each other. Why? Why did he have to be so possessive? What happened to him that would cause so much darkness to infiltrate his soul and blacken his heart? Derick had such amazing qualities about him, and she had seen true goodness within. But the evil inside him defeated any chance the light had of taking over. He would've made a wonderful man and partner for someone if he ever learned to purge himself of that evil.

Amarah hated what she had to do, what her heart knew was the right thing. She wished with every ounce of her being that she could help him, but he was too far gone. He'd never let her go, never allow himself to get help because he saw nothing wrong, and that left her with no other choice but to end him.

Derick released her chin and took hold of her hand as he escorted her from the bathroom. "Lay down on our bed." He spoke in a husky voice. She shifted her features into a calm mask and did as she was told.

CHAPTER 40

Lying down atop the bed, Amarah watched in fear as Derick unbuttoned and removed his long-sleeved black plaid shirt and sent it pooling on the floor. His naked torso was sun-kissed and packed with lean muscles as he bent down and started placing soft kisses from the inside of her ankle up her leg as he slowly climbed further onto the bed.

"You have no idea how long I've waited for this moment," he said in between kisses. "I would've gotten to you last weekend when your tires went flat. But your… savior… had to pull over to help you, just in the nick of time."

"You sabotaged my Tahoe?" Her body went rigid beneath him. He *had* been out there. That feeling of being watched was real, not a delusion her paranoia created. Were the other times real as well? When she got the feeling outside the coffee shop and twice in the parking garage at Godrik Enterprises?

"It's alright though, I have you now. We're together and nothing will come between our love again," he said in a sweet tone that was at complete odds with his actions and behavior. "Now, relax, and let me worship you like the goddess you are."

By the time he reached her knee, he was too lost in lust to focus on her movements. Amarah's vision shifted to the tray of dirty dishes and the knives that still rested atop the dresser, then to the vase of flowers that sat beside their bed. She'd been pondering ideas all afternoon about what she could do and how she could get herself out of this cabin. Derick was larger, stronger, and faster. She knew she'd never beat him in a fight. She had to be smart and strategic with her plan.

When her gaze kept observing the flowers he so rudely butchered and murdered from their peaceful home in her garden, she knew there would be nothing more poetic than repaying the favor. She just needed to find the right way to steer this, so he was on his back, and she was straddling him. That would give her the most advantageous position to grab the vase and smash it down atop his head.

She was the weaker opponent. That knife was her only chance. She prayed the hit would knock Derick out, but if it only stunned him, she'd make every second count. As hard as it would be, she would have to play along so he wouldn't suspect something was up. The thought made her hate herself, but she pushed it aside. Survival would be her sole motivation.

Derick kept peppering the inside of Amarah's leg with kisses as he began to reach her upper thigh. He gripped the hem of her nightgown and pushed it up her body to pool around her navel. He continued further as he reached her core, placing a gentle kiss on the outside of her underwear, and continued up her stomach, over the hint of exposed cleavage, and up her neck until he nestled himself down between her parted legs.

He propped himself up on his elbow and placed a large hand on the side of her face. "I know your first time might seem scary, but don't fret, my touch will be gentle. I can't tell you how much it means to me that you saved yourself. I'll be the only touch you've ever known, the only touch you'll ever need." He raked his heated gaze down her exposed body and back up again before crushing his mouth against hers.

Derick wasn't her first touch nor would he be her last. Liam claimed those, someone she knew who truly deserved them. She kept her thoughts to herself because if Derick ever found out Liam took her virginity, she feared he might kill her in retaliation. The thought of Derick having anything of hers had her stomach churning. If this happened a month ago, she would've considered allowing him to claim her. What a wrong choice that would've been.

Derick nibbled on her bottom lip and his tongue sought entrance. Reluctantly, she parted her lips, and their tongues played the familiar dance they once did before he turned on her. His free hand trailed down over the thin fabric of her nightgown and grabbed a handful of soft tissue as his fingers played with her nipple.

It was hard to believe that at one point in time, she wanted his touch, craved it even. But now, all it did was disgust her. Her body repulsed him, no matter where he touched her. And all she could do to get through this was replace Derick with Liam, imagining it was him doing these things to her.

Amarah forced herself to stay focused. Now was her chance. She had an opening to make her move. If she'd pushed him onto his back and climbed on top too soon, he wouldn't have believed it. It would've put him on alert.

However, waiting too long would risk him being inside of her before she could climb on top, and like hell if that was going to happen. She may be willing to go this far, but Liam would be the only man to ever be inside of her.

Amarah gently placed a hand on Derick's chest as she started to guide him to his back. He was far too lost in lust to think clearly. Good. But the next thing they knew, the room went completely dark. They both froze. Did they blow a fuse? Did a storm knock the power out? Derick let out a frustrated groan.

"Stay here. I'll go check the breaker."

Amarah sat up and fixed her nightgown, so she was fully covered again, straining hard to contain a sigh of relief. As he left the room, he closed the door behind him, and the sound of a soft click followed. *Did he... Did he just lock me in here?*

Once she heard the creaking of the stairs, a sound confirming his retreating presence, she got up and quietly checked the door. Yep, locked. God must be smiling down on her, and she wasn't about to waste this opportunity. She quickly grabbed one of the knives and crossed the room, tucking it beneath her pillow. When Derick returned, she'd be ready.

She padded across the hardwood floors to the French doors, seeing the full moon's light cast a bright glow through the woods below. Not a storm cloud in sight. She peered out across the lake and saw lights from buildings and other homes, so she knew it wasn't a power outage either. Most likely the breaker. She jiggled the handles, praying they would be unlocked but she wasn't that lucky. She didn't know why she expected them to open. A commotion coming from downstairs pulled her out of her thoughts.

Amarah rushed toward the bedroom door and put her ear against it as she tried to hear what was going on. Two muffled male voices came floating up the stairs from the living room. Hope sparked in her chest thinking Liam had come for her, but another thought entered her mind just as fast, and it quickly squashed her newfound hope. What if it wasn't Liam, but someone whom Derick was working with—a silent partner she knew nothing about?

Just then, gunshots rang out through the cabin, causing her to jump back from the door and cover her mouth in terror.

Fuck this! she said to herself.

She didn't care who was down there. She had to get the hell out of there. Now! Amarah turned on her heel and sprinted towards the French doors. She spotted Derick's discarded shirt on the floor and picked it up as she wrapped it around her fist tightly.

Once her hand was fully protected, she punched the pane of glass, sending her fist clean through to the outside. She ran her hand around the edges, clearing any glass from her path. Then she pulled her hand back through and removed the fabric from her fist. A soft clinking sound drew her gaze to the floor, and her eyes widened. A small brass key lay at her feet. Hysterical laughter bubbled up her throat and shook her shoulders as she thanked God for extending his blessing to her. It must've fallen out of the small chest pocket of his flannel. She reached down and picked it up. Before she unlocked the door, she retrieved the knife from beneath her pillow.

Reaching her hand back through the now windowless glass pane, she slid the key carefully into the lock. With a twist of her wrist, a soft click signaled her freedom. She flung the door open and sprinted onto the balcony, careful not to step on the shards of glass that littered the ground.

The balcony was almost fifteen feet deep and ran the entire span of the back of the house, with a waist-high railing made up of small logs. She quickly turned her head from side to side and spotted a large staircase that would take her down to the backyard. She wasted no time, and before she knew it, her bare feet were on the well-manicured grass, running toward Derick's car.

Please, please, please let it be unlocked! She jerked at the handle, but it didn't budge. *Shit!* More gunshots thundered through the cabin. She turned toward the woods and flew across the lawn as fast as her bare feet would take her. She didn't dare stop as she entered the cover of the dense forest.

CHAPTER 41

Liam rounded a curve as Lake Ouachita came into view. He knew he was close. He would've preferred to take the company jet, but it would've taken at least half an hour to fuel and ready it for takeoff. The flight would be minimal but he would've been left with finding a nearby landing strip and a rental car, and that was an entire headache he wanted to avoid. It was easier for him to take his own truck and break numerous traffic laws by speeding like a madman down the interstate.

He pulled his truck over onto the shoulder of the road as he reached into the pocket behind the passenger seat and pulled out an atlas. He flipped through the pages and stopped when he reached the one that contained Lake Ouachita and all the roads that surrounded it. Placing one of his fingers in the general vicinity of the cabin, he looked for the best route that would take him there.

He selected his best option and pulled back onto the paved road, turning off onto a small gravel drive barely wide enough for two vehicles to pass on. Liam quickly shut his headlights off as he slowly crept down the road before stopping a short distance from the cabin, careful not to make his presence known.

He grabbed his binoculars and continued the rest of the journey on foot. As the cabin came further into view, he took cover behind a large tree, crouched down, and brought the binoculars up to his eyes. The spot gave him a clear view of the property, and he spotted an older model Toyota Corolla parked in the driveway.

He removed his cell phone from the pocket of his vest, pulled up Detective Trenton's contact, and pressed dial.

"Mr. Godrik," Detective Trenton answered after the second ring.

"I remembered Amarah telling me that Derick's family owns a cabin at Lake Ouachita in Arkansas. I can't confirm the license plate, but the same model of car he was seen driving in the security footage is parked outside. I think it's safe to confirm they're here." Liam kept his voice low and calm.

"Hold on, Arkansas? Why are you telling me this now? You had, what, a four-hour drive in which you sat on this information instead of notifying me right away?" The frustration was heavy in his voice.

"I wanted to confirm my hunch before I sent you hours away out of town." Liam kept his voice neutral.

"Uh huh, sure." Detective Trenton let out a sigh. "Ok, I'll notify local authorities and take a chopper to your location. Can you drop me a pin?"

"Yeah, hold on," Liam said as he pulled the phone away from his ear, pulled up his GPS, dropped a pin, and sent it to the detective in a text message. "Sent it."

"Got it, thanks." The detective hesitated before continuing, "Liam… be careful."

Liam knew that Detective Trenton had to watch what he said. Phone records might be pulled as evidence, especially if the detective was asked how he knew about the location of the cabin. But Liam caught the hidden meaning in his warning. Be careful how he went about getting her back.

"Always am." He hung up.

He had roughly ten to fifteen minutes to handle this before the cops arrived. He secured his phone and binoculars in the pockets of his vest as he continued his way to the house under the cover provided by the dense woods. He reached the tree line and peered across the lawn, not a soul in sight.

Liam kept his body low as he sprinted across the large yard, stopping at the glass back door. He gave the knob a gentle turn and found it locked. He dug into one of his vest pockets, pulled out a small lockpicking kit, and got to work.

A few seconds later, a soft click sounded as he opened the door, slipped through, and closed it behind him, making sure to lock it again. His eyes made quick observations of his surroundings as he took in the spacious living room that contained a couch, a coffee table, and two chairs opposite the couch. The seating area was centered in front of an open, double-sided fireplace, the backside of which pointed toward the foyer and front door.

An open staircase descended into the corner of the living room. To his right was open to the dining room and kitchen. He kept his steps light, not making a single sound as he crossed the space and stopped at the front door to unlock it completely. He turned and retraced his steps as he stealthily crept around a large wooden dining table. His gaze spotted a door in the back of the kitchen that should lead him to where he needed, the utility room.

Liam popped open the breaker box and flipped the main switch, killing the power to the cabin. Quickly, he closed the box and made his way out of the kitchen and into the dining room in time to duck behind the table as Derick came down the stairs.

It took every ounce of willpower for Liam not to confront Derick and snuff out his life as he watched the man pad across the space. *All in good time*, Liam told himself while taking a slow, deep breath.

Derick made his way through the kitchen and into the utility room, muttering curses under his breath the whole time. He reached the breaker box and used his phone's flashlight to inspect the inside.

"What the hell?" Derick's confused voice drifted through the all too quiet main floor.

He flipped the switch back on, and light flooded the cabin again. Derick began to make his way back to Amarah, only to be stopped dead in his tracks when he found a rather large man standing in the middle of his living room. Derick's body went rigid as he glared at his unwelcome guest.

"Where is she?" Liam asked in a flat tone.

"Upstairs in my bed waiting for me. You… interrupted us," Derick said as a sly grin spread across his face.

Liam peered down Derick's front, taking in his appearance now that the power was back on. He was shirtless, barefoot, and sporting a bulge in his jeans. Clearly, he did interrupt something. Anger welled up inside of Liam like a dam about to burst.

Not at Amarah, as he knew she wasn't a willing participant. Instead, he was angry at Derick for all the violations the man had done and continued to do to her, all the fear and pain he'd put her through over the past few weeks. Enough was enough. It was time to end it.

"That's unlikely. She'd never willingly let you touch her. You repulse her."

"She didn't seem too repulsed when I kissed all over her sexy body and laid between those legs she spread so eagerly for me."

"You can bait me all you want. But I don't play games with little boys. I know you love her, but it's one-sided." Liam forced his mind to lock up his emotions so he could remain calm and rational.

"For you to come all this way, it seems I'm not the only one who loves her," Derick said, holding Liam's gaze.

"You're correct," Liam stated simply. A silver piece of metal caught his attention, and his vision narrowed on a ring Derick wore on his right ring finger. He perched a black brow high on his forehead in amusement. "For a Ranger, you're pretty observant."

Surprise flashed across Derick's face. Not many people recognized his Army Ranger's ring, and the ones that did were fellow service members.

"What branch were you in?" The surprise faded as Derick's face went serious, and his jaw ticked in annoyance.

Liam knew Derick was observing him more closely now. The gear he wore, the way he held himself, and the look on his face. It was a look that all service members who've seen action had.

"Navy SEAL," Liam informed him.

"Fucking Frogman," Derick muttered as he shook his head from side to side. Liam heard it, and a grin tugged at the corner of his full lips. "You have horrible timing. I find it funny that you've known her for so long, yet you wait until now to try and claim her. You couldn't stand to see her happy with me, could you? So, you took it upon yourself to worm your way between us."

"That's where you're wrong. I've loved her for years," Liam confessed.

"You could never give her the love she deserves. Not like I can," Derick spat.

"Your idea of love sounds more like an obsession. That's the difference between you and me. You can't stand to be away from her. You think that loving her means you have to keep her so close that you suffocate her with your presence. Controlling every aspect of her life because you think you know what's best for her. But it's not. If you truly love something, you set it free and know that if it loved you in return, it would never leave. You must have the confidence to let her be her own person, make her own decisions, let her live her own life, and have the faith that even with all that freedom, she still chooses you." Liam paused, letting Derick fully hear his words. "You're afraid to let her go because you know she wouldn't come back."

"And what makes you think she loves you?" Derick seethed through gritted teeth.

"Because no matter how much distance I put between us, she kept choosing me, each time more powerful than the last, until we couldn't stand to be apart any longer."

"That's a bunch of bullshit! You've used your friendship to manipulate her mind and heart. She's *mine!*"

Derick grabbed a table lamp next to him and threw it at Liam. Liam threw his arms up and blocked it, sending it shattering against the hardwood floor. He straightened back up and found himself staring down the barrel of a pistol.

CHAPTER 42

Liam threw himself to the floor behind the couch as Derick opened fire on him. *It seems I'm not the only one with hidden weapons in their home. Well played.* Liam unholstered his pistol as he returned fire, causing Derick to seek shelter behind the double-sided fireplace.

Liam counted each shot that sounded from Derick's gun. He doubted Derick had time to grab an extra magazine when he reached for the Ruger 9mm. Liam recognized the weapon and knew it was a single-stack pistol, which meant that Derick had no more than eight bullets to work with.

"Fuck!" Liam heard Derick curse as the shots ceased.

A grin pulled at one side of Liam's lips. Now was the time to move before Derick could get to another hidden weapon.

Liam stood and was in the middle of raising his gun when Derick leaped over the couch and tackled him, sending the two men crashing against the hardwood floor with a hard thud. Derick controlled the hand Liam gripped the pistol in and slammed it against the floor twice rapidly, causing Liam to drop the gun. It clanged against the floor, and Derick sent it sliding across the room, so neither man could use it.

Liam sent his left fist into Derick's face, knocking the man off balance before he sent his boot into the middle of Derick's bare chest, knocking him backwards into the bullet-ridden couch. Both men scrambled to their feet and began to slowly circle each other.

"I was starting to worry this wouldn't be a fair fight. It's been a while since my skills were truly tested," Liam said, unable to keep the excitement out of his voice. Excitement and anticipation for a good fight.

"This doesn't have to be this way," Derick warned. "Leave now and I won't have to kill you."

"Let me leave with Amarah and you've got a deal," Liam countered with a sly grin.

"Not happening," Derick growled as he sent a bare foot toward Liam's head.

Liam blocked it and sent another fist into Derick's face. Derick faked another kick, and as Liam put his hands up to block it, Derick sent a left hook into Liam's side. He grunted at the impact, but recovered quickly. Liam unsheathed his knife and flipped it around in his closed fist so he could throw punches and slice at the same time. Derick's eyes widened slightly at the sharp blade as it glistened in the light.

Liam swung his right arm out toward Derick's face. Derick blocked it but the knife slashed across his tanned skin. Derick hissed in pain but shook it off. The men traded punches and kicks, some landing while others were blocked. Liam had also landed a few more strikes with his knife.

The few slashes across Derick's arms and chest were now leaking trails of crimson down his naked torso. Liam faked a punch and went in for a double leg takedown, sending Derick's back smacking into the hard ground. Liam got between Derick's legs and sent a left fist into Derick's face, then another.

"Didn't the Army teach you to never fight with your emotions?" Liam taunted.

"Fuck you!" Derick spat as he caught the third punch and grabbed the wooden leg of a nearby side table.

He hurtled the piece of furniture toward Liam, sending shattered wood falling around them. Derick kicked Liam off him and reached his hand under the couch. He pulled out another hidden pistol and took aim at Liam. He kicked the gun from Derick's hand, sending it flying across the room. Derick swung his leg and kicked out Liam's foot from beneath him, sending him crashing to the floor.

Derick scrambled to his feet and took off running, taking the stairs two at a time. As he reached the top step, he quickly unlocked the room Amarah was in, relocked the knob, and shut the door behind himself. His gaze bounced frantically around the room and stopped when he saw the French door open to the balcony.

"Damnit!" he cursed in frustration.

He rushed over to a nightstand, threw open the drawer, and placed his thumb on the fingerprint scanner. The lid clicked open, and he pulled out the pistol residing within as he took off out the glass door.

"Ah, fuck!" he cursed as he stumbled onto the balcony and raised his hurt foot.

Blood dripped from it as he dug out a few sharp pieces of glass. Derick hesitantly set his foot down, testing to see if there was any glass he missed. After he was sure he got it all, he took off down the stairs. The sound of twigs snapping in the woods nearby sent him running toward them. Derick spotted small bare footprints in the forest floor. He picked up his pace and followed them, knowing the only person who could've left them was Amarah.

Liam got up, sheathed his knife, and retrieved his gun as he followed up the stairs. Not knowing which room Derick and Amarah were in, he slowly made his way around the top floor, gun aimed and ready to fire if he saw Derick.

Liam had cleared most of the rooms upstairs as he came upon the last shut door. Jiggling the knob, he found it locked. Without hesitating, he sent his foot hurtling forward with all his strength. The door flew open, banged into the wall, and bounced back.

Liam slowly entered, clearing all the corners as he went, not knowing where Derick could be hiding. After clearing the bathroom and the closet, he made his way to the open French doors. He took in the broken glass and noticed blood on the floor of the balcony.

He quickly followed the drops that led him down a flight of stairs. Liam paused at the base of them and glanced around. He stood completely still and focused intently on his hearing, trying to pick up anything that would signal which way they went. A snap of a branch had his head whipping up in the direction of the woods and off he ran.

Amarah ran as fast as her bare feet could take her. She weaved in and out of the dense trees, vaulted over fallen logs, and took care not to step on anything that would damage her feet. Even though her lungs were screaming at her to stop, she pushed through the pain. She had to get as far away from Derick as she could. She came to a stop only when she felt like her heart would explode if she kept going.

She gasped for air and rested against a tree as she clutched her hand to her chest. She closed her eyes and willed her breathing under control. After a few minutes, she was feeling better, and her breathing was starting to normalize again. She was about to continue when she heard a familiar voice call out from somewhere close by.

"Love, that savior of yours is really starting to piss me off."

Fear washed through her, and the hairs on the back of her neck stood up at hearing Derick's voice. How had he found her? How had he caught up so quickly? Then what he said fully sank in. At first, she was confused, not sure who he was referring to. Then hope blossomed in her chest as she figured it out.

"Liam!" Amarah shouted.

She knew Derick was hot on her heels in those woods, but she also knew Liam was close behind Derick. Shouting would lead Derick right to her, but it would also lead Liam to her as well. A risk she was willing to take. She crouched behind the tree she was resting against and willed her breathing to be as silent as possible.

Branches snapping around her signaled that she was no longer alone. Her knuckles were white around the knife she clutched, the only weapon she had. All too soon, the footsteps drew closer.

"Come on out, love. Haven't you realized by now that you can't hide from me?"

The menacing voice sounded as if it were right behind her. Amarah closed her eyes and took a deep breath as she mustered up the courage to stand and stepped out from behind the tree, tucking her knife behind her back. She froze when she observed the gun Derick had raised in her direction.

CHAPTER 43

Amarah took in Derick's busted lip, the slashes across his arms and chest, and the slight bruising starting to color his tan cheek. Panic spiked deep within. If Derick looked like this, what did Liam look like?

Only after a few seconds did he finally lower his weapon and stalk towards her. He stopped and brought her into a tight hug. After a moment, he stepped back and backhanded her across the face.

"That was for leaving me… again!" he seethed, his words laced with hurt.

"I heard gunshots! What the hell did you expect me to do? Wait around to get shot?" she spat back, holding a hand to her stinging cheek.

Derick grabbed a handful of her sunny strands as he yanked her head back, so she was forced to look him in the eyes. "You will never raise your voice to me again. Understood?" he growled in a low and dangerous tone that sent every hair on her body standing up.

"Fuck you," Amarah whispered with all the hatred in the world.

"What did you just say to me?" He had a crazed look in his eyes.

"I said, fuck you. No matter what, I will never submit how you want me to. I will never love you. I will never be yours!" she finished, each sentence coming out stronger than the last. She had reached her breaking point.

"You. Don't. Have. A. Fucking. Choice!" Derick seethed as he brought his face mere inches from hers.

Without saying another word, still with a fistful of her hair, he started tugging her violently in the direction of the boat dock. A way that would get them across the lake and far enough away from Liam.

They only made it a few feet before a voice boomed from behind them. "Let her go!"

They spun around to find Liam standing a few feet away with his gun aimed right at Derick's head. Without missing a beat, Derick threw Amarah in front of him, held her in place with an arm across her chest and his hand gripping her neck tightly, his own gun trained on Liam.

Despite the strong hand cutting off her air supply, relief washed through her at the sight of Liam before her. Her eyes raked over his face, taking in the damage he sustained from his fight with Derick. He had slight bruising starting to form on his face, and his left brow was split open with dried blood caked around it. Her eyes locked on his and there was a silent promise that swirled heavily in his bright greens. A promise that told her everything would be ok.

"You can't shoot me without hitting her. Toss over your gun," Derick said from behind her.

"Hiding behind a woman, that's rich. And here I thought you couldn't become any less of a man. Yet again, you proved just how much of a pathetic waste of space you are," Liam said flatly.

"Toss over your gun, or I'll shoot her!" Derick threatened as he turned his gun towards her head instead.

Amarah's body locked up. She'd never had a gun pointed at her before. Was this it? Was this how she died? She only prayed that Liam would be quick enough to end Derick's life, too. She would die happy if she knew that the psycho was no longer walking this earth.

"You won't do it. You love her too much, in your own psychotic way. You won't kill her." Liam spoke calmly.

"You may be right. But I'd rather her be dead than let you have her," Derick spat at him.

Amarah mouthed Liam's name, the movement catching Liam's eye. His vision shot to hers, and time ceased to exist. Slowly, a shaky smile tugged one side of her lips up, and she winked at him. She watched as he shifted his gaze down to her hand and caught sight of the knife she gripped tightly. His vision glowed with pride.

Liam looked back toward Derick, who was oblivious to the silent moment they just shared. "I've already had her. Multiple times, in fact. Might I just say, she's fucking delicious!" He slowly lowered his gun, creating the distraction Amarah needed.

"What?" Derick choked out, cocking his head to the side, devastation and disbelief filling his eyes.

With all the strength she could muster, Amarah jammed the knife deep into the front of Derick's quad, slicing through fabric, skin, and muscles like butter, only stopping when the blade hit bone.

"Ah! You fucking bitch!" Derick roared in pain, releasing her as he staggered back.

She threw herself to the hard dirt-covered ground and took cover right as Liam raised his gun back up without hesitation and emptied three rounds right into Derick's chest, his grouping no larger than the size of a quarter. Derick staggered back a few more steps, too stunned and full of adrenaline to fully process the pain and reality of the bullets now residing deep within the cavity of his chest.

Numbly, Derick brought up his left hand and touched the holes in the center of his chest. Pulling his hand back, he looked at the fresh blood dripping from his fingers. Slowly, he brought his gaze up, watching Liam's emotionless face. He tore his eyes away and turned his head to the side, looking into the horror-filled eyes of Amarah, who was staring up at him.

Derick pulled his brows together in confusion as hurt crossed his face. "But... I love you?" he choked out as his mouth started to drip blood.

Finally, Derick collapsed to the ground, his back hitting the forest floor with a loud thud, his now lifeless eyes staring blankly at the night sky.

The ground was cold beneath Amarah as she pushed herself up by her hand and took in Derick's fate through watery eyes. It was over...

It was finally over. A magnitude of emotions rocked through her as she couldn't tear her eyes from her stalker's corpse.

A part of her was relieved, glad that it was finally done, that Derick had been stopped, and she wouldn't be forced to look over her shoulder anymore, waiting for a boogeyman to get her. Another part of her was thankful that both she and Liam would be walking out of this alive. Yes, they both gained some external and internal wounds today, but they were alive.

However, she felt ashamed as well. Ashamed of those previous feelings, but she also found herself sad. Sad that this had to end with Derick losing his life. Could he have been saved from the demons of his mind? Or had the Devil taken such a strong hold over him that there was never any chance for salvation or redemption?

Liam holstered his weapon and exhaled softly. Taking a life was never easy, no matter how many times you've done it. Yes, with each time, you learn to numb yourself to the effects, but a piece of your soul is damaged with each life you snuff out, whether you feel it or not. He didn't regret what he did, not one bit.

Derick had hurt the woman he loved in more ways than one, and he would be lying if he said seeing Derick's lifeless body made him unhappy. If losing a small piece of his soul was the price he had to pay to keep the love of his life safe, he would gladly pay it a million times over.

He glanced over to Amarah and his heart broke at the sight before him. He didn't have to be a master at reading people to know she was fighting a battle inside that beautiful brain of hers. Fighting between multiple emotions that tried to take over and the guilt of having those feelings. Calmly, he walked over and put himself between Amarah and Derick's body. He crouched and placed a finger beneath her chin, gently lifting her head, and forcing her to shift her gaze from Derick to him.

"He couldn't have been saved, Cupcake. Don't do that to yourself." He kept his tone soft. "If he wasn't stopped, he would've just found another innocent woman to torment. People like that can't change because they don't want to."

Amarah didn't respond, just nodded in understanding. Liam stood up and outstretched a hand. After staring blankly at it for a few heartbeats, she took it, and he helped her to her feet. She threw her arms around his neck and buried her face in his vest as she began to sob.

"It's over, Cupcake. You're safe now." Liam cooed as he pulled her flat against his hard frame and wrapped her securely in a tight hug. A hug that promised her safety. A hug that promised he would never allow harm to befall her again.

CHAPTER 44

The sounds of sirens wailing in the distance pulled Amarah and Liam back to the present. Their sounds gradually grew louder the closer they got. She pulled away and swiped the backs of her hands across her tear-stained cheeks. He released his hold around her as he took her hand in his.

"I'm glad you're here," she said in a weak voice. "I would've gotten lost and probably died in these woods."

"Nah, you're pretty resourceful. I'm sure you would've found your way out in no time." He gave her a kind smile.

"The amount of faith you have in me is scary sometimes." She shook her head and kept her gaze on the forest floor in front of her.

They made their way back through the woods. Amarah was shocked at how long it took them to get back. The distance she ran in the thick of things felt shorter than this. They finally broke through the tree line and crossed the lawn to the cabin.

Faint red and blue lights illuminated the forest in front of them as the cops made their way down the gravel road. Still hand in hand, they took a seat on the staircase that led to the second-story balcony as they waited.

A few moments later, four squad cars pulled up, sending brighter lights dancing off the exterior of the cabin and the surrounding area. An ambulance and a fire truck arrived right behind them.

"Hold your hands up so the cops know we aren't the threat," Liam informed Amarah as multiple officers climbed out of their squad cars with weapons drawn, not knowing what they were walking into. She didn't argue with that logic.

Liam raised his voice to make sure the officers heard him. "We aren't the bad guys. We'll wait here until Detective Trenton arrives in a chopper and can fill y'all in on what exactly is going on."

If Liam was keeping his mouth shut, so was she. Anything you say can and will be used against you in a court of law, right?

A while later, the sound of helicopter rotors filled the air and the wind started picking up as a police chopper landed in the large open field by the cabin. Detective Trenton hopped out as the pilot worked to turn off the chopper.

"Do you mind if I have a word with these two, officers?" Detective Trenton asked as he flashed his badge and greeted the cops guarding Liam and Amarah.

The two Arkansas officers shared a look, then glanced back at the detective. "More power to you. We couldn't get them to talk." They turned and walked back towards the squad cars.

"I was hoping y'all would keep quiet until I got here," the detective said as he squatted in front of them. "First off, Amarah, are you ok? Are you hurt? Have the paramedics looked you over yet?"

"Calm down, sir." She couldn't help but laugh a little. "Yes, they've looked me over already. A few cuts and bruises but nothing major."

"And you?" Detective Trenton said, turning his gaze on Liam.

"All good," Liam said with a curt nod.

"Ok, good," Detective Trenton said, sighing deeply and running a hand through his chocolate hair. "I need to hear it straight—everything that happened, exactly how it happened, so I can try to swing this the best I can and get y'all home as soon as possible without facing any charges. Wait, where's…" He turned his head around as if expecting to find Derick in the back of one of the squad cars or handcuffed, sitting on the lawn somewhere.

"Dead," Liam clipped.

"Shit… Ok, lay it on me."

They took turns telling him what happened. Amarah went first, explaining how Derick threatened her and kidnapped her from the restaurant, waking up in the cabin, and what he did to her before Liam got there. The whole time she was retelling her story, she never once looked at Liam. She couldn't face seeing the pain she knew would be in the greens of his eyes, the pain she caused him with her actions. Then she went on to say how she heard gunshots, how she escaped through the balcony doors and ran off into the woods, and explained what Derick said and did to her when he caught up to her.

Then Liam stepped in and told his side of the story, how he knocked on the front door, how Derick let him in, and they got into an argument that led to Derick throwing a lamp and drawing a gun on him. Detective Trenton cocked his head as if confused by the start of Liam's story.

However, Amarah knew the truth. Liam had told her everything on their walk back to the cabin. How he picked the lock to the back door and relocked it, then made sure to unlock the front door. He made sure there was no sign of forced entry, so when the cops did their investigation, that's how they would say he entered the home. She had to give the man credit. He was smart in his planning.

Liam continued with everything that happened after: the fight, going upstairs, following the blood trail down off the balcony, and hearing Amarah call for him in the woods, which let him know which way to go. And lastly, about what happened when he caught up to them, how Derick held her at gunpoint, and how the man met his untimely demise.

"Can you lead me to where the body is?" the detective asked.

"Yes," Liam answered simply.

Amarah stayed on the steps as Liam led the detective through the woods, right to Derick's body. She knew what they'd find. A steak knife protruding out of Derick's leg and three gunshot wounds to his chest. All of which would line up with their stories.

Upon returning to the cabin, Detective Trenton spoke with them privately again. "I will ride with y'all down to the local police station. Y'all will give formal statements, and I will collaborate with them on everything I have against Derick already. With the prior assault charges and all the evidence we already have, this should be an open-and-shut case. Just don't alter your stories, and don't add anything new you didn't already tell me. Understood?" They both nodded and made their way to one of the waiting squad cars.

CHAPTER 45

After a few hours at an Arkansas police station, Amarah and Liam made the drive back to Oklahoma. She only made it a few minutes into the drive before she fell asleep. The next thing she knew, she was being carried into his house, glad to find herself enveloped in the warmth of the man she loved. She draped her arms around his neck and watched as he carried her right into her bathroom. He stood her gently on her feet before turning on the shower to let the water start heating.

"May I?" he asked, standing in front of her.

He motioned with his hands to her torn and dirty nightgown. She answered by raising her hands above her head so he could take off the ruined fabric. He held the shower door open as she stepped inside. Liam stripped off his own clothes and climbed in behind her.

Silence fell between them as he grabbed the loofah, soaped it up, and began rubbing small, gentle circles all over her body. Dried dirt flaked off her skin and fell to the shower floor, where it turned into mud before it was washed down the drain. She rinsed off as he scrubbed himself up next.

Once done, she turned to exit the shower, only to be stopped by his hands gently on her waist. He cupped her chin and met her gaze. "Why won't you look at me?"

"Because I can't bear to see the pain in your eyes that I've caused you." Fresh tears welled up in Amarah's deep blues, but she fought hard not to let them spill over.

Liam peered at her in a look of utter confusion. "What pain have you caused me?"

"What I did before you got there. Letting… Derick… do that stuff to me." It was hard for her to get out. Even harder for her to say his name.

"You think I blame you for that?" he asked gently.

"How could you not? I stripped and showered in front of him. I let him touch me and kiss me. I kissed him back…"

Her tears fell freely at this point. There were too many to keep them contained. He slid his thumb across her tanned cheek, wiping her tears away.

"Oh, Cupcake…" Liam sighed as he rested his forehead against hers. "He had you restrained. The only way to get out was to prove you would obey him. You had no idea I was coming for you. You had no idea if or when anyone would come to rescue you. So, you took matters into your own hands to make sure you stopped him. You found a way that would keep you alive in the end. I do not blame you for the plan you came up with or the actions you carried out. I know you love me, and you wouldn't have done those things if you had another choice."

He held her as she cried. She cried from the guilt she felt, cried from how understanding he was about this, cried from what happened to her in those woods, cried with relief that it was finally over, and cried because she was frustrated with herself for crying so much. She finally calmed down enough to look him in the eyes.

"Tell me something to make me feel better. Something that will get my mind off things for a while."

Liam grabbed her arms and brought them up around his neck. He placed his hands on her hips and let his thumbs rub small, lazy circles across them as he thought for a moment.

"You know my gate code?"

"Yeah," she answered hesitantly.

"It's not a bunch of random numbers. It's the day we met. The day I first came over to your house after befriending Travis and met you."

Amarah was speechless, her mouth slightly parted.

"That's not all. You know my phone password?" All she could do was nod at this point. "That spells out Cupcake in T9 texting. Do you know why I call you Cupcake all the time, even though you hate it?" Again, all she could do was shake her head. More tears threatened to spill—joyful ones this time. She may act like she hated the nickname, but she secretly loved it. "It's because you're as sweet as one, and it's what you were eating when I first met you. A red velvet cupcake with white frosting and dark red sprinkles."

Amarah remembered that day. They'd just celebrated her father's birthday, and instead of a cake, he wanted cupcakes. Red velvet was his favorite. There were only a handful left, and her mother allowed her to have one after getting home from school because she had gotten straight A's on her report card.

She couldn't utter a single sound, even if she wanted to. Instead, she smashed her lips against his as he pulled her body in close to his and deepened that connection. Liam rested one hand on the small of her back and ran the other through her hair to rest on the back of her neck. His tongue slid across her lips, and she was happy to oblige as she opened her mouth and met him with such intensity it had her toes curling.

Liam turned off the shower without breaking the kiss. He cupped her ass and hoisted her up as she wrapped her legs around him in agreement. There was no time to dry off, not when they needed each other so badly at that moment. They needed to be one, to be connected in the most primal and intimate way possible.

He strode into the bedroom, climbed on the bed, and gently lay her flat on her back, easing himself down between her legs. Both of their hands were now free to explore each other's wet and naked bodies. Finally breaking the kiss, Liam made quick work of giving Amarah's neck some attention, placing kisses and small bites on her sensitive flesh.

He lifted his hips just enough to reach down and positioned his hard cock at her warm entrance, running the swollen head along her slickness. Unable to stand another second outside of her, he thrust in.

"Fuck…" Liam drew the word out, groaning in pleasure.

Amarah's gasp turned into a moan at the sudden fullness she felt, his thickness stretching and filling her in the most delicious way possible. Instantly, her hands were on his ass as she urged him to start moving. She didn't need time to adjust. She needed him working inside of her that very moment. He didn't argue as his hips rocked back and forth, pulling out to the tip and burying himself completely each time.

There was no hurry in his movements, nothing rough or animalistic about it. They went slow, making each motion precise and deep, letting the love flow between them. Her hips moved with his as she tried to pull him further into her. He grabbed her ass in both hands and rolled onto his back, to where she was now on top, all without ever pulling out.

Amarah instantly started to grind herself against his cock. The new angle allowed him to go deeper inside of her. Her movements were slow and precise, just like his. His large hands ran up her wet body and cupped her full breasts as he massaged the soft tissue.

"So fucking beautiful," Liam spoke as his intense gaze raked over her soft curves.

Amarah laid her chest against his as she brought her lips to his. One of his hands snaked into her wet hair as the other cupped her ass. She began to raise just her hips until only the tip of his cock was left inside of her. Then she slowly sank back down until their hips connected again. Those slow deliberate moves had her feeling the tightening in the base of her spine that she knew would bring her immense pleasure.

She picked up her pace, bouncing on his cock faster, impaling herself over and over again as he grabbed handfuls of her ass to help guide her.

"I'm so close," Amarah moaned as she closed her eyes and rested her forehead against his.

"Don't stop, Cupcake. You're going to make me spill inside of you," he growled, lust heavy in his voice.

That sentence struck a chord within her, knowing she was doing that to him, making him feel so good. Knowing her movements were bringing him to his climax made hers arrive with his.

As her orgasm erupted through her, he elevated her hips up so he could thrust into her, extending her finish as well as bringing his own to the surface as he pumped every bit of his seed deep within her.

Amarah collapsed onto Liam's chest as she tried to catch her breath. She slowly lifted herself off him, instantly missing the feeling of him inside of her as he pulled her down to lie next to him, her head resting on his inky chest as he wrapped his arms around her.

"Look at me," he said softly. She craned her neck up and peered into those bright eyes of his. "I love you," he stated, emotion thick in his voice.

A large smile broke out across her angular features, brightening her sapphire eyes. She'd waited a decade to hear those words. She'd lost count of how many fantasies she'd imagined where he finally confessed his love to her, and this, with his finish buried inside of her, took the cake. To hear those three little words spoken from his lips made her the happiest woman alive. If she died right then, she'd die with a smile on her face. She didn't have to think if she should say it back. She'd said those words to him in her mind for years, and she couldn't wait to voice them into reality.

"I love you too." She crushed her mouth against his and started kissing him hungrily. He matched her energy as he rolled her onto her back.

A few hours and a few more rounds later, Liam and Amarah collapsed, completely exhausted, onto their bed. "Let's get cleaned up. Travis and Sandra will be here shortly." He smiled as he kissed her forehead.

After washing each other, they got dressed and finally left their bedroom just as the doorbell echoed through the home. Liam peered through the peephole before unlocking it.

"Come on in—" he started to say but was shoved out of the way by Sandra as she rushed into the home.

"Where is she? Is she alright? Amarah!" Sandra shouted as she searched frantically around the living room.

"Calm down sis, I'm right here," Amarah responded as she rounded the corner, gliding into the room.

"Oh, thank God!" Sandra cried as she ran and threw her arms around a laughing Amarah. They held onto each other tightly.

Travis and Liam came into the room a second later, shaking their heads at the crazy redhead. Sandra pulled back from the hug and wiped tears from her freckled cheeks as Amarah locked eyes with her brother. Relief swirled through Travis's eyes as his shoulders relaxed. He wrapped her up tightly and placed a soft kiss on the top of her head.

"I'm so glad you're ok," Travis whispered, his voice cracking with emotion.

"Alright, I don't know about y'all, but I could use a drink." Sandra blew out a breath as she made her way into the kitchen.

The rest followed behind as they all gathered around the large island. Sandra opened the fridge and pulled out four bottles of beer. She popped the tops of each one and handed them out before taking a rather large gulp, then walked around to stand next to her husband.

Liam leaned his waist against the counter and pulled Amarah's back flush against his chest as he wrapped his free hand around her waist. Amarah leaned into him, loving the warmth his body radiated as she took a drink from her beer. She paused and took in the scene playing out in front of her, not realizing how much she missed this normalcy.

A few hours later, things were wrapping up. Sandra, Travis, Amarah, and Liam bullshitted about random stuff, caught up on how the kiddos were doing, ate some greasy takeout, and just enjoyed one another's company. It was the best form of therapy Amarah could ask for. Detective Trenton had called to inform them that the detectives in Arkansas had ruled the incident as self-defense.

The rest of the weight Amarah was carrying lifted off her shoulders. She could finally put Derick behind her, start her healing process, and move on with her life.

They all stood at the front door as Liam and Amarah bid their goodbyes to Travis and Sandra. She couldn't help but laugh at her brother practically having to throw his wife over his shoulder to get her to their vehicle because she didn't want to let Amarah out of her sight, afraid she might disappear again. Liam shut and locked the front door before turning to her and scooping her up in his arms.

Amarah squealed in surprise at the gesture as she snaked her arms around his neck. "Where are we going?"

"To bed."

"But I'm not tired." She stuck her bottom lip out in a pout.

"Who said anything about sleeping?" A wicked grin slid across that beautiful face of his.

Butterflies took flight in her stomach and her core heated as she smashed her lips against his in a hot and passionate kiss.

THE END... FOR NOW

DON'T MISS OUT!

Here's a sneak peek at book 2 in the Desire Series –

Desire's Blessing

CHAPTER 1

FRIDAY – 13 DAYS TILL DEPARTURE

The brutal August heat had let up a little, allowing a nice breeze to cool the Oklahoma night air. With her radio set to a classic rock station at almost maximum volume, Serenity rolled down the front windows of her newer cherry-red Honda Civic and sang along.

Completely lost in the second verse of "Summer of '69" by Bryan Adams, the loud, high-pitched sounds of emergency vehicles eluded Serenity. Her only indication that something was wrong was the faint glow of red and blue lights that illuminated her darkened neighborhood. She pinched her black brows together in confusion as she muted the radio, the sounds of sirens replacing her music, growing louder the closer she got.

She prayed no one was severely injured as she reluctantly turned down her street. The sight before her had her heart stopping, her stomach churning, and her face draining of its usual tan color. A few cop cars, an ambulance, and two fire trucks were parked in front of her house, which was completely engulfed in bright yellow and orange flames.

4 HOURS EARLIER

"Do you have a date for the wedding yet?" Addison asked around a mouthful of a tortilla chip that she had dunked completely in her small bowl of white queso.

"Not yet." Serenity sighed heavily as she took a rather large gulp from her frozen strawberry margarita, pinched her brows together, and squeezed her bottle-green eyes shut to try and fight off her oncoming brain freeze.

Every Friday night after work for the last four years, the two best friends had met up at a restaurant for dinner and drinks. This week's choice was Mexican.

Serenity *had* a date for Addi's wedding. She and Noah, her boyfriend of two years, had everything planned out. Plane tickets were bought, and a luxurious room at the resort had been booked for the entire weekend, but that was before she found him in bed with another woman. She valued trust more than anything in a relationship, so the moment Noah broke that trust, there was no going back. She dumped him right then and there.

It had been over three months since that dreadful evening, and she still heard from him. Too often for her liking. Sometimes he would call and leave a voicemail saying how sorry he was. Other times, he would text her how much he loved her, that it would never happen again, and ask her to take him back. Because she never responded, she'd found him waiting for her on her front porch one evening after work. That led her to threaten him with a potential restraining order just to keep him away, but that didn't stop the periodic calls or texts.

"Renny, we leave for Hawaii in thirteen days. If you don't find a replacement date by then, you'll end up having to spend the weekend with my cousin trying to hit on you the whole time," Addi teased with a half-laugh, her dark brown eyes full of amusement.

Addi was getting married to the man of her dreams, who just so happened to be a highly renowned criminal defense attorney and was rather wealthy. Jack wanted her to have the wedding of her dreams, which is why they were getting married on a white-sanded beach in Hawaii at a beautiful five-star resort.

"It might be easier for you to find a new maid of honor before I find a new date," Serenity joked as she dunked a tortilla chip in her queso and popped it into her mouth, the chip crunching loudly under her straight pearl teeth.

"I would cancel my wedding before I found a new maid of honor." Addi spoke in all seriousness, pointing a manicured finger at her friend.

"Well, we can't have that now, can we? So, any ideas? I'm open to suggestions."

Their waitress brought out their steaming fajita platter and the savory smell of fresh tortillas, peppers, rice, and beans filled the air around them.

"Have you tried online dating? A girl at my gym met her boyfriend on one. It's called Desire, I believe." Addi wrapped up her chicken fajita and took a large bite, moaning slightly at the delicious taste.

"There is no way I would be able to find someone in such a short time. Well, someone that doesn't want to murder me and wear my skin, that is."

Though she was joking, she could not stop the chill that rolled down her spine at the image she'd accidentally created in her mind. She'd heard some horror stories of online dating. Not all were happy tales.

"How about you try a type of 'speed dating?'" Addi put up air quotes with her fingers.

Two creases formed between Serenity's brows as she spoke around a mouthful of food. "I'm listening."

"Ok," Addi said, setting her half-eaten fajita back on her plate and wiping her mouth with her napkin. "You scroll through profiles, pick out like seven or eight potential guys. Each day, go on a date with a new one. Get to know them, talk to them, and see if they give off any creepy vibes or not. The ones who pass the test go on a list. The ones who fail… Well, just forget about them." She waved her hand dismissively. "After you've dated them all, go back over the list and make a final selection. Hell, you could even go on a second date with them if you want to be *extra* sure. Then ask them to go with you to my wedding."

Serenity perched a brow high on her forehead. "Even if this goes well, which is highly doubtful, you expect me to take a random stranger on a weekend getaway?"

"No one said you have to sleep with them, Renny. Unless you want to." Addi's thick brown brows wiggled with mischief. "Make that a stipulation up front so they understand your rules and boundaries. Tell them it would just be a fun weekend away on a tropical island, all expenses paid. People put out ads like this on Craigslist for companions for occasions such as these."

"You really are trying to get me murdered, aren't you?" Serenity shook her head, laughing. The action sent her long raven hair dancing across her back.

Addi reached across the table and placed her hand gently over Serenity's. "Come on, sweetie, it's been months. You deserve to have a little fun."

The image of Noah's betrayal flashed through her mind, causing a jolt of pain to ache deep within her chest cavity. She had tried hard to scrub her brain clean of that horrific scene, but it's as if it had been seared to the organ with a branding iron.

Not wanting to ruin her girl's night out, she shook her head clear, took a deep breath, and willed all things Noah-related from her mind. She was hesitant to indulge Addi's bizarre idea, but if she were being honest with herself, she didn't want to attend this wedding alone.

Serenity pointed her fork at her friend. "Ok, ok, fine. But if I get a creeper and end up dead, I'll come back and haunt you for the rest of your miserable life."

"Deal!" Addi threw her head back with laughter, sending her brown and blonde hair spilling over her shoulders.

After finishing their dinner, Serenity and Addi moved to the L-shaped bar in the restaurant so their table was free to seat more hungry customers. A few hours and a few more drinks later, they called it a night, hugging each other and parting ways to head home.

Serenity pulled over and parked next to the curb across the street, got out, and rushed over to a cop who was standing by his squad car.

"Oh my God! What happened?" she asked frantically.

The cop quickly stepped in front of her with a hand held out, blocking her path to the danger ahead. "Ma'am, it's not safe over here. We need everyone to stay back until the fire is out."

"That's my house," she said in a half-daze.

Her voice was barely loud enough to hear over the roaring of the fire. She peeked around the officer, her eyes following the chaotic dance of the enormous flames.

"Does anyone else live in the home that could still be inside?" the cop inquired.

Without removing her eyes from the blazing inferno, she answered. "No... No, I live alone."

Shock and disbelief were starting to take hold of her as she watched thousands of gallons of water being sprayed into what used to be her house. The cop took down her information for the police report and directed her to wait by her car across the street until the fire was completely extinguished.

This can't be happening...

Serenity numbly walked over and leaned against the hood. It was gone. It was all gone. Everything she owned was in that house. She had renters' insurance, thank goodness, and they would cover everything she lost, but that was beside the point. Unfortunately, not everything could be replaced: keepsakes, photo albums from her childhood, and other sentimental objects that were irreplaceable and priceless to her.

She pulled out her cell phone from the back pocket of her blue jeans. Her thumb moved hurriedly over the screen as she dialed her friend.

"Addi..." She trailed off, her voice cracking with emotion.

Addi's tone turned serious. "Renny, what's wrong?"

"My house… It's gone… A fire," she choked out between the soft sobs she was fighting desperately to keep in.

"Oh, fuck… I'm on my way, sweetie. I'll be there in five minutes!" Addi spoke quickly before hanging up.

Serenity tucked her phone back into her jeans and turned her attention toward the collapsing structure that used to be her home. Thankfully, the flames were getting smaller with each passing second.

The sound of an approaching car pulled her from her thoughts as she turned to see Jack's shiny new black Corvette with a single blue racing stripe across the top pull to the curb behind her car. Addi barely waited for him to stop before she threw open her passenger side door, ran over, and threw her arms around her friend.

"Oh, Renny," she said, her voice filled with sympathy. "How are you holding up?"

Addi pulled away and turned to the house that was badly charred and half-standing. Her eyes widened with horror at the sight before her.

"I'm ok," Serenity said with a soft smile as she quickly wiped her cheeks to hide any evidence of the tears that betrayed her by falling.

Serenity turned her head and watched Jack approach. He wore a grey polo shirt that was tucked into a pair of black slacks and a pair of black Italian leather shoes. He brought up a muscular arm wrapped in a gold Rolex and ran his fingers through his wavy brown hair.

He walked straight up to Serenity, wrapped his strong arms around her in a tight hug, and pulled her against his lean frame.

"I'm so sorry, Renny. Are you ok?" He pulled back enough so his deep emeralds could gaze into her mossy greens.

Serenity tried to give him a believable smile. "Yeah, as ok as I can be right now."

Jack broke the hug and leaned against her car as they waited. Another ten minutes passed before the fire was finally lifeless. The ambulance and fire trucks made their way back to their stations while the cop approached Serenity again.

The officer asked, "Do you have a place you can stay at tonight?"

Serenity opened her mouth but then closed it again, unsure of how to respond. The only family she had nearby were her parents who lived an hour away and were out of the state on vacation. So, their place was out of the question. A hotel, maybe?

Addi spoke up, deciding for her. "She'll be staying with us."

The officer spoke with the utmost sincerity as he handed her a copy of the police report for her records. "I'll have a team out here first thing tomorrow to investigate the cause of the fire. I'll give you a call once the investigation is complete. I suggest calling your insurance company right away to start your claim. I'm glad no one was hurt."

Serenity thanked him and watched as the cop got back into his squad car and drove off.

Jack turned toward the girls. "Well, it's late and Renny has been through a lot. Let's go home and get some rest."

Everyone got into their vehicles, Serenity following in her car back to Jack and Addi's place.

CHAPTER 2

Serenity pulled into the gated community where Jack and Addi lived. She couldn't help but practically drool at the massive newer homes. Jack had already owned the property when he started dating Addi a few years back and she had been living with him for almost seven months now.

Each of the homes in the neighborhood was a different combination of rock, brick, or both, and each sat on an acre of professionally manicured lawns. A variety of expensive cars, boats, and RVs that probably cost more than she made in a year filled the driveways.

She followed behind Jack's Corvette as he pulled into a long, paved driveway that led to a massive single-story house covered in rock. Large windows framed with black shutters lined the front and it was topped with a black metal roof.

After parking, Serenity followed the couple into the house. She couldn't help but sigh in relief at being in a calm, familiar place. The entire drive over, she was on the phone with her insurance company through her car's Bluetooth, letting them know what happened. She gave them the information from the police report, and they said that once the investigation was completed and they received the paperwork with an itemized list of every possession that burnt in the fire, a check covering the expenses would be mailed to her. She was mentally exhausted at this point.

"Come on, I'll get you some clothes and get the guest room ready for you," Addi said as she walked down the hall toward her and Jack's bedroom.

The home was completely open-concept, updated, and clean. Everything had a place, and everything was in its place. Various photos of the happy couple hung sporadically along the tan walls. Addi walked over to her wooden dresser and withdrew a pair of shorts and a tank top. She turned and handed them to Serenity before she escorted Serenity down the hall to a guest bedroom and bathroom.

"You sure you're ok?" Addi asked as she turned down the ocean blue covers on the bed and turned the ceiling fan on to help circulate the air.

"Really, I'm good. Everything can be replaced. On a happy note, now I have a legit reason to go clothes shopping without getting buyer's remorse." Serenity laughed, though it sounded a bit hollow.

She did love shopping and couldn't wait to rebuild her wardrobe. Good thing she had a plush savings account. She would have to use that until she got the check from the insurance company.

"Ok, well, we're right down the hall if you need anything." Addi smiled, kissed her lightly on the cheek, and left, shutting the bedroom door behind her.

Serenity walked into the attached bathroom and immediately turned on the shower. While the water warmed up, she got undressed and stepped in, closing the glass door behind her. A soft moan escaped her lips when the hot water fell against her tensed muscles. She closed her eyes and lost herself in the warmth for a while, just letting the water roll down her body, feeling the tension leave her muscles with each passing minute.

After getting washed up, she climbed out, toweled off, and got dressed. Thankfully, her best friend kept this bathroom fully stocked with everything anyone could ever need. She ran a brush through her wet raven strands before braiding it back, turned off the bathroom light, and closed the door behind her. Exhaustion was weighing on her as she yawned and crawled into the queen-sized bed. After snuggling into the fluffy covers, it took no time for sleep to take her.

Addi walked into her bathroom where she undressed and started up the shower. After climbing in, Jack entered and started to shed his own clothes. She couldn't help but watch the man reveal every inch of his six-foot body packed with lean muscles to her. Even though she had seen it a thousand times, each time was like the first all over again.

Jack climbed into the shower behind her, wrapped his arms around her middle, and pulled her back into his front while the hot water fell over them both.

"I can't believe that happened." She spoke as she leaned her head against his strong chest.

"I know, but Renny is a strong woman. She'll bounce back quickly," he reassured her, placing a soft kiss against the top of her wet hair.

"She will. That I have no doubt. Just what are the odds, you know? I wonder what caused it." She closed her eyes, loving the feel of his body against hers. Need quickly flooded her core.

"It could've been a number of things honestly. I'm just glad it happened when she wasn't home." Jack pulled her flatter against himself, sensing the shift in her breathing.

"I wish there was something we could do for her."

He began to place kisses down the column of his fiancée's neck. "Well, she could always stay at my parent's old house until she finds a new place. That way she can take her time with a proper house search."

Addi opened her eyes and craned her head up to meet his gaze. "You mean that? You would do that for her?" Hope and admiration began to fill her voice.

"Of course. She's your best friend," he said, not letting up on the kisses he placed against her creamy skin. "Besides, that house has been empty since they died. It's about time someone used it."

She spun around and wrapped her arms around his neck, her full and heavy breasts pressing into his hard chest. She could feel his fully hardened erection pressing into her stomach and the thought of it had her squeezing her thighs together to relieve the ache between her legs.

"I love you." Her bright smile fully touched her chocolate eyes.

"I had a feeling," he said with a wicked grin as he crushed his lips against hers, their mouths instantly parting, their tongues dancing together in a familiar rhythm.

Jack ran his hands down her back and over her full ass as he gripped the back of her thick thighs and hoisted her up, turned, and pinned her against the tiled wall. She paid the cool mosaic no mind. Her attention was solely on the man about to enter her.

She reached down between them and gripped his thick cock in her hand. Her fingers and thumb lightly touched around his girth as she stroked the entirety of his long shaft slowly a few times, causing pre-cum to bead on the swollen tip before aligning it at her wet entrance. He groaned and with a single thrust, buried himself inside of her, causing her to moan loudly and himself to grunt in approval.

With his head buried in the crook of her neck, he quickly began to thrust into her in a hard, rough manner that they both craved at that moment. Addi brought her hand down, grabbed a handful of soft tissue, and began to massage it and rub her thumb over her hardened nipple. That combination had an orgasm building fast inside her.

"Harder!" She moaned in approval. "Yes, just like that!"

"You like when I fuck you against the wall like this?" Jack growled against her sensitive skin as he pumped harder into her.

"Oh God, yes!" She tipped her head back and closed her eyes, focusing solely on the euphoric feeling.

After a few more violent thrusts, she came undone, her core convulsing around him tightly. Her orgasm rocked through her as she screamed his name and clawed at his back, leaving bright red scratches across his lean muscles.

Not letting up on his pace, he kept moving inside of her, chasing his own finish. With her tight muscles constricting around him in a death grip, he spilled deep inside of her. He groaned as he milked every last drop before pulling out and gently setting her back down on shaky legs. They both breathed heavily as they got cleaned up and climbed out of the shower. After getting dressed, they crawled into bed and held each other closely until they fell asleep

FOR MY READERS

Thank you for reading Desire's Curse. I hope you enjoyed Liam and Amarah's love story as much as I did. I would love to hear your thoughts about it so please leave a review and follow me on social media to stay up to date on my latest writings.

P.S.A. Please, be careful with online dating. If you take anything from this story, let it be that there are real creeps in this world, and unfortunately not all stories end as happily as this one did.

Facebook: Maricca Wood - Author
Instagram: mariccawoodauthor
TikTok: mariccawoodauthor
Website: www.mariccawood.com
Newsletter: www.mariccawood.com/newsletter

ACKNOWLEDGMENTS

First and foremost, to the Most High—Your unconditional love and grace gives me the courage to chase after my dreams. Philippians 4:13 "I have the strength for everything through him who empowers me."

To my husband—This book would've never happened if it weren't for you. You pushed me every time I started to second-guess myself. Thank you for believing in me more than I believe in myself sometimes.

To my mother and best friend—Thank you for forcing me (quite literally) to give reading another chance. You've opened the entire world to me, real and fictional, and I'll be forever grateful.

Next, to my editor, The Havoc Archives—Thank you for the amazing input and for polishing my book so it can be the best version possible. You're truly incredible.

Also, to my beta readers, Samantha and Shelby—Thank you so much for taking the time out of your busy schedules to give my book a shot. I appreciate your honest feedback and am grateful to have friends like y'all.

Last but certainly not least, to my readers—I do all of this for you. I hope you enjoyed Liam and Amarah's love story as much as I did. Thank you for giving my book a chance. I can't wait to write more stories and share them all with you!

ABOUT THE AUTHOR

Maricca Wood is a hopeless romantic who, believe it or not, used to loathe reading growing up. Now, she finds it hard to put books down. She writes contemporary romance, some darker than others, and fantasy, all with plenty of angst, relatable characters, and of course, spice!

She lives in Oklahoma with her family and possesses an associate degree in Entrepreneurship. She enjoys reading a wide range of genres, playing video games, watching anime, doing puzzles, and building Lego sets. She can count on one hand all the people who have ever pronounced her name correctly the first time. Good luck!